CLAIMED BY THE ELVEN KING

ELVEN KING SERIES BOOK ONE

CRISTINA RAYNE

The characters and events portrayed in this book are fictitious. Any similarity to real persons, living or dead, is coincidental and not intended by the author.

Published by Fantastical Press

ISBN -10: 0692240793
ISBN-13: 978-0692240793 (Paperback)

ALSO BY CRISTINA RAYNE

Elven King Series

Shadows Beneath the Falling Snow Novella

Claimed by the Elven King

Claimed by the Elven Brothers: Decision and Fate

The Elven Realms

(Sequel series to the Elven King series)

Memories of an Elven Prince

To Love an Elven Prince *coming soon

Riverford Shifters Series

Tempted by the Jaguar

Accepting the Jaguar

Rescued? by the Wolf Novella

Tempted by the Tiger

Tempted by the—Lion?

Suspecting the Lioness Novella *coming soon

Dragon Shifters of Elysia Series

Where Sleeping Dragons Lie

When Fire Dragons Fall

What Stubborn Dragons Want

What Fire Dragons Treasure

Lords of the Vampire Underground

Tales from the Vampire Underground: A Prequel Collection

A Whisper in the Darkness *coming soon

Incarnations of Myth

Seeking the Oni

Falling for Enma *coming soon

Fractured Multiverse

(Writing as C.G. Garcia)

The Supreme Moment: Kairos

The Supreme Moment: Externus *coming soon

Black Crimson *coming soon

The Golden Mage

(Writing as C.G. Garcia)

The Kingdom of Eternal Sorrow

The Man Within the Temple

The Last Stone Cast

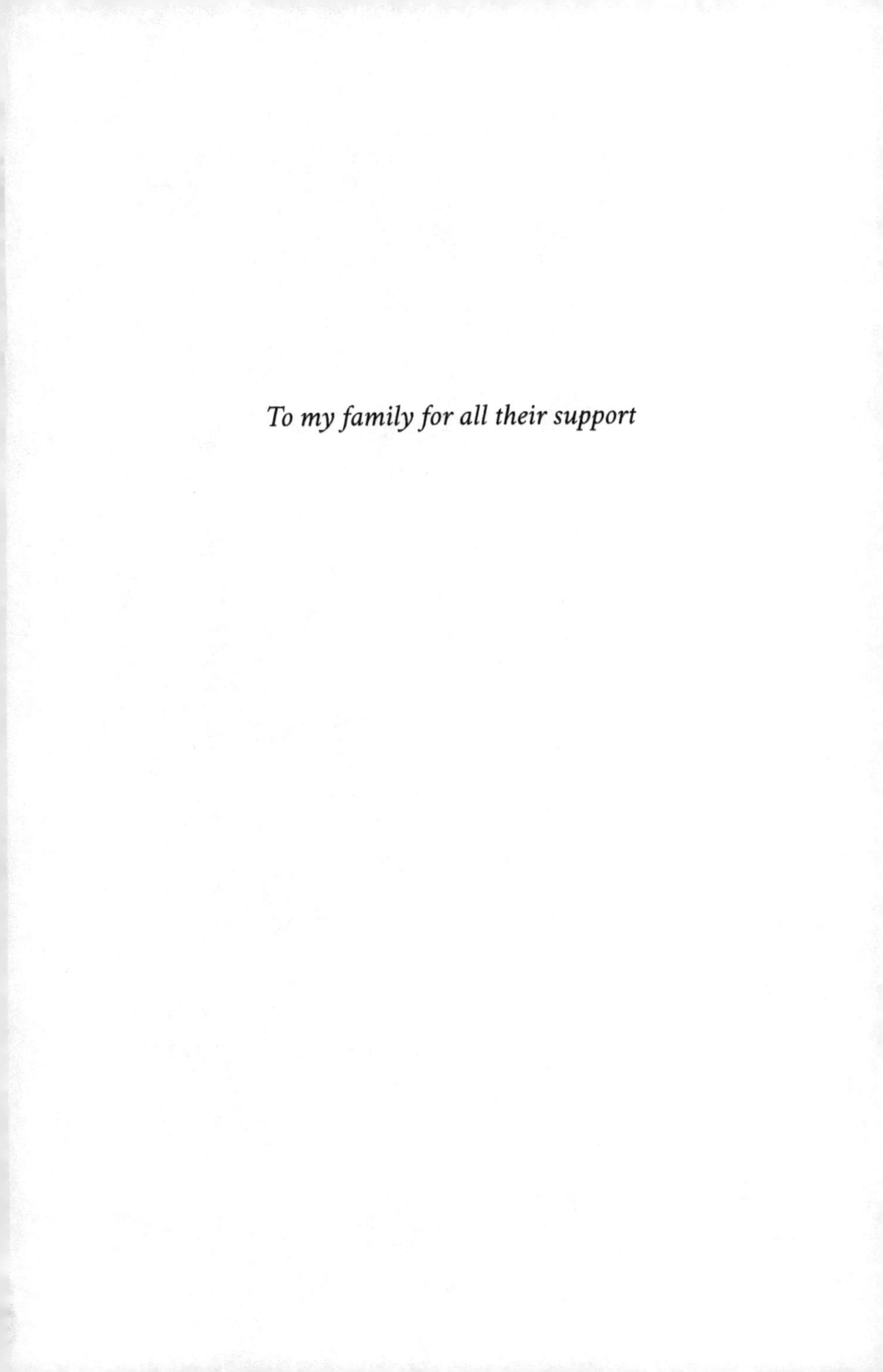

To my family for all their support

CHAPTER 1

It was the middle of the night when they came for me. Even now I can't be sure of the time, whether they waited for me to have been asleep long enough to ensure that I would be super confused if accidentally awakened, or if they had waited until after midnight when my roommate usually headed out for her graveyard shift at the hospital. I can't even be sure if all the fantastical things I experienced afterward really happened or was the mother of all delusions that is still ongoing. A small part of me has never been able to let go of that small fear. All I know is that it sure felt damned real to me that night.

Being a light sleeper, I immediately awakened, at first not certain why. I felt them that night. I know that now, but back then it was as if I had awakened straight into a nightmare. I didn't even have time to blink the sleep from my eyes before the shadows of my room seemed to come alive, forming into human-like shapes and surrounding me as silently and ethereally as fog approaching a coastline.

Before I could make a sound, I felt the shock of several cold hands on me, lifting me from my bed, and it was suddenly as though the chill of their touch entered my body in a sudden, shocking burst that washed completely through me. My lungs seized painfully and left me unable to breathe for a few terrifying seconds. As I gasped frantically for air, the little sight I still possessed in the darkness abruptly winked out until all I could see was a blackness so absolute it was as if I had suddenly gone blind.

What was happening to me? Yet, for some reason, it never occurred to me to scream. Maybe it happened too quickly; maybe I was in shock or thought that I was still dreaming. I didn't even struggle.

I could feel their hands binding my arms like living manacles, others holding my legs as if I was a log to be carried away between them. Then there was a sensation of traveling very rapidly, of wind blowing in my face as though I had just stuck my head out the window of a car going seventy down the interstate, though I could almost swear none of us had actually moved. I still couldn't see, and at that moment, that was more terrifying than the realization that I was being abducted.

Then the wind abruptly ceased, and it was over. Just like that, between one breath and another.

The shock of feeling something solid, smooth, and cold on my bare feet was akin to being doused with ice water. I had been set down on my feet, it seems, and had the shadow hands not have still had a firm grip on my arms, I would have surely collapsed.

Only then did I find my voice, but all I could manage to ask was, "What?"

I still can't believe that I had been so brainless at such a crucial point, but I guess I'm as human as the next person after all. I had always fashioned myself the type to think quickly on my feet and always ready to react to whatever crisis life would throw at me, but it turns out I'm just as prone to freeze in the face of danger just like the majority of people. A major blow to my ego, for sure, but in my defense, the possibility of waking up still very much existed because what was happening was just too crazy to believe.

Adding insult to injury, my kidnappers didn't even bother to answer my confusion. I was simply forced to walk forward, the hands imprisoning my arms gently, but insistently, pushing me onward.

Blinded, I saw no gain in resisting, so I walked for

what seemed like hours before the hands holding my arms pulled me to an abrupt halt that nearly sent me to my knees. My captors still didn't speak or make any sound. I couldn't even hear any audible breathing, which completely creeped me out and made me begin to wonder whether I was still even alive.

I heard the creak of a door swinging open, and I was once again urged forward. I immediately noticed the sound of running water, but I had no time to contemplate what this meant before I was thrust into the hands of others, and I felt the satin material of my nightgown being swiftly lifted up my body.

"What are you doing!" I cried, finally finding the fight in me. I struggled uselessly against the surrounding bodies imprisoning me like iron bars. "Why are you... where *am* I? Why can't I see?"

"You will not be harmed," a soft, melodic female voice near my ear assured me. The shock of hearing someone speak silenced me into immobility. Hearing a woman's voice was as out of place as a clap of thunder in a cloudless sky.

"Why?" I pleaded helplessly, unable to put my confusion into words.

My captors refused to say anything more, but they quickly removed the rest of my clothing. At this point, I knew it was pointless to resist them. Where would I run? I was freaking blind!

I gasped when I was lifted into something warm. It took a moment for my frightened mind to realize that it was water. My confusion increased when I felt my captors begin to wash me with something that felt both coarse and soft, like sponges. No inch of my body escaped them—my ears, my breasts, my groin. I knew I should have felt violated by what they were doing to me, but I couldn't really think straight, as though everything happening was as surreal as a dream. Yet some deep voice within had finally started to shout out through my confusion that all of this was very real.

I was removed from the water, dried, and clothed in what I could only guess was a lightweight robe that glided over my skin as cool and smooth as silk, although they didn't bother with any undergarments. I was placed on a flat, but still somewhat soft, surface, and what happened next was something that I shudder to remember now even after so many years.

Pain!

From one moment to the next, my whole body was saturated with pain. It was as if a million tiny needles were stabbing into my body simultaneously and trying to tear me apart. Even then, I didn't scream. I gritted my teeth and suffered my agony in silence. I did it for a sense of control, even though I knew that screaming was a release that would help ease a little of my pain. I had no clue why I had been taken, what my captors were doing to me that was causing every single nerve ending in my body to light up with pain, but I would be damned before I gave the bastards the pleasure of hearing the torment they were inflicting. "You will not be harmed" my ass!

I could feel tears streaming down my cheeks, scalding against skin that had gone ice-cold despite the warm bath. My body felt as if it were being torn apart atom by atom.

Only when the excruciating pain abruptly ceased what felt like two eternities later did I realize that the thing I was gripping tightly was someone's hand, though there was something wrong with it. The skin was too soft, feeling as silky and pliable as the garment I wore.

I felt a hand with the same texture as the one I clutched rest on my forehead as if checking for fever. The natural reaction should have been to flinch away, but instead, I felt a curious peace flood my body, spreading a pleasant warmth and washing away the lingering spasms of pain throughout my body.

"You are strong. That's good," I heard that same woman say somewhere behind me.

"For what?" I whispered, muddle-headed and feeling as if I were waking from a half-remembered daydream.

"Soon."

Someone lifted me from the surface where I lay and carefully placed me onto my now extremely unsteady feet.

"Why can't I see?" I anxiously asked again, then frantically grabbed onto the arms of the person still holding me by my upper arms before my wobbly legs could give out.

I suddenly felt like a newborn foal taking its first steps. My chances of escape were quickly falling towards zero.

"Soon," the woman repeated maddeningly.

They once again forced me to walk down what felt like an endless maze of corridors, my legs still weak and unsure. What was going to happen now? Why was I taken, and by whom? What had my kidnappers done to cause me so much pain? To what end?

I never cry just for the sake of crying, but by the time they brought me to a halt, I was damn near tears. But I didn't give in. I nearly gave myself a headache holding my tears back. I would stay in control of at least my emotions if nothing else. At this point, it was either that or go mad with fear.

Distracted by my internal battle to keep my

emotions in check, it took me a few moments to realize that I was looking at a large door of ornately carved wood. My sight had returned!

I immediately turned my head to catch a glimpse of my captors, but my head was instantly turned back forward before I could see anyone. One of them knocked on the door, so quickly that I didn't even have time to turn my gaze to see the action.

"Enter," a deep, muffled voice called.

The door swung open as if on its own accord, and I was ushered through so abruptly that I stumbled a bit as I crossed the threshold. I saw the figure immediately, sitting in a large armchair before a blazing fire, but still somehow almost completely hidden in the shadows. Only the light of the fire illuminated the room.

"Leave us," the person said, turning his head.

I still couldn't make out anything other than the figure had the build of a man, a useless observation when his deep voice had already given his gender away.

Rooted in place, I was watching him so closely that I didn't notice that my captors had released me until I heard the door shut behind me. However, I couldn't take my eyes off him to take advantage of this fact as I watched him rise and step out of the shadows.

CHAPTER 2

"*Sidhe*," I heard someone whisper as I stared at the entirety of the man before me with a mixture of awe and alarm—then startled, realized it was *me* that had just spoken.

The man's expression was also surprised. "Interesting," he said, a smile lighting up his face. "To know my people—I had not anticipated this."

At that moment, I couldn't have spoken to save my life. What I had unconsciously named him was more commonly known as an elf—and he was the most beautiful being I had ever laid eyes on. His hair was a golden blond that spilled loosely over his shoulders to mid-torso, the dancing flames behind him casting a contrast of orange hues and shadow throughout the ludicrously long locks that was almost hypnotic in its beauty. His eyes seemed to glow yellow-orange in the gloom that surrounded him, but I couldn't tell if it was just a trick of the light from the flames. But what really captured my attention were the two pointed ears that were peeking through his hair.

This had to be someone's bad idea of a joke. There's no *way* that elves could be real, that the ears I was currently looking at weren't prosthetics. There's no way this beautiful, impossible creature that was now staring at me curiously could be real in anything other than my dreams…

To this day, I couldn't tell you what he had been wearing. Once my eyes had latched onto his face, it was as though all previous thoughts and memories had been seared away by the sheer realization that I was looking at a being straight out of a fantasy story.

"Do you know why you have been brought here, Emily?" he asked.

My heart seized hearing my name coming from that mouth. This had to be a dream because there was no way he would know my name otherwise. Right…?

I swallowed thickly. "I have a pretty good idea," I replied more steadily than I thought possible.

And I did have a good idea. One quick glance around the room was all I had needed. Why else would I have been brought to his *bedroom*?

To my surprise, he chuckled. "Perhaps," he said. "Come to me, Emily."

I began to steadily back up until I felt the door handle press sharply into the middle of my back.

"I'd rather not," I said tensely.

Then quick as lightning, I reached my hand behind me, clumsily grabbed the handle, and tried to jerk the door open. It didn't budge an inch.

I dropped my hand and looked down in defeat. Honestly, what would I have done had it turned? I had been taken to Fairyland, or Underhill, or to freaking Middle Earth for all I knew. Where would I have gone?

My eyes slowly rose to look at the elf who still stood a few feet away. Despite my escape attempt, he had not moved closer, nor had his expectant expression changed. No way out, there was only one thing left to do —I boldly obeyed his command, refusing to show him my fear. Up close, his resulting smile was like a punch in the gut, it was so stunning.

"You are a rare one, indeed," he said softly, raising his hands to encircle my face. "Do not fear. I won't hurt you."

An elf's hands really did feel like silk. That inane thought ran through my head as I raised my hands to his chest to feebly attempt to push him away, as successful as trying to move a brick wall since from the moment he had touched my face, a strange lethargy had begun to creep into my body. It was more reflex than anything.

He responded by lowering his head until his lips firmly pressed against mine.

The abrupt kiss was like hitting me in the face with a sledgehammer. My knees gave out, and I would have definitely fallen on my ass had he not caught me. I felt my mind slipping away further, my eyes closing, even as I felt myself instinctively open my mouth to accept his kiss.

What was happening to me? His touch, his very presence was so overwhelming that it was like standing on the surface of the sun.

I felt him lift me until I was cradled in his arms, seemingly as weightless as a feather, his lips never once leaving mine. His tongue aggressively twined with mine before it could shy away in surprise, coaxing me to join its sensual dance. Then the next thing I felt was an incredible softness at my back, and I knew that he had taken me to his bed.

"It's your choice now," he whispered in my ear, making the hairs on the back of my neck stand on end. "Will you allow me to bed you, to fully experience my touch with a clear mind, or do you wish to fall into oblivion and wake tomorrow in your own bed as though from a barely remembered dream?"

I couldn't think; my mind was so hazy that his words flowed through my awareness like a whisper in the distance. Somewhere in the back of my mind, I knew that he had done something to me. I wasn't sure if it was intentional or something that was just a part of his elven nature, but I knew I would have been seriously freaking out about my current position without it. Even if the elf *had* fuzzed my mind out a bit to make things easier for me, not knowing what was going on *at all* wasn't something I would ever want.

This is a dream, anyway, so what does it matter? my mind offered up with a mental equivalent of a shrug, and for some stupid reason, at that moment, I really believed it. *I'm going to wake up alone in my room like always no matter what I say here, so I might as well enjoy this utter insanity while I can.*

"Touch me," I murmured, and just like that, my mind cleared so completely that I finally was able to appreciate the fact that the elf was looming over me, yards of golden hair spilling down to tickle my face and neck.

He was as large, beautiful, and majestic as an angel.

"I did not expect this either," he said, sounding delighted.

He then proceeded to open my robe-like garment until my breasts were revealed. It took every ounce of self-control I had within me not to cover myself out of shyness; yet, I couldn't look away from the intensity of the eyes I could barely see in the darkness, either.

I felt the fingertips of one hand slowly, teasingly glide up my stomach until those same fingers curved around my right breast and squeezed playfully. However, instead of feeling aroused, I felt an almost overwhelming terror course through me.

Although I'd had a handful of boyfriends over the years, this wasn't something I had ever really done—lying so utterly bared and submissive to my partner, never mind be comfortable with any of them to even *consider* sex. I knew that all I had to do was ask for oblivion, to go home, and the elf would grant my request. However, for some inexplicable reason, despite my fear, I also felt that I would die if he stopped or I lost this experience.

I closed my eyes tightly. Something definitely had come loose in my brain during the last few minutes...

But then I felt the rose petal-like skin of his full lips firmly cover mine again, and the terror simply ceased. I hesitantly raised my hands and tangled my fingers in his hair. The delicate strands were softer than even silk, feeling almost like water flowing through my fingers. I felt him smile against my lips, and that simple gesture made me shudder with pleasure.

I was careful not to touch his ears. I don't know

why, but something about them made me feel that touching them without his permission was a big no-no, the equivalent of it being taboo for a stranger to grab a random woman's boobs or a man's crotch. Considering what we were doing right now and the inevitable sex that would follow, it was a stupid thing for me to worry about, but I felt I shouldn't do it, all the same.

I could feel his thumb brushing lightly over my nipple over and over until it hardened. I moaned involuntarily and squirmed a bit as he teased the sensitive nub while devouring my lips as if they were a delectable meal and he had not eaten in months.

It was then that I became keenly aware of the weight of his body over me—and that he was completely nude. Where one of my hands had been tightly gripping a handful of cloth at his shoulder, my fingers were now digging into soft, bare flesh. When had he taken off his clothes? I couldn't remember a time he had paused long enough to remove anything.

He shifted slightly, and my thoughts were derailed by the unmistakable feel of his hardened cock against my inner thigh. That's when I realized that I, too, was completely missing the robe he had only opened and drawn aside earlier.

I pulled my mouth away with some difficulty and

gasped out, "Wait! Wait—what happened to our —*mmph*!"

Apparently, my soon-to-be elven lover was in no mood for talk as his tongue effectively cut off my words and a rough thrust of his hips that managed to rub perfectly against my clit shot a shocking burst of pleasure through my body, effectively short-circuiting my brain. My thighs instinctively tightened around his hips as he continued to thrust between my legs in a series of slow, drawn out slides against my now thoroughly wet sex. The delicious friction made me throb and shiver like never before as I writhed and moaned beneath him with abandon.

He drew his mouth away with a final brush against my swollen lips and a teasing nip on my bottom lip that probably should have stung but only left a pleasurable throb in its wake, and then proceeded to suck and lick his way down my jaw. Propped on one forearm, he stopped to pay special attention to several newly discovered sensitive points on my neck with teeth and tongue that had me throwing my head back and offering my throat to him as if in submission to another beast.

The elf's free hand reached down and began to fondle my thus far neglected breast. Both nipples were long past reacting to my excitement, hardened pebbles that were so sensitive now that they were beginning to ache. I sucked in a sharp breath as he pinched my nipple a little more firmly than I had expected, the sensation somewhere between pleasure and pain.

Licking a path down my breastbone to the top swell of my other breast, I suddenly felt his mouth latch onto it, a hot, slippery tongue laving and rolling over the nipple while his mouth began to roughly suckle, and I couldn't have formed a coherent thought to save my life. I moaned and arched my body closer to his mouth, pressing his head down with both my hands in the same instant.

My hand accidentally brushed against the point of one of his ears, and suddenly I just *had* to touch them, my earlier apprehension about needing his permission nowhere to be found. I delicately ran a fingertip slowly from the tip of one pointed ear down along its outer edge. It was as silky as the rest of his skin and as firm as a human ear.

I squeaked—yes squeaked—when his teeth suddenly bit down hard along the edge of my areola as he very nearly jumped out of his skin, and a sharp pain erupted from my chest. He immediately jerked his head up with a wild expression, a shocking smear of bright red staining his lips from the obviously unintentional bite. Who would've guessed that elves had such razor-sharp teeth!

The tips of both of his ears twitched as if in agitation. "Sorry!" I said quickly before he could open his mouth, afraid that I had just made him angry.

He shook his head, and my eyes widened when he very deliberately licked my blood clean from his lips instead of just wiping it off with his hand or the blankets or *something*. My pulse sped up as I watched that pink tongue lap up the last remnants of blood along his lower lip in a slow glide. That had to be one of the most erotic things I had ever seen, and I couldn't for the life of me understand why. What was wrong with me? Shouldn't that have disgusted me? I mean, what if he—

I let out a muffled exclamation of shock as his lips crashed against mine in the sloppiest, wettest, *hottest* kiss I had ever shared with anyone, and the full weight of his body pressed me down deeper within the softness at my back. It *should* have been uncomfortable, but the added weight, as well as the mild throb along my breast where he had bitten me, only seemed to make my pulse quicken even more. Who knew biting could be so stimulating?

I could vaguely taste something metallic on his tongue. Was that it? Did the blood excite him? Wait—don't tell me the elf was a *vampire*, too!

That settled it. This was all definitely a dream. I had to have gotten plastered after work, and I was absolutely never going to drink again if this convoluted delusion was the result! Then he did something amazing with his tongue, and any worries about vampires or elven taboos were instantly thrown to the wayside.

For what felt like hours, we sucked on each other's tongues while his hands seemed determined to search out and skillfully caress every spot on my body within reach that made me shudder and moan. His rock-hard erection was equally determined to stimulate me into a frenzy as he sensually rubbed himself almost teasingly against my pelvis.

Then before I knew it, his considerable girth was inside me, stretching my virgin passage almost to the point of tearing, and he was thrusting into me as if he were trying to drive me completely through the mattress to the floor beneath. It was a testament to how completely gone my mind was at that point that I couldn't even remember the moment when he had penetrated me for the first time.

The sensations I experienced were phenomenal. Shockwave after shockwave of pleasure shot up my spine with every heavy, deep thrust until my toes curled, and I all but screamed. Nothing I had ever experienced in my twenty-three years of life could even come close to the pleasure the elf gave me that night.

I wrapped my legs tightly around his hips and

wantonly thrust my own hips up to meet each of his thrusts almost as if compelled, clinging to his firm, muscled back as if it were a lifeline. His body was so perfectly made that it was unreal. It *had* to be unreal...

I climaxed after only a couple of minutes at most, so startled by that sudden, unimaginable explosion of ultimate pleasure that all the conflicting emotions I had been futilely trying to keep in check abruptly shattered, and I began to sob in earnest even as my body shuddered in ecstasy.

"It's all right," the elf whispered against my ear, turning to gently lick one of the tears trailing down my cheek. It was a shock to just hear his voice. "The pleasure will only overwhelm in the beginning. Let yourself go—set your spirit free, and everything will balance itself out as it should."

To this day, I can't understand how he could have spoken so calmly while never once losing his rhythm. He moved over and within me with all the grace and power of a blond panther, his hips driving his cock so deep into my passage that the force of it was almost bending me in half. That fantastic tension was building in my sex again even as it was still tingling pleasurably from the first explosion. I tightened my legs around him in an attempt to increase the friction between us as I desperately ground my hips upwards against him, feeling as if my brain would melt if I didn't come soon.

When I finally crashed over the edge again, I came twice within seconds of each other, the last orgasm so powerful that it bordered on painful. It was as if every nerve ending in my body just *sang*. I very nearly blacked out as the stimulation really was more than my body and mind could handle, especially when my elven lover was still thrusting powerfully within me while relentlessly attacking my nipples with both tongue and those sharp teeth.

As my body shuddered and writhed with spasm after spasm of pleasure, he gave one last, heavy thrust that seemed to almost reach into the center of me, and the warmth of his climax nearly sent me over the edge again. He lay atop me with his full weight for a few moments, kissing my neck with more energy and aggression than I felt should have been possible after the wild ride he had just taken me on, then lingering on my lips with a little less alpha male and more tenderness.

He then carefully withdrew his cock from within me, making me gasp as I felt one last throb of arousal from my over-sensitized tissues, and rolled onto his side, pulling me with him into a tight embrace of incredibly soft skin and tangled limbs.

With my body tingling like mad and still overwhelmed with emotions, I began to sob again, burrowing my face into the damp muscles of his chest. I felt my elven lover kiss the top of my head, and then he slowly began to run his fingers caressingly along my scalp and through my hair in an unmistakable gesture of comfort.

"Sleep now," he said. "Leave all your fears and questions for a time, and tomorrow, I promise the answers will come."

"What's your name?" I murmured as my mind began to fog.

Before I lost consciousness, I heard him whisper into my ear, "Sethian."

CHAPTER 3

Waking up, I felt as if I had been asleep for years.

My body felt heavy, stiff, and every one of my muscles seemed to throb—and not in a good way. There was a dull ache in both my temples and the back of my neck that spiked with pain every time I moved my head. It was like waking up after going on a five-day bender of hard liquor and no sleep. Not that I had any firsthand experience, mind you, but I did have a few wild friends during my undergrad days and had often witnessed the absolute train wreck of misery and self-hate that had always followed.

It took me a lot longer than usual to shake off the lethargy of sleep, but once my mind had cleared a bit and my eyes had focused completely on my surroundings, I don't think I have ever been as wide-awake as I was at that moment. The room I was in was *not* my own, the bed a far cry from my twin-sized bed. I lay in the center of a bed large enough to sleep at least ten people comfortably. I bolted upright, wincing when my head throbbed sharply in protest, and my hands immediately went to my body.

They met silk.

Almost afraid of what I would see, I forced my eyes downward and saw the robe-like garment the *elves* had dressed me in—the robe *he* had removed.

Sethian.

"Not a dream," I said aloud, probably just to hear a voice, to hear something so familiar.

It was no wonder I felt as though I had a hangover. I *had* been drunk last night—drunk on the type of sex that shouldn't have been possible in the real world.

Then I noticed my arms.

The color was wrong was my first thought, but as my mind unfroze from that initial moment of shock, I realized it was much more than that. Not only was my summer tan gone, but my skin was unmarked, unblemished as if I had never exposed it to twenty-three years of the sun. I could compare it to a baby's skin, but it would be like comparing apples to oranges. No one's skin was that perfect—no one's except Sethian's, the other elves'...

"Oh my God," I whispered in horror, staring at the living marble my arms and hands had become.

I jumped out of bed, my eyes searching not for a door, but a mirror, a window, *anything* with a reflective surface. My gaze stopped on what looked like an ornate dressing table, except this one didn't have the usual mirror. However, I immediately found what I was looking for in the form of a silver hand mirror laid out beside what looked like an old-fashioned porcelain basin and pitcher.

One look at the stranger staring back re-convinced me that I had to be dreaming. It was me, but at the same time completely *not* me. My hair was still the same dark chestnut-brown, though twice as long and more glossy and healthy than I have ever seen it. My eyes were no longer the color of milk chocolate. They were a shade of green that had an almost preternatural glow, filled with an inner fire I had never seen them reflect.

My face had lost its roundness; my cheekbones were much more prominent, my eyebrows thinned and more slanted.

It was me and not me.

Then a frightening thought occurred to me, and my free hand shot to one of my ears. Round—no, they were unchanged. Breathing a brief sigh of relief, I tugged at the upper ties of my robe and instantly felt what little blood that remained in my cheeks drain away once I had drawn the folds open.

My ears were the only thing unchanged, it seemed.

Although I have never been what people would consider chubby, I haven't been even remotely close to supermodel-thin either, and with graduate school eating up most of my time, the gym wasn't exactly high on my list of priorities. Now, as I examined my body with increasing alarm, I could see that every ounce of fat was gone. Just—gone, my boyish figure replaced by pleasing feminine curves and a hint of muscle.

My eyes zeroed in on my breast where a certain bite mark was conspicuously absent. I had felt the pain, seen the blood on his lips...hell, had even *tasted* it on his tongue for God's sake! How could it be *gone*? No scab, no scar, just—nothing but that strange new, airbrushed-looking skin?

Feeling an invisible hand begin to squeeze my racing heart painfully, I forced the whole disturbing thing out of my mind and turned my attention to my legs. I raised the ankle-length robe with a sense of dread, finding that my trepidation was indeed warranted.

I hadn't noticed it when I had stood so close to Sethian that first time, but now I could clearly see that the length of my legs had increased significantly. From what I could remember, the top of my head had come to his shoulders, so taking into account my new height, I guessed Sethian's height to be at least 6'5", making me now about 5'10" or 5'11", a far cry from my previous 5'0".

I now understood the cause of the excruciating pain I had suffered. I had felt as if I were being torn apart bit by bit, atom by atom. The supporting evidence was quite literally now staring me right in the face. The elves had somehow *remade* me. I didn't know whether to thank them or to be furious and insulted.

While I had always considered myself passably pretty in a girl-next-door kind of way, I was nowhere near cover model material. They had changed a good many things that had bothered me about myself over the years as if they had plucked the information from my mind. However my eyes—they were my one feature that I really liked, and now the elves had taken that away without so much as a "may I" and replaced them with something that was alien, and honestly, scary as hell. Who the hell was this strange girl staring back at me with wide eyes, looking a breath away from completely freaking out?

I let the mirror fall back to the dressing table. I didn't

want to see anymore. I needed to *think*. God, I needed a chair!

Looking around, I spotted a small, square table with a couple of wooden chairs against the far wall. I stumbled over to it and all but collapsed into the chair facing the door. I wanted no more surprises.

For a while, I just sat there staring at the door, trying to calm my racing heart. Questions milled around my head, so jumbled that the only coherent thought that emerged was "why?"

There were only a few things since I was awakened by the "shadows" within my room back in my apartment that I was fairly certain were true. One was that I had been abducted by elves, another that they had physically changed me. The "how" was still a mystery, though. That I was also brought for Sethian's pleasure was another, but I wasn't at all sure I was seeing the whole picture with that one. Sethian had implied as much after our—lovemaking.

I could feel my cheeks heat up at the thought of him. Dream or no dream, I didn't understand how I could have so willingly given to him, my abductor, what I had never given to another man without putting up at least some kind of fight, even if I knew it was no use. I knew I couldn't really blame it on his overwhelming presence, either. He had given me a choice, and I had answered without much, if any, thought. It had just felt right, somehow.

He was a complete stranger, a man that I hadn't even known his name, yet I had slept with him as if I had known him all my life. The real kicker was I knew damn well that I would still make the same decision if presented with the same choices right now when my head was clear, even as my theory of this all being a dream was becoming less likely by the second.

I sighed and cradled my head in my hands. It was too much to think about. I raised my eyes wearily and scanned the room for a distraction, any distraction. There were no windows, making me suddenly feel uncomfortably boxed in even though the room was large and spacious, like a comfortable cage—no! I wasn't going to let myself go there. Not now. My eyes landed on a couple of built-in bookcases in the wall beside the bed, filled from ceiling to floor with books.

Perfect.

I rose immediately, trying to unsuccessfully ignore the throbbing soreness deep inside of me I had never experienced before as I gingerly walked over to the closest bookshelf. I pawed through a few, finding that most of the titles on the spines were written in a script I had never seen, one I suspected was unknown to all humans, all connected half-circles and random-looking squiggly lines.

I selected one of the few with a title written in Latin that, with its warped spine and cracked leather covers, looked old enough to have been read by Plato. I had studied Latin for a couple of semesters as an undergrad, so I hoped I could piece through it. I was convinced there were answers to be had within its yellowed, ancient-looking pages.

However, after plowing through a few pages, I realized things wouldn't be so easy. The Latin was so archaic that it might as well have been written in Sanskrit for all I could decipher it. Plus, the person who had transcribed it had atrocious handwriting. It was difficult to even make out each letter, much less a word.

I was so intent on my translation that it was a while before I sensed that I wasn't alone anymore. I stiffened and slowly raised my eyes to the door, my heart suddenly in my throat.

"You do not disappoint, my Emily," Sethian said, stepping up to the table.

CHAPTER 4

He was dressed just as I imaged an elf would dress within an elven court, flowing navy-blue tunic-like robes of silk all embroidered in silver and gold filament straight out of a costume designer's wet dream.

I started to get up, to do what, I didn't know, but he shook his head.

"There's no need to rise," Sethian said gently, his eyes boring into me so intently that I could almost feel his gaze as something physical.

Even though I knew my face was probably nuclear red, I refused to look away out of pure stubbornness as I sank back down into my chair, trying not to wince when I accidentally irritated the soreness between my legs. I gestured to the chair across from me.

"Will you sit?" I asked, surprised I could speak at all.

The elf bowed his head slightly in acceptance and complied. He was not tense at all, the bastard. Where my movements were stiff and cautious, Sethian seemed as though he was performing an intricate dance, his movements so fluid and relaxed.

"So…am I supposed to be your concubine now?" I rushed out, hating myself for asking, but I had to know the truth. Running away had never gotten anyone anywhere, after all.

His smile was all teeth. "Based on our first meeting, I know it would seem so. Concubines are for humans. For the *Sidhe*, there are only lovers and life-mates."

"And I'm which?" I said quietly, pushing my book aside.

"Our relationship is a bit more complicated, I fear. I did not expect you to be so compliant, so accepting, even though your strength and spirit were the reasons why I chose you."

I stiffened. "Chose me for what?" I demanded more harshly than I had intended.

He nodded. "Last night I promised you answers, and you will have them, but first I would wish answers from you."

I was relieved that my earlier tone didn't seem to have offended him in the least, but it did nothing to alleviate the enormous knot tightening in the pit of my stomach.

"What do you want to know?" I asked, swallowing against my now raging anxiety.

"What do you think of all of this?" Sethian asked, gesturing at the room, then at himself.

It was becoming increasingly more difficult to concentrate the more I looked into his eyes. Although exactly the same shade of green as my new eye color, his irises were a bit larger than a human's, making something primal in my brain squirm uncomfortably.

"To tell you the truth, I-I wouldn't know where to start. This could be one of my dreams, albeit one of the weirder ones, except for what happened between—" I stopped, unable to go on. I could feel my cheeks blazing again.

My embarrassment only seemed to amuse him more. "Are you expecting to wake up?" he asked curiously. "Is that why you have accepted everything so quickly?"

"Not anymore," I admitted, to both him and myself. "I already woke up, and everything is still the same." I paused. "Sethian—is that really your name, or did I dream it?"

"It's my name," he confirmed, "although you probably will rarely hear it spoken. My people address me differently. I suppose that is as good of a place as any to begin.

In private, you may address me as you wish. When others are present, 'my lord' will suffice."

He paused suddenly and stared at me for a long, uncomfortable moment. I almost forgot how to breathe.

"Or, you may address me as 'my lord husband.'" He was watching me very carefully.

"Husband," I repeated dumbly. Then it dawned on me. "Last night—"

I couldn't finish, but I didn't need to.

Sethian nodded approvingly. "Our joining was more than what you humans so fondly call 'a roll in the hay.'"

"How can you be so casual about it?" I blurted out, embarrassed to the point of tears, but I wouldn't cry. I *don't* cry. As far as I was concerned, crying last night after the elf had so thoroughly made a mess of me didn't count.

"My dear, so innocent," he said teasingly. He looked way more amused about it than was decent. "Perhaps last night was not enough to bond us into a state of familiarity. Perhaps there is too much table between us now."

He pushed his chair back. "Come, have a seat," he said, patting his lap.

I didn't move, afraid of what I was feeling, of how much I instantly wanted to jump up and obey him. His smile deepened, and I almost lost my resolve.

"I only nip when it's appropriate," he assured me, making me stiffen even more when I remembered last night's accidental bite. "Trust me; this will help matters. I do not wish to see you so conflicted."

God, I have never been so afraid of anyone in my life. I prided myself on my control, but this being sent every ounce of my control to the four winds. I was also afraid of myself, of what I was feeling.

Sethian waited patiently, saying nothing while I struggled with myself. I didn't want to go to him, to be so near. I did; I didn't…

A single tear fell from my right eye as I rose from my seat and took a step closer to him. It was the only moment that I truly hated him, not for making me come to him, not even for abducting me, but for making me show him once again what I considered the ultimate weakness—tears. However, only that single tear fell.

"I'm so confused," I whispered.

I don't know why I said that. Even now I still don't know. I hadn't meant to say anything at all. That my soul felt compelled to utter such an admission felt like a betrayal.

"Come to me, Emily," he coaxed gently, holding out his hand. "You need not be confused any longer. I will do my best to put your mind at ease."

That was what finally decided me. I wanted to be

near him, to touch him, but what I really wanted more than that was answers, for the conflict within me to end. I needed *control.*

My hand was shaking as I accepted that perfect hand. I honestly felt that I had sold my soul the moment I felt his hand encircle mine. I was now utterly his; I felt it down to the very marrow of my bones.

He gently pulled me towards him, his free arm moving to encircle my waist as he set me gently onto his lap. I almost lost myself completely at that moment. I felt a sensation flood through my being very much like fitting two pieces of a puzzle together. This was so *right.* God help me, it was so right.

"Sethian..." I said, hearing the fright in my voice, even while in such a mentally fragile state.

The elf's arms tightened protectively around me. I turned my head and gazed at him with frightened eyes. He bent his head nearer, so slowly that I had all the time in the world to pull away—no doubt his intention. An eternity later, I felt the shock of his warm lips on mine, and all of my fear was just—gone. Forgotten. Or perhaps even banished. He was an elf, so there was no telling what he could or couldn't do. At this point, I was ready to believe anything.

Sethian pulled away almost immediately and smiled

his charming smile. "Feel better?" he asked in that maddeningly casual voice.

"Yes." I couldn't hide the surprise in my voice. My trembling had even stopped.

"You see; I told you all would be well. You are already beginning to relax, and that pleases me immensely."

He was right. The tension had all but melted from my body. I felt strangely at ease as well. Maybe it was because the conflict within me had finally been satisfied rather than anything magical the elf had done. I was exactly where I wanted to be.

Boldly, I laid my head onto his shoulder. Not even the mind-blowing ecstasy of last night compared to the peace I felt from such a simple gesture.

"Are you ready to hear the rest?" he asked into the silence.

"Yes." And I was.

"I should really start with who I am, my standing within the elven realm," Sethian began, sounding thoughtful. "As I said, last night was more than a night of pleasure. When I brought you into my bed, you became my wife. I'll explain why this was necessary in a moment. For now, I believe knowing your husband's true identity is the most important thing.

"You knew the name of my people, the *Sidhe*, but we are very much different than any account you may have heard. We exist in the same multi-dimensional space as humans, just slightly a degree or two out of phase. I know you understand what I mean because of your astrophysical studies."

I involuntarily twitched. How in the world did he know so much about me? Had he been spying on me somehow? Reading my mind? I was anxious to ask him, but I didn't want to interrupt him when the information he was giving me was so fascinating.

"The reason humans cannot perceive our world, or even *us*, is that our various types of energies vibrate at a different frequency. It's like trying to see the color ultra-violet with human eyes alone. It's not possible. The *Sidhe*, on the other hand, can easily see your world as clearly as humans see it, can even reach into and interact with your world partially."

"That's why the elves that appeared in my apartment looked like a bunch of animated shadows," I said with sudden realization.

"Yes, and that is also why in order to bring you here, my servants had to change a portion of your body's energies to match our vibration since a purely human body cannot interact in our plane of existence at all. You would have experienced the change as something like a cold wave flowing through your entire body. That is also why you seemed to lose your eyesight for a time. A 'side-effect' is the word you would use, I believe.

"However, what my servants did to you in your apartment was only a temporary fix. The natural laws of our dimension are very different from yours, which meant even *you* had to be almost completely altered in order to keep the correct level of vibration. You may have noticed how much you now resemble my people. It was necessary, and could only be done because our two worlds are essentially, to borrow another human phrase, 'two sides of the same coin.'

"But I really have strayed from my initial point. Myself, I am what you would call a 'king' in your world, but that word is inadequate, really. My status is so much more, but I won't get into that right now."

A king… It figured. Just what had I gotten myself into?

"You say I'm your wife," I said hesitantly. "Then what does that make me?"

"Just that—my wife," he replied simply. "Our hierarchy does not work the same as some of those in the human world. I have another wife. She is of a different race of *Sidhe* than I—there are four altogether in this realm—and is the queen of all the elven realm just as I am its king. She has been the queen since her birth. Our marriage is only a technicality, a symbol of unity between our two peoples."

He laughed suddenly. "Truth be told, she really does not care too much for me. As far as elves go, I am not much to look at, I'm afraid. The queen is a very vain creature, beautiful. I honestly cannot remember the last time she was in my bed. A century, perhaps, and only because it was her duty to produce heirs. However, she never did conceive, and that is where you come in."

"Huh?" I said cleverly. I was still trying to deal with the fact that he already had a wife, never mind the utter incomprehensibility of someone as exquisite as he believing that he "wasn't much to look at."

"Every few centuries, we must choose human women to bear our children," Sethian continued. "We are not a very fertile race. In contrast, humans are exceedingly fertile. We need your human genes in our children, or else sooner or later, our women are born barren. This is such a time. An elven child has not been born in over five centuries."

The fear returned again, as did the tension. "You brought me here to have your *children*?"

"Yes," he replied, his voice maddeningly calm. "You will bear my heirs. That's why marriage was necessary between us. My heirs must be legitimate."

"But—but what if I don't *want* to have a baby?" I stammered, pulling away from him.

The thought terrified me. What kind of life would we create?

"You may already be with child," Sethian said pointedly. "You were very fertile last night."

"Oh God," I moaned.

I wanted to jump off his lap, to run, to just get away. Instead, I collapsed against his chest and began to cry softly. It was the last straw, and I didn't know what else to do.

Sethian said nothing, merely stroking my hair in an attempt to comfort me.

"No," I said suddenly, pushing away from his shoulder, "I *won't* cry." I wiped at my eyes angrily. "I need to understand this. Why me, Sethian? Why choose *me*?"

"Let me ask you this," he countered, raising a hand to my face and deliberately wiping a stray tear from my cheek. "If I were to allow you to return home now, would you really want to?"

His question caught me completely off guard, and I answered before I could stop myself, "No."

What had I done? Both the elf and I knew it was the truth. All that was waiting for me back home was an empty apartment where my best friend and roommate worked so much and at different hours than me that we might as well have been living in different apartments. Most of my friends had scattered to the ends of the earth or dropped off the edge completely after graduating college, and those that didn't, I rarely saw anymore.

With both work and graduate school taking up the majority of my time, I hadn't been on a date in at least a couple of years. As far as family, both my parents had died before I had even finished my sophomore year in college, and I was an only child just as both my parents had been. No aunts or uncles; no cousins my age.

I was alone.

"I did not think so," Sethian said with a smile that was more a smirk, "and that seems to answer your question as well. It seems I chose wisely with you. You will instill good qualities into our children."

"Our children," I repeated dully. "I don't know what to think or feel anymore."

"You need not think or feel anything about any of this if that is truly what you wish," he reminded me quietly. "That is still a choice I give you—will *always* give you."

I sighed and lay back against him. "That's something I'll never choose. So what happens now?"

"Now," he said, turning my face towards his, "we make love."

CHAPTER 5

I didn't try to resist him. What was the point when I really didn't want to anyway. He found my lips parted and welcoming. However, it was a quick kiss, not exactly the rough, tongue-wrestling affair I had in mind.

"Let us find our marriage bed," Sethian said.

As I watched with astonished eyes, the room began to change—into the same bedroom I had initially been taken to last night. We were also no longer sitting in the chair. Sethian now stood in the center of the room with me cradled in his arms.

"How did you do that?' I asked curiously.

"Always the scientist," he laughed. "Now is not the time for explanations. We will have countless millennia for that."

My new elf husband wasted no time in carrying me to the bed, then tumbling us both onto the coverlet. He had been calm and serious before, but now his demeanor was completely playful. That made him all the more appealing.

Feeling the entirety of his weight pressing my body into the bed was its own ecstasy. I wrapped my legs around his torso and sought his lips while my hands threaded into his hair. I would never get tired of running my fingers through that unique silkiness.

He chuckled delightfully and said, "I guess removing our clothing the usual way is out of the question."

And in the next second, I felt his skin against mine where cloth had been earlier. More elven magic, I supposed, but I didn't care at the moment because Sethian had chosen to forgo foreplay and had entered me to the hilt with one powerful thrust, instead. Last night, I had not experienced his initial penetration since my mind had been mush at the time, so I wasn't prepared for it at all.

I gasped at the unexpected amount of pain. Apparently, I was a lot more sore from last night than walking around earlier had revealed, but I welcomed the pain. It was my anchor to reality, the thing that told me this was all real. In all my dreams, never once had I felt any kind of physical pain.

My elven lover moved slowly within me, perhaps aware of my slight discomfort. I closed my eyes tightly, afraid that I would start crying again. Immediately, I felt his fingers lightly caressing my face. I opened my eyes, and I swear that all time stopped. His eyes weren't just looking at me; he was *looking* at *me,* everything I am, was, and will be—the very essence of my being.

That realization was earth-shattering enough, but it was the dew on a blade of grass amidst a raging hurricane compared to what occurred next. I seemed to leave my body momentarily, and another presence filled me—Sethian—every bit of emptiness within my soul had become saturated with his essence. No—*bonded.* Joined, connected—our souls had somehow become one.

It could have been a second, an hour, a year, a hundred millennia; all were correct. The first thing I saw when my wits returned was the utter shock in Sethian's eyes. It had been my thought that the experience was the elf's doing. His expression was telling me I couldn't have been more wrong.

He lay over me, all movement completely stilled, almost as if he feared he would shatter something precious with something as mundane as breathing. Even in such a short time of knowing him, I had already become so accustomed to the elven king's seemingly unbreakable calm. To see that calm shattered completely was like leaning against a brick house and it suddenly falling over onto its side.

"What did that mean?" I asked softly.

He didn't pretend to misunderstand.

"I'm not certain," Sethian admitted, his eyes staring intently at my own. "It could mean nothing—or everything."

Slowly, he withdrew from me and rolled over to his side, pulling me into a tight embrace as if reluctant to have me even an inch away from him.

As I lay silently in his arms, a maelstrom of emotions swept through me—curiosity, puzzlement, excitement, worry, fear…

…and I realized that they were not my own. Confusion and anxiety were the only emotions I felt in any large quantity. Those other emotions seemed almost alien, except that they left the "feel" of Sethian in their wake.

I glanced at Sethian and found him looking down at me. It was apparent that he had been staring down at me for some time.

"Why are *you* afraid?" I asked on a whim.

"You feel that, do you?" That seemingly impenetrable calm had returned.

"I feel it," I confirmed. "I don't understand how, but I'm sure it isn't my imagination. Elven magic?"

He shook his head. "It's not that simple. I do not wish to get into metaphysics with you at this time. You are confused enough. Plus, I do not fully understand how this happened myself. Between *Sidhe* and human…never mind. Perhaps the best approach is to simply allow things to continue without speculation."

I gasped as I suddenly found myself on my back again, a grinning elf hovering above me, his forearms bearing most of his weight.

"What are you—" I stammered, feeling my cheeks getting warm as I realized the flutters I was feeling throughout my body was the elf-king's amusement.

His smile widening, Sethian bent to brush his lips lightly over mine, just enough to make them tingle, followed by a teasing swipe of his tongue along my bottom lip that made me quiver with pleasure.

"I'm curious," he said, his mouth only an inch from mine, "about what this new, deeper connection between us will add to our physical joining." He gazed down at me knowingly. "Especially since such a mild emotion from me causes such a reaction within you."

By now my face was burning so hotly that I imagined flames were consuming my cheeks. Yet, somehow I managed a shaky smile and a murmured, "We *were* interrupted…"

His enormous cock slid into my slick passage once

again, stretching my delicate tissues to the brink of what I could comfortably handle, and my feelings of excitement and arousal exploded exponentially. I moved to wrap my legs around him, but before I could, he dug his arms beneath my back and lifted us both up until he was sitting back onto his haunches and I was straddling him across his lap. His cock reached even deeper into me so that I felt that it was almost splitting me in two.

I wrapped my arms around his neck as he cupped my ass and lifted me up a bit, urging me to move. Having never done this, I rocked onto his member with a slow and uncertain movement, his scalding hands quickly guiding me into a faster rhythm as he bent his head to fasten his equally hot mouth onto the point where my shoulder and neck met. He sucked so hard that I dug my nails deep into the flesh of his back and cried out in both surprise and pleasure.

I had the sudden urge for him to bite down, and in the next second, I felt the sting of his teeth shallowly pierce my skin, causing me to suddenly climax so hard that I nearly bit my tongue in half. A rush of salt and metal flooded my taste buds as waves of pleasure crashed throughout my body.

Sethian grabbed my trembling hips in a bruising hold and began to thrust up into me almost violently, capturing my lips again in an equally bruising kiss. My tongue stung a little as he slid his tongue over and over the slight injury I had inadvertently caused myself, tasting, and I had a fleeting thought that I had never asked him if drinking my blood was just a particular kink of his or something darker. Then Sethian slammed up into me with a particularly deep and brutal thrust that made me cry out in a strange mixture of pain and increasing arousal, and I lost the ability to think at all.

As he bent to take one of my breasts into his mouth, a faint noise made it past the haze of pleasure that had filled my mind, and I instinctually opened my eyes to look over my elven lover's shoulder.

A woman was standing in the doorway across the room, an elf I realized, pointed ears poking out of hair so platinum blonde that it was almost white. She was staring expressionlessly at us from a face that was so alien, yet beautiful, that it couldn't be real.

Mortified at being seen in such an intimate moment, I started to say Sethian's name to alert him to our unexpected visitor, but my vision suddenly blurred and everything instantly faded to black along with my consciousness.

CHAPTER 6

Confusion was quickly becoming the norm for me upon awakening as I once again found myself with no clue about what was going on for those first couple of minutes after opening my eyes. Then I realized that the unfamiliar room I was in really wasn't so unfamiliar, and I bolted up in bed, looking around for Sethian but not really surprised when I found myself alone for the second time in a row.

For a long moment, my memories of before I had fallen asleep were hazy, as if I was trying to see something clearly out of the corner of my eye. Then after a while of hard thinking, I was pretty sure that we had made love—if nothing else, the fact that I woke up naked, along with my still-throbbing vagina and sore nipples, confirmed my fragmented memories of riding him. Had I passed out during the act? It had almost happened before, so it was completely possible.

I grimaced. How embarrassing if that turned out to be true!

A folded piece of clothing at the foot of the bed the same color of blue as the elven king's robes caught my eye, and I wasted no time in slipping it on, though dealing with the multitude of ties along the side were somewhat aggravating. Despite all we had already done, the last thing I wanted was for Sethian to suddenly walk into the room and find me naked. Nudity was all good and well while having sex, but I could only imagine how vulnerable I would feel trying to have a normal conversation with him while only he was fully clothed and leering down at me. Not that I've ever seen him leer…

I ended up leaving the bottom three ties undone out of frustration and made my way over to the door Sethian had entered through, wondering with a sick feeling at the pit of my stomach whether or not it was locked. There was another door on the other side of the bed that either led to a closet or bathroom, so keeping me locked in was completely plausible.

My hand hesitated briefly over the handle before I mentally berated myself for being such a wuss and grabbed it with more force than was necessary. Even so, I almost went weak in the knees with relief when the handle turned easily, and with a soft *click*, the door opened.

Feeling almost like a prowler, I stuck my head through the partially opened door and peered into the room beyond, not really sure what I was so nervous about finding. From what I could see, it was a large, high-ceilinged room filled with several cream-colored couches in the center that were bookended by a couple of small tables with a pair of rather ornate and old-fashioned-looking lamps resting in the center of each. Several wooden, high-backed chairs were pushed up along one of the walls. A sitting/living room by the looks of it.

Pushing the door open farther, I cautiously stepped into the room, half-expecting someone to jump out at me like some sort of cheesy horror movie, but not a soul was in the room, the only sounds my shallow breaths and the rapid beating of my heart thrumming in my ears. There was a door across the room directly facing the bedroom door, and two others on the left and right. To the left was also a large picture window that was covered by only a couple of thin, nearly transparent white curtains.

I made a beeline to the windows and pushed the curtains aside. That the sky was a familiar blue made the huge knot of tension in my chest loosen just a bit.

However, a sense of vertigo washed through me when I looked down and was greeted by the sheer drop of a jagged cliff face, the rocks and crashing waves at the bottom so far down that they were barely distinguishable. The drop must have been at least a couple thousand feet. Startled, I immediately jerked away from where I had been leaning against the window, my heart suddenly in my throat.

Why in the hell would someone build a structure so close to the edge of the cliff? One small earthquake or weathered edge suddenly becoming unstable and someone would earn a one-way ticket to the last terrifying ride of their life. It was completely disconcerting to know that someone could be *me* if this was where Sethian intended for me to stay from now on.

I stepped back from the window and looked over to the bedroom door, wondering if I should just go back inside and hide under the blankets until Sethian returned. Then my stomach growled, and I was suddenly reminded that I hadn't eaten in who knows how long. Was there a kitchen somewhere nearby? I wondered if I was in something like an apartment, or if the king of the elves lived in a castle or palace and this was just one of several of its wings. Maybe the door across the room to the right of the bedroom led to a kitchen, or at the very least, a dining room. I really hoped I wouldn't have to wait for Sethian to show back up to get something to eat.

Walking over, I paused only briefly in front of a pair of French-style doors that I hadn't noticed initially that opened out onto a wide and spacious balcony with tables and seating. Although I wasn't exactly afraid of heights, there was no way I was going out there alone without first asking Sethian about it. For all I knew of the elven realm, it could be a windy season or something and not safe to step out onto it right now.

The first thing that greeted me when I opened the next door was a wall of books. A library was all I had time to think before my eyes fell on the long-haired, blonde person seated on one of the many overstuffed chairs in the room, an open book in their lap. A young female elf, I realized with a start as I stood frozen in the threshold and stared while her green eyes blinked over at me in surprise. She was incredibly beautiful, her features much narrower than a human woman's but delicate and perfectly proportioned as if they had been sculpted by one of the Renaissance masters.

With something akin to panic, I wondered if this ethereal girl was the queen. She looked a lot younger than I would have thought, but she could've been a thousand years old for all I knew about the longevity of elves.

I sure as hell wasn't ready to meet Sethian's other wife, especially when I was in essence "the other woman." He had said that the queen didn't care for him at all, but that didn't mean that she would be all that happy about him bringing another woman into the household. I'm ashamed to admit that the thought of just backing out of the room and running back to hide in the bedroom crossed my mind before the elf woman smiled—and it was a genuinely friendly smile without a sharp edge to be found.

"Hello," she greeted, closing her book and placing it onto the small table beside her before standing up. "I'm sorry I wasn't there when you awoke, my lady. You must walk on cat feet as I did not hear you at all! My name is Lariel, of the family Elerdir, and I am a servant of the royal household. My Lord King has assigned me to be your lady-in-waiting."

Feeling the tension drain from my shoulders, I flashed her what I hoped was an equally friendly smile and replied, "It's nice to meet you, Lariel. I'm Emily."

I didn't give her my last name, unsure of what the proper etiquette was for introductions now that I was considered one of the king's wives. Just thinking the "w" word made me squirm inside. At that moment, I very much felt like a fish out of water. I didn't need to be from the elven realm to know that it was probably dangerous to commit a social *faux pas* even with a servant. I mentally winced. I didn't like the sound of that word at all and resolved right then and there to never call anyone a servant but to think of them as hotel staff, instead.

"Are you sure you should be up?" she asked worriedly. "His Majesty expected that you would not wake for several more marks, yet."

Her eyes fixed on my stomach for a brief moment, and I had an uncomfortable suspicion that I knew what she was worried about. The problem was that I couldn't really say she was wrong, given that I had already slept with the king twice. To make matters worse, I felt my cheeks heat up at the thought of everyone in the whole damned elven realm knowing that I had just spent the last day being screwed into the mattress by their king. I had always been a very private person, but it was beginning to look as though complete privacy would no longer be an option.

"I'm fine," I assured her quickly. Then hesitantly, "Maybe a little hungry. My—lord husband—" I almost choked on the word. "—hasn't had a chance to show me around yet. Is there a kitchen, or is there someplace specific I'm supposed to go to eat?"

Lariel inclined her head gracefully. "I will have a meal prepared and sent up. His Majesty sends his apologies, but he will not be dining with you for the midday meal. Perhaps you would like to visit the royal baths while you wait?"

Probably a good idea since I likely smelled like sex and sweat. I felt myself blush again as I nodded. Just how good was an elf's sense of smell, anyway? For all I knew, I probably reeked to high heaven, and Lariel was just too polite to say anything until now.

To my dismay, the large door I had figured earlier to be the main exit had been locked after all—and from the other side, no less. Lariel had to call out to what I presumed to be guards standing just outside to unlock the door. I decided to pretend that it didn't bother me at all. The last thing I needed to do was to start the rumor mill before I could even get the lay of the land, so to speak.

Two guards were waiting on the other side of the door, both looking as narrow-faced as Lariel, yet somehow a thousand times more alien than either her or Sethian even, though they were beautiful in their own right. However, unlike when I looked at Sethian, when I looked at them, something deep inside my psyche shivered in alarm rather than awe. I was rather relieved that after giving me a cursory glance, neither one of the guards looked at me again.

"Saeria of the family Maelenas and her younger

sister, Rinwen, will be joining us sometime past midday," the elf girl chatted as we, along with one of the door guards, walked down a series of narrow corridors that all looked identical.

They would probably be as difficult to navigate as a maze on my own—which was probably the idea, now that I thought about it. Extra security and all that. "His Majesty has also assigned them to serve as My Lady's ladies-in-waiting."

Being addressed in such an archaic way was driving home the reality of my situation, and I found my anxiety levels rising again. I was now the wife of a freaking elven king and was expected to bear his heirs. The thought of it was infinitely more terrifying in the light of day without a mind overwhelmed by mind-blowing sex.

The royal baths was an area straight out of an expensive spa brochure, all marble pools and a low-lighted ambiance made possible by several small oil lamps littered throughout the huge chamber. However, I had very little time to absorb the extravagance of the place because I finally noticed that Lariel was staring at something ahead of us—and her whole body had visibly tensed. My eyes followed her gaze, and I saw that someone with white-blonde hair was lounging in one of the smaller side pools while four female elves hovered at the edges nearby.

Looking closely, I suddenly went positively rigid when I realized that it was the face of a woman I had seen before. I *remembered.* I remembered with a clarity that was almost as shocking as it was mortifying. How could I have forgotten the incident, even for a moment?

It was *her*—the elf that had been standing in the door of Sethian's bedroom watching us while Sethian had been doing his best to screw me into oblivion. With a sinking feeling, given where she was now and that she had been able to walk into the king's bedroom, I realized there was only one person she could be.

Silently, the probable queen met my gaze, her face just as expressionless as the first time I had seen her.

CHAPTER 7

Lariel bowed and said something in a musical language that, just by its tone, must have been an apology, but I didn't need to understand her words to have my suspicions confirmed. Her bow said it all.

Unsure if I was supposed to bow, too, I decided not to do anything. If she was offended, I figured I could probably use the stupid-human-doesn't-know-anything-yet excuse and apologize later. Might as well milk my ignorance for all it was worth while I still could.

Even when Lariel had spoken, the queen didn't take her eyes off me, acting as if she hadn't even heard the young elf speak. It took everything in me to keep a neutral expression on my face and not to outright scowl at her. She was acting as snooty as I had feared, which definitely didn't bode well for me. Pissing her off here would only make matters worse.

The queen suddenly spoke sharply in what I assumed was Elvish, and two of the four elves with her hurried over to an alcove where piles of what looked like towels and other various garments were neatly folded on several rows of shelves. They returned with several of each just as the other two elf women were carefully helping their mistress out of the pool.

She then posed with her arms slightly out and raised, seemingly unconcerned about displaying her nudity to everyone in the room, while two of the elves dried her as carefully as if she were a delicate figurine that might shatter. Not that she had any reason to be concerned. Every part of her body was a masterpiece.

Through it all, I stood rooted to my spot, silent and feeling extremely awkward. Lariel also stood silently beside me. It was apparent by her worried eyes that she had no idea what to do in this situation, had probably not even expected the queen to be here, and I immediately felt a kind of kinship with her. From Sethian's earlier explanation, I figured it had probably been several hundred years, if even more, since a king might have needed to take a human wife. We were both treading unknown waters here.

And one of the biggest sharks in the ocean is heading right for us, I thought in a sudden panic as the queen, dressed in exactly the same robe I was wearing, seemed to almost glide across the marble floor until she stopped only an arm's length away from me.

This close, I could see that Sethian was right. She was extremely beautiful, but unlike Lariel's delicate beauty, the queen's beauty was utterly alien, bringing to mind power and coldness in the sharp angles of her face. There was nothing soft or delicate about her. She reminded me of a well-honed, well-crafted sword that just happened to have an exquisite jewel-encrusted hilt. It was almost as though she had been bred to be a warrior.

Sethian had said that she was of a different elven race. I wondered if the rest of her people's women shared the same sharp, warrior-like characteristics.

I was drawn out of my thoughts when I realized that the queen was examining me as well, her eyes moving critically up and down my body several times. She even tilted her head to look at me from several different angles, giving the impression that she was a judge examining the quality of an animal at a stock show.

I flashed her a small smile even though I was internally gnashing my teeth at the way she was treating us and said a short "hello." Sethian had implied that she held just as much power as he, both elves the ruling representative to their different peoples, so antagonizing the elven queen here would be worse than stupid. Hopefully, me talking to her first wasn't a social misstep or even worse, against the law.

As soon as I spoke, the neutral expression on the queen's face melted into something between a sneer and a look of disgust, making her appear even more alien. I couldn't help the shiver that ran down my spine and hated myself for being the one who had blinked first.

"So *you* are to bear our future king," she said, her eyes still doing their best to bore twin holes through my face. I wasn't altogether sure she *couldn't*. "I should not be surprised that a mongrel would choose a mongrel, but..."

I swear I could hear my spine crack, I had grown so stiff with suppressed outrage, but I merely stared back at her neutrally without a word. She was clearly trying to get a rise out of me, and damned if I would give the elf-bitch the satisfaction.

She sniffed and then uttered a few words in the musical elven language she and Lariel had spoken earlier that made Lariel suddenly twitch as she walked past me without another glance. Her ladies-in-waiting hurried after her, flashing me a few curious looks as they passed, but saying nothing.

"What did she say?" I asked my new companion once I could no longer hear the faint footsteps of the queen and her entourage.

A flash of panic showed momentarily in the elf girl's eyes before she could completely hide it. She tried to cover it up by smiling brightly and urging me towards the largest pool in the chamber with a gentle pat to my back.

"Don't worry about it, My Lady," she said airily. "The queen is still adjusting."

Translation: "The queen just called you a dirty whore; but that's only because she's jealous, and she really, *really* doesn't mean it..."

I decided not to force the issue and allowed her to lead me to the steps of the main bathing pool. While I removed my robe, she went to fetch me some soap. The pool was pleasantly warm and wasn't as deep as I had thought along the edges, coming up to just below my shoulders. A natural stone ledge beneath the water had been carved and smoothed out into a bench, allowing me to sit comfortably with my head above the waterline.

Lariel returned with the soap as I was dunking my head beneath the water in order to thoroughly soak my hair, and she immediately insisted on being allowed to wash my hair. I let her have her way without a fuss, but flat-out refused to allow her to wash anything else, telling her it was a "human" thing to allay any possible hurt feelings. Remembering how I had been washed by all those unknown elves while still blind and clueless about my fate made my skin crawl just thinking about it. I wondered if this was the pool where it had happened.

After bathing, she directed me to one of the smaller pools towards the back of the chamber just like the one the queen had been soaking in. I wasted no time in getting in, extremely uncomfortable with even walking that short distance while completely naked even if the only one to see me was Lariel. The pool was a bit hotter than the one I just left but not quite hot enough to count as a hot tub.

"Relax your body here within this pool for a time while I go alert the kitchens about having your midday meal brought to your personal rooms," she said. "If you need anything before I return, you need only call out to the guard at the entrance, and he will send one of the bath servants immediately."

Bath servants? It had never even occurred to me that there were other elves around! I quickly scanned the room, but except for us, the large chamber appeared empty. "Where—"

"Don't worry," Lariel said quickly. "They would not dare intrude on the Royal Wife unless called."

Never mind Lariel calling me "My Lady," I *really*

didn't like this newest form of address, for more than the obvious reasons. For me, titles had always seemed to dehumanize the person being called them, building walls between them and the person speaking, no matter how necessary they may seem. Lariel was certainly friendly, but as long as she insisted on calling me by honorifics, I would always be the "Royal Wife" and she the "lady-in-waiting." If the elven realm was where I would be spending the rest of my life, then I would at least want to have a few real friends.

However, now was definitely not the time to bring it up, not when I still had very little clue as to what was in store for me.

"Thank you," I said with as sincere a smile as I could muster.

Alone again, my thoughts couldn't help but wander back to the new title the young elf had just called me—Royal Wife. It reminded me once again of why Sethian had stolen me to the elven realm.

"You will bear my heirs."

A baby was utterly the *last* thing I wanted right now, especially when I was still so confused about my feelings for Sethian. We hardly knew each other, never mind what my stupid, sex-muddled brain thought of the matter. Hardly the ideal situation to raise a child, especially if my new elven husband only saw me as a baby factory, a pleasurable means to an end. The thought of the elven king only tolerating my company just for the sake of—breeding made something deep inside my core twist painfully, leaving me feeling cold despite the warmth of the surrounding water.

But then there was that weird—incident—that had happened the second time we were having sex that Sethian had yet to explain properly to me. Not that he'd really had the time to explain even if he had wanted to, I suddenly realized. We had started making love again almost right after, then—

I made a face. Then the *queen* had walked in on us and instead of saying something, gasping in shock, *anything*, she had just stood there and watched us go at it like some kind of damned voyeur! That I apparently had passed out just when I was about to say something to Sethian about her was probably no coincidence.

The only question was which of the two royals had been the culprit?

CHAPTER 8

A pair of arms abruptly slid over my shoulders from behind and hugged my neck, and I yelped in sudden shock until the familiar laugh next to my right ear had me falling completely still instead of fighting against the unexpected hold. I couldn't believe that I had been so deep in thought that I hadn't even heard him step up behind me!

My cheeks flaming in embarrassment, they got even worse when Sethian slipped into the pool beside me, and I was treated to a full-frontal sideshow of hot, wet muscles and a thick cock that was already at half-mast. My eyes frantically darted towards the entryway, afraid that Lariel had accompanied the king inside, but not a soul was in sight, not even the guard that had accompanied us here. No one would have ever accused me of being an exhibitionist back home, and it didn't take a genius to figure out why Sethian had sought me out here. I sure as hell wasn't about to prove them wrong.

My eyes turned back to Sethian with some trepidation, but other than slipping an arm around my waist and drawing me closer against his side, the elf didn't try to initiate anything sexual at all. I ruthlessly squashed the tiny part of me that was just a little bit disappointed. This was a truth that I had been better off not knowing about myself.

"You are still afraid," he said. I could hear the frown in his tone.

"I'm just unsettled," I clarified. "This has all happened so fast, and I really didn't expect to have to meet the queen so soon—"

"You met the queen?" he interrupted sharply, his eyes flashing with an emotion I couldn't quite decipher.

I nodded hesitantly, suddenly unsure if I should have told him about it at all. Even if the queen had acted like a bitch, I didn't want to make trouble for her.

"She was soaking in one of the pools when I got here."

Sethian narrowed his eyes angrily, and I suddenly wished I could go back in time and tell myself to keep my big mouth shut because the being sitting next to me was suddenly the most terrifying thing I had ever seen.

His whole body seemed to radiate *power,* and it was at that moment that I finally understood what he had meant when he told me his role as the elven king embodied much more than that of the human kings I was familiar with.

I instinctively shrank away from him, and when he saw that, he instantly clamped down on the fireworks until he no longer looked or felt so scary.

"I am sorry," he said, actually sounding contrite as he gave my body a squeeze of comfort. "It wasn't my intention to frighten you. I was merely displeased that Limira ignored what was custom. It is rare that a queen and a Royal Wife should meet, and it never should be done out of the presence of the king. Taking a human wife is a delicate enough situation, as it is often painful for the elven wife to know that her husband will have the child she could not give him with another woman."

"Is that why I keep waking up in a different bedroom than yours?" I asked.

"Yes," he said, and I suddenly felt as if I had been stabbed in the heart even though it was an answer I had expected. "Keeping both wives in separate households tempers the pain, somewhat."

I guess I shouldn't tell you about her calling both *of us mongrels,* I thought uncomfortably. Instead, I said with a bit of embarrassment, "Then she must've been pretty upset about walking in on us earlier..."

"She was told to keep her distance for the time being," he replied, sounding unapologetic, "something that she normally does on her own on any given day. She had been quite dismissive when I initially brought up the idea of me taking a human wife, as though she could not be bothered at all with it. I should have known better. Did she say anything to you?"

Crap. I really didn't want to tell him about the mongrel thing, but I also wasn't sure if Lariel would rat me out if pressed by her king. "She made a comment about me being the one to bear the next king. That's all," I lied, deciding at the last second to take a chance on a lie of omission.

The queen obviously already hated me enough as it was, so why open that explosive can of worms if I didn't absolutely have to? I could always just apologize later if caught out, anyway. I was quickly becoming the Queen of Later, it seemed.

I let out a cry of surprise as I was suddenly pulled onto his lap. The feel of both the warm water and his silky member simultaneously gliding against my naked sex as I turned to straddle him properly was utterly indecent. I grabbed onto his shoulders tightly and looked at him with wide eyes. Apparently, *that* conversation was over.

He grinned mischievously and lowered his head until his face was buried into my neck. I felt him take a deep breath through his nose before planting a soft kiss against my damp skin.

"I never knew that humans could smell so good," he murmured before taking another deep whiff of me. "Where elven women are sunlight and air, you are rain and flowers and earth. It is quite intoxicating."

He slowly slid his cheek along the skin of my collarbone, and I gasped when he playfully nipped at my shoulder.

"Do elves like to bite?" I asked a bit breathlessly even though we hadn't even kissed yet.

"This one does," he said with a growl as he lowered his head farther down and bit down a little harder into the softer flesh of my breast before moving to take my nipple into his mouth.

Sethian's tongue quickly had my already hardened nub aching almost painfully with sensory overload as I closed my eyes and began to rub myself slowly against his swelling cock, wanting to pleasure him, too. He hummed in encouragement and cupped my buttocks to pull me tighter against him, allowing for more friction as the sensual rocking of my hips automatically began to speed up to match my rising excitement.

He released my breast with a wet *pop* and roughly claimed my lips, seemingly trying to suck out all the breath from my lungs while his fingers playfully kneaded my ass cheeks. I eagerly sucked on his tongue as my thrusts against his sex became more erratic and firm.

Then his hands suddenly seized my hips, forcing me to still my movements. He lifted me up slightly from his lap and abruptly thrust his cock up into me all the way to the hilt, swallowing my sharp gasp of surprise.

I pulled away from the kiss as he began to thrust and breathed urgently, "Wait…!"

I saw concern flash briefly in his eyes as he immediately stilled, but I smiled and brushed my lips gently against his. "Let me," I said, my voice low and soft, and sounding completely unlike me.

His answering smile was so beautiful that I think I lost myself in the sheer magnitude of it for a moment, but a soft caress of his fingers against my cheek brought me back to the here and now. The elven king was making me fall hard for him, and at that point in time, I really wasn't sure if that was a good thing.

Our last coupling had been somewhat frenzied and rudely interrupted. If this incredible being was to be my one and only husband, then I wanted to take my time getting to know his body, to watch his expressions. I wanted to experience something akin to the glow of excitement a newlywed couple experienced because I didn't know how long I could have him. I didn't know how he really felt about me. That strange window to his emotions I had experienced before was conspicuously absent right now, so I only had my eyes to rely on.

Once I was pregnant, would he still want to spend time with me?

I slowly rolled my hips while impaling myself on his hard cock over and over again, forcing myself to look into his rather intense eyes before he half-closed them in an expression of pleasure and leaned over to taste my lips once again. I slipped my fingers through the hair spilling over his shoulders, following the long strands down his back and then teasingly tracing the curves and valleys of his muscles back up to his shoulders with the pads of my fingertips. He shivered, and something within me seemed to tighten with a tangle of complicated emotions.

Even at this slower, more tender pace, I came rather quickly, squeezing his member tightly in reaction to the pleasurable spasms of my orgasm and making him groan. I swallowed that sound greedily as if it were ambrosia. However, I didn't feel the expected flood of warmth from his release, and for a moment, I was upset that I hadn't managed to make him climax as I had intended. But then he suddenly stood up with his arms still wrapped tightly around me, and all thoughts fled as I hastily wrapped my legs around his waist and grabbed onto his neck to keep from sliding off both his lap and his member.

With his cock still a hot iron bar within me, Sethian waded over to the center of the pool where the water was a little deeper, reaching up to the top of his shoulders. His hands lowered down to grab my ass again, and my eyes widened at his first, powerful thrust. The water around us began to slosh and splash noisily with each forceful plunge into my tight warmth, and I threw my head back and cried out with abandon, the buoyancy of the water making me feel as if I was literally floating on cloud nine.

His huge cock seemed to reach even deeper into me in this position, hitting and rubbing against sensitive areas I had never known I possessed. Shock after shock of pleasure zipped through my body like an electric current with every thrust, making me inadvertently dig my fingernails into his back until he winced—something I would feel guilty about later when my entire being wasn't so drunk on pleasure. When I could *think*...

I soon climaxed again with a shout that I would definitely be embarrassed about later, but even at such a brutal pace, I marveled that my elven lover still hadn't been satisfied, that he still hadn't had enough of my body. He continued to plow into my passage with a rather intense look on his face as if suddenly determined to make me cry out like that again.

Even as my body was still shuddering in the aftermaths of my orgasm, a pointed ear caught my attention while Sethian sucked hard on my neck, and I couldn't resist reaching my mouth up to nip the tip.

As before, the elf jerked as if he had suddenly been tasered. The look in his eyes when he lifted his head was almost scary, his pupils so dilated with lust that only a sliver of green was still visible. The next thing I knew, Sethian was moving us over to the nearest edge of the pool. He pulled me off his cock, turned me around, and bent me over until the hard rim pressed a bit uncomfortably into my stomach, my arms splayed out in front of me.

He wasted no time in roughly thrusting back into me from behind before I could even really secure my footing, his fingers digging into my hips so strongly that I was positive I would have bruises later, and proceeded to pound into me as if he was suddenly desperate for release and had lost all reason. My fingers scrambled frantically over the slick marble trying to find something to hold onto as my body was pushed forward over and over with each deep, powerful thrust.

The elf's behavior should have scared me to death, but once again, my traitorous body decided his sudden loss of control was hot as hell, and I felt my arousal building towards an explosion for a third time. When that explosion finally did happen as Sethian gave one last, brutal thrust, I'm pretty sure I blacked out for a minute or two because the resulting spasms had gone beyond pleasure into the realm of something very close to pain. I suddenly found myself gasping for air that didn't seem to be there anymore and crying while Sethian had already withdrawn his member from me and was in the process of pulling me up and back into his arms.

I immediately turned around and buried my face into his wet chest, scrunching my eyes tightly in an attempt to stop my tears and gain control of myself. I was trembling so hard, it was almost as if the water surrounding us had abruptly turned ice cold.

His arms tightened around me. "Come," he said softly. "Let us sit and talk for a moment."

I nodded and allowed him to lead me back towards the underwater bench we had started out on.

"I apologize," he said as he cuddled me against his chest.

I had calmed down considerably now that I was sitting comfortably sideways on his lap, and with both his warm, silky arms and the warmth of the water enveloping me, I was feeling drowsy and pleasant.

I shook my head and looked up to see him frowning down at me, his eyes almost glowing in their intensity. "But it was my fault, wasn't it? Because I touched your ear?"

"It was my fault alone for not explaining the—consequences of touching them."

"But it's not like you hurt me!" I protested.

He raised an eyebrow. "You were crying," he said pointedly, his frown deepening.

"I was just—overwhelmed," I insisted, feeling my cheeks heat up in embarrassment. "Before you, I've never experienced anything close to…" I trailed off with a shrug, still shy even after everything we had done.

He sighed. "Once aroused, it is very easy for me to forget that I am bedding a human, more so if my ears are involved. A *Sidhe's* ears are extremely sensitive when we are already sexually aroused, even more so than our sexual organs. Touching my ear with your mouth was very much like taking my cock into your mouth, only doubly so. The instinct to mate becomes overpowering."

I covered my face with a moan. I *knew* I shouldn't have touched his ears.

"I'm sorry," I blurted out through my fingers.

Sethian gently pulled my hands away from my face and kissed me softly, a sweet, closed-mouth press of his lips. "You mustn't think I am angry." He grinned mischievously. "In fact, I am flattered that you find my ears so fascinating that you could not resist touching them. Limira, well, it is not something she has ever done for me."

Once again, I felt my chest tighten with a surge of jealousy. I really didn't want to think about Sethian sleeping with the queen—ever—but especially not right now after Sethian and I had just finished having the most incredible sex ever.

He sighed again, and absently rubbed his hand gently over my abdomen. "I should have been more careful. You could very well already be with child, and taking you so roughly could have endangered you both."

I stiffened, reminded once more of the very large, neon-pink elephant in the room. "Do you really think it's going to happen so soon?" I asked quietly.

"I certainly hope so," he replied, his sincerity and excitement stabbing into me like twin knives to the heart.

That he rubbed his hand affectionately across my stomach again was just the sour icing on the cake. I closed my eyes tightly, wondering for the thousandth time how my life had ended up so convoluted and out of my control.

Perhaps sensing my turmoil—maybe even quite literally—he seemed content to just sit there cuddling me in the pool. A peaceful silence fell over us, and despite all the questions I had wanted to ask from the moment I had awakened alone in that huge bed, I was content to just leave things as they were for the moment.

After all, there was always tomorrow…

CHAPTER 9

The equivalent to a human earth month later, I would have given anything to be having that unsettling conversation again.

As soon as Sethian had escorted me back to the rooms that were now essentially my new apartment, he had left to attend to his duties, leaving me to have lunch with only Lariel. Although I was more upset about it than I had wanted to admit, I was happy that I at least had Lariel to keep me company until I could see him again.

The only problem was that he *still* hadn't come back.

Lariel told me not to worry, that the king had many duties that often kept him away from the palace, that the passage of time was perceived differently by the *Sidhe,* but I was still irritated that he hadn't at least sent me a message or something to let me know that he wouldn't be back for a while. As the days turned into weeks, my irritation gradually shifted to mild anxiety, then finally to full-out worry that my initial fears of being no more than a viable womb to the elven king were only too warranted.

I struggled not to let my fears show to Lariel, instead, trying to distract myself from my growing anger—and if I were completely honest, despair. I asked her and the other two elf sisters that had arrived to serve as ladies-in-waiting a little bit after I last saw Sethian as many questions about the elven realm and its many protocols and customs as I could. They had also begun to teach me the elven language, a dialect so incomprehensible and unpronounceable to my human tongue that I despaired of ever learning it. I had never been good with languages.

It helped immensely that the three women were genuinely friendly and quite curious about the human realm in return. Otherwise, I probably would have curled up into a ball of misery after only a few days alone with only my dark thoughts and fears to keep me occupied.

Today we were having an elven version of tea out on

the balcony. After assuring me that the wind wouldn't be a problem, it had become my favorite place, other than the private garden that the king had apparently given me as a marriage gift, to visit with the elf women whom I now considered as friends. The balcony had also become a favored place to think (worry) when I was alone.

"So next year, you won't have to work *at all*?" I asked Lariel in disbelief.

She nodded seriously. "It's custom. Long ago, our families tied themselves to the fortunes of the royal family. In exchange for our service, we are allowed to set up residence within a single wing of the palace, itself. Starting at age twenty, we begin working in whatever position we have grown up preparing to fulfill."

"One year of service. One year of rest," Saeria cut in. "At least for those who serve within the royal household. The pact is different for those who wish to serve in governance or in one of the many trades."

She was the more outspoken of the two elf sisters. They looked like identical twins, but Saeria had just laughed when I had asked and said she was two hundred years older than her sister, Rinwen. The admission had floored me as the elf sisters looked to be around sixteen years old, as did Lariel. I still hadn't worked up the nerve to ask any of them their true ages. For all I knew, all of them, even Sethian who looked to be around mid-twenties at the most, could have been thousands of years old. Sethian had certainly spoken of centuries as if they were nothing.

Of course, I was going by human standards of aging. So far I hadn't met more than a handful of elves, just my ladies-in-waiting, the queen, a couple of bath attendants, and a few rotating guards—not an ideal pool to draw a comparison.

"You *wanted* to serve the king's wife?" I asked, finding the idea incomprehensible.

The three girls exchanged a confused look. "That you are human makes no difference to us," Lariel said, grabbing my hand and gently squeezing it as if to comfort me.

I shook my head and said, "That's not what I meant. I'm just trying to understand your choice of jobs. You made it sound as if you chose to be someone's lady-in-waiting as a child rather than be assigned the duty."

If anything, they looked even more confused now.

"To serve at the side of the Royal Wife, to help in the rearing of the next king and his royal siblings, is something many of us desired," she said. "His Majesty has told you about our difficulties in conceiving, yes?"

Lariel looked so sad that I suddenly felt like an idiot.

Even with my trepidation of becoming a parent in such an uncertain situation, I could completely see how heartbreaking it would be if no one were able to have children.

I nodded. "He told me an elven child hasn't been born in the realm in at least five hundred years."

"And that last child was me," Lariel said with a small smile. "Ever since my mother told me this, I have been determined to be by the side of the woman who would bring life back to our people."

Hearing that, not only did I suddenly feel like the lowest person alive, I suddenly felt the weight of an entire people crash down onto my shoulders. How had my life come to this?

"But I'm not the only human trying to conceive an elven child right now, right?" I asked, trying to keep the panic out of my voice.

"You are," Rinwen said, sounding proud. "The heir must be born first. Thereafter, one male from each elven family is chosen to take a human wife to continue the family line."

"I'm not sure how many men you're talking about," I said slowly, "but somehow I don't think a bunch of women suddenly going missing all at once in my world like I did will go unnoticed."

Lariel shook her head. "You were chosen specifically

by His Majesty, himself," she said. "That was not how it was done by our ancestors. During the last Plague of Infertility, doorways were set up throughout the human realm near most, if not all, human settlements that would allow our two races to meet in a dimensional space between our two worlds should a human woman wander inside. They were then offered a choice to join us in the realm. It is something that will happen slowly over a great length of time."

Her unexpected revelation hit me like a ton of bricks. I did not at all like the tiny surge of hope I suddenly felt that my elven husband truly did want me for me if I had been the exception to the rule. If this had happened thousands of years ago, I could very well imagine what those women thought when they saw an elf for the first time. Depending on their beliefs, they probably had mistaken them for gods. Nowadays, people would either know immediately what they were like I did thanks to popular media, or they would mistake them for aliens or maybe even angels. Either way, I didn't think it would be quite so easy to find willing human mates this time around.

"Just the fact that you are here, Emily, has our elder brother and his wife excited about the possibility of children in the near future," Saeria added. She laughed suddenly. "His wife, Irdes, has asked me every day since the night of your Consummation whether there have been any signs that His Majesty's seed has borne fruit. I haven't seen the ladies of the court this excited in quite a while."

I quickly looked down uncomfortably at my hands. While they still wouldn't come right out and ask, during the last four weeks, all three women would often drop a hint of their desire to know whether or not I thought I was pregnant here and there in seemingly unrelated topics of conversation.

"I don't think it happened this time," I said quietly. If anything, the light period I'd had over a week ago took care of the uncertainty even though I had kept it from my friends, having not been sure if I could keep my relief from my expression.

Once again, Lariel took my hands between her own. "Please don't let it worry you," she fretted. "No one thought you would conceive so soon. I suspect it will take many moon-cycles, or perhaps even years. The old texts are quite clear on that."

"Besides," Rinwen added, "your days of fertility will begin again tomorrow. Just in time for His Majesty's visit."

My head instantly shot up. "He's coming to see me tomorrow?" I said, wincing internally at the eagerness in my voice. Dammit...I really *had* fallen for him, hadn't I...

"That's what the messenger said this morning," she confirmed. "We were instructed to have dinner prepared and waiting for you two in His Majesty's personal chambers tomorrow evening. I believe he will come for you, himself."

CHAPTER 10

I was exhausted when Lariel came to wake me up the next morning, having gotten very little sleep that night out of both anticipation of seeing Sethian and nervousness. It had been so long since I had last seen him that I felt it would be like meeting a stranger. Every other time he had come to see me, we had progressed to sex fairly quickly, and I didn't want that this time. I wanted us to just hang out together for a while and just talk, maybe out on the balcony if he wasn't in the mood for a walk in the garden—something I'm ashamed to admit to daydreaming about.

Yes, I really did have it bad for the elf, but instead of being happy about it, it only made me angry at myself. I had always thought I had more common sense than to invest so much of myself into a relationship as uncertain as this one right from the beginning. Who knew that all it would take was a few kind words, a hot body, and mind-blowing sex to win me over so thoroughly?

However, I was determined not to let my traitorous body get in the way tonight. After everything the girls had told me, I had a month's worth of questions for him, and I would demand answers to at least some of them before going anywhere near a bed.

After a visit to the royal baths, I was sitting in my bedroom at the dressing table brushing out my hair and snacking on a bowl of grapes while I waited for Lariel to return with the Maelenas sisters and my breakfast when the nausea hit. It came on so suddenly and violently that I almost fell out of my chair in shock.

I clamped a hand over my mouth and an arm around my stomach and scrambled towards the *en suite* bathroom, whose door I had thankfully left open. I barely made it in time to drop to my knees in front of the elven version of a toilet—what amounted to a marble aqueduct of perpetually flowing water that spanned the entire length of one of the walls in which a person would squat or hover over to do their business. I then proceeded to spew everything I had just eaten and then some until my throat was raw and I was reduced to dry heaves.

Once I was sure my stomach was finished rebelling,

it took every ounce of the meager strength I had left to keep from falling face-first into the water stream and pull away to lean my back against the cool marble instead.

I looked over and up to the ledge against an adjacent wall where a pitcher of water sat. As awful and weak as I felt, it might as well have been miles away rather than a few feet, but if I didn't rinse the sour taste of bile from my mouth soon, I feared I would start to dry heave again.

Yet, what I really wanted to do was curl up into a miserable ball and cry because even though there were several different explanations for my sudden sickness, I knew damned well which one was correct.

"In contrast, humans are exceedingly fertile."

Sethian's words echoed through my mind almost mockingly as I wrapped my arms around myself in an effort to control my sudden shaking. Sethian would be ecstatic. My friends would be ecstatic. The entire elven realm would probably be ecstatic, but the only thing I could feel in that moment of realization was complete panic.

Despite all the previous signs that had pointed to the contrary, I was probably pregnant, and all I could think was, *Sethian can't know!*

My husband was finally coming to see me tonight

after being gone and out of touch for a whole freaking month, and fate had chosen *today* of all days to drive me to my knees with morning sickness! Once Rinwen had told me about Sethian coming, deep down I had figured the timing of his visit corresponding with the start of my ovulation cycle wasn't coincidental at all. Once he found out that I was probably pregnant, would he even have a reason to visit me except maybe to occasionally check on the progress of the pregnancy?

I had to stop shaking and wallowing in misery on the floor. Lariel would be back any minute now with everyone, and there was no way I could let them find me like this. They would know immediately what was "wrong" with me, and nothing short of the end of the world would keep them from running immediately to their king with the glorious news.

I needed time—time to sort out my feelings about having a child in the first place, something I had been spending the last few weeks trying *not* to think about at all, which, given my current predicament, was about the stupidest thing I had done since our "wedding" night. I needed time to talk with Sethian and figure out what kind of relationship he wanted with me. Now that my pregnancy was all but confirmed, things would definitely have to change, the first being that the elf-king couldn't just leave me here waiting without a single word until he either got an itch for sex or I was fertile. There was no damned way I was just going to sit in this royal apartment and spit out babies for him like a damned machine.

Maybe it was because I hadn't been in Sethian's overwhelming presence for so long or the panic of realizing I could very well be carrying an elven child within me, but for the first time in a long while, my mind felt clear and wide awake. For the past month, I had lived my life as if I were moving within a dream, accepting things as they had come along without thinking too hard about them, if at all, but now I was determined to never let myself fall into that deceptive spell ever again.

If I was going to bring a child into this world, then dammit, it was going to be a *family* effort! And the only way I had a chance of making that happen was to work on establishing a deeper relationship with my *husband* other than as his occasional bed-warmer.

An image of the queen's sneering face flashed into my mind, and I scowled. If that was the way she acted with Sethian, then maybe my goal wouldn't be as difficult as climbing Mt. Everest in the middle of winter.

No—I just have to get through tonight without ever letting on how sick I'm feeling, I thought in despair.

It would have to be an Oscar-worthy performance, and unfortunately, I was never a good actress at the best of times. Having to *eat dinner* with him with a queasy stomach would be absolute torture!

Even so, I needed to talk with him without a baby clouding the issue. I didn't want to ever feel as though he was just humoring me because he didn't want me upset for the baby's sake. That would be infinitely worse than completely ignoring me. I didn't want one of the most important relationships of my life to be a lie.

But first things first—I had to get off the damn floor before Lariel and the others could find me!

Just climbing to my knees almost had me hurling again, but I just gritted my teeth, and using the marble ledge of the toilet/aqueduct as a crutch, climbed back onto my feet with a stubbornness I had only exhibited a handful of times in my life. Don't cry when the schoolyard bullies pull on your double braids as if they were reigning in a horse; don't cry at your mother's funeral or you may never stop; don't hurl just because an elven king knocked you up and you now have a little morning sickness…

Once on my feet, my nausea subsided enough that I felt I could walk over to the pitcher of water across the room without sending me running to the aqueduct again. Finally being able to rinse out my mouth also improved my level of nausea to where I felt I might just be able to ignore it and act fairly normal after all. The only problem would be the breakfast I would be expected to eat in a few minutes.

I frowned thoughtfully. Maybe being forced to eat breakfast wouldn't be the tragedy it seemed. If I became queasy again, then maybe I could convince them that it was just nerves and that I had no appetite as a result. Lariel had remarked before that I always seemed to be in a perpetual state of anxiety and that she wished I would relax more, so there was definitely a precedent established.

If anything, it would at least give me the practice I needed before my dinner date because if I couldn't manage to fool my ladies-in-waiting, then there was no way in hell I would be able to fool Sethian. I knew better than to hope that my nausea would subside by this evening; life had never granted me any favors, and I really doubted it would start now at the moment when I really *really* needed a favor.

I splashed some cool water over my face, hoping it would add a little color to my undoubtedly pale face before I carefully left the bathroom and headed back to my dressing table. It was a relief to be sitting down again as my stomach decided to give another unpleasant lurch at that moment as if to remind me who really was the one in charge. After taking several deep, shuddering breaths to keep the dry heaving at bay, I pushed aside my bowl of grapes as far from my sight as possible and grabbed my hand mirror.

Did my complexion still look a little green? Were my eyes dull or a little too bright? In the low light of a single lamp in my windowless bedroom, I couldn't really tell. Maybe I could pass off looking a little sickly as nerves, too. Thank God Lariel had already seen me before I had puked my guts up. If I had gotten sick during the night, there would have been no hiding it from her, no passing it off as nerves. I swear elf ears could hear a pin drop ten miles away…

"I can do this," I muttered to my reflection, but I didn't look very convinced.

The front door to my apartment suddenly clicked open, and I instantly went rigid. Unfortunately, the sudden rush of adrenaline instantly triggered a humongous cramp in my stomach, and I very nearly lost it again as I doubled over momentarily before I could stop myself.

A wash of female chatter that was distressingly close made it past the thundering sound of my own panicked heartbeat in my ears. I only had seconds to pull myself together!

I can't let him find out.

I can't let him find out.

I can't let him find out...

CHAPTER 11

The three elven women found me sitting stiffly at my dressing table, a brush in hand and staring off into space as though deep in thought when the truth was my performance had already begun. It was only sheer will that was keeping my nausea down to a manageable level at this point. I knew there was no way I would be able to eat breakfast without puking right now, so rather than force myself to try, I needed to show them my very real anxiety of meeting Sethian again after such a long absence.

The best lies were the half-truths we told.

One of them placed a hesitant hand on my shoulder, and I purposely jumped a little before slowly turning to face them.

"Is everything all right, Emily?" Lariel asked, a slight frown already beginning to stretch her lips.

I nodded and gave her a tiny smile. "It's nothing. I'm just being silly, really."

"About…?" Rinwen prodded, her eyes briefly darting to first my hands, then to my midsection.

I cringed inside. She always did that whenever the subject of my imminent pregnancy came up. It was as though she expected me to inadvertently give my pregnancy status away by cradling my belly or rubbing it or something. I was beginning to suspect that she was even more excited about the prospect of a royal baby than even the baby-obsessed Lariel.

"About seeing my lord husband again," I replied with a sheepish shrug. "I haven't seen him in so long, so…" I looked down with what I hoped was a shy expression and shrugged again.

"Ah," Saeria said sagely. "It's easy to forget that you are still very young, even by human standards. Come. You will feel better after you have eaten something."

The mere mention of food made my stomach turn, and I quickly shook my head. "I tried eating some grapes earlier, but I really don't have an appetite this morning. Let's just have some tea and chat out on the balcony. I could use some fresh air."

"Are you sure you are all right?" Rinwen persisted. Was that suspicion in her eyes? "Your face looks a little pale this morning..."

My throat tightened briefly in panic. Why was it always the quiet ones who caused all the trouble?

"If you are not feeling well, just tell us," Lariel added, a grin suddenly threatening to split her face in two even as her eyes lit up as if the sun had just risen within them. "Don't feel as though you have to keep quiet until you see His Majesty this evening. I promise we won't tell him that you told us first. He probably even expects it."

For a split-second, I stared back at Lariel in shock before I covered my face in my hands with a groan and exclaimed through my fingers, "It's not what you think! I'm just—" My mind was suddenly coming up quite empty on excuses, nearly causing me to have a full-blown anxiety attack right then and there until one thankfully popped into my head before my pause could become too awkward. "—just *scared* to see him again!"

"Scared?" Lariel echoed, sounding utterly surprised as she gently, but firmly pulled my hands away from my face. She kneeled down before me and squeezed my hands between her own. "Whatever is there to be scared about?"

"That he's changed his mind about me," I blurted out

in my panic and wished at once I could take it back. That was one truth I had never wanted anyone to know, least of all the three women before me.

Lariel sucked in a sharp breath. "Why would he do that?"

"I'm just an ordinary human," I answered miserably.

If I was going to stick my foot in my mouth, might as well swallow the whole leg and be done with it. The way my stomach was churning right now with more than just morning sickness, I would probably just puke it up later, anyway.

"I can't for the life of me understand why an elven king chose *me* out of billions of other human women to have his children. What if the reason why he's stayed away for so long is that he's having second thoughts about me?"

"But he hasn't been away overly long at all," Lariel insisted. "Oh, you poor thing! You should have told us you still had these fears sooner. It's no wonder you have no appetite; you have worried yourself sick!" The concern in her eyes abruptly melted into sadness. "My earlier misunderstanding must have been terribly troubling, as well. Forgive me. It was never our intention to put so much pressure on you concerning a royal heir."

If I wasn't already feeling so ill, then her words

would have definitely made me feel sick to my stomach with guilt. At that moment, I wanted to tell them I thought I was pregnant so badly. It would have been such a relief, but in the end I just couldn't do it. I trusted that Lariel had meant every word of her promise not to tell Sethian that I had told them about my pregnancy, but what I couldn't trust was their ability to lie to their king if he flat-out asked them.

Even though I had only lived within the elven realm for about a month, the information I had absorbed from my many discussions with the three elven women made me understand that the king's word really was law in the strictest sense of the word. I was already acting selfishly as it was; I wasn't about to endanger the lives of my only friends for something as petty as easing the guilt I was feeling. The guilt I *should* be feeling.

I needed to keep this secret for as long as possible. The performance *had* to continue…

"You haven't," I assured them. "This is just me being stupid, I guess."

"We just haven't explained things well enough," Saeria said firmly. She reached down and tugged on my arm. "Come. You need fresh air and sunshine. We cannot let His Majesty see you so pale and distraught."

I grimaced. "Yeah, I don't want him getting mad at

any of you because of something that's totally my fault." I considered the state of my stomach, what standing would do to it, and then added tentatively, "You might need to help me up. My stomach's so tied in knots right now that I'm not sure I can do it without making it worse. The last thing I want to do is puke all over the floor."

Even with both Lariel and Saeria's help, the moment I stood, my stomach cramped badly, and I very nearly started to retch again. Only the fact that both women were supporting the majority of my weight saved me from that indignity as it allowed me to completely concentrate on controlling the urge to gag. The smart thing would have been to just have them rush me to the bathroom and just be done with it now that I had given them a very good reason for being nauseous, but once my stubbornness kicked in, it was as though all my good sense took a vacation.

"You need to practice" my mind kept telling me, and like an idiot, I listened.

"I'm—okay," I said after a long pause, opening my eyes to three nearly identical skeptical expressions. What they must think of the weak human now…

"Perhaps it would be better for you to just return to bed," Saeria said. "I know so little about the intricacies of human illness. It has been centuries since a human was last brought to the realm. Thus the study of them by our healers has only just resumed in response to His Majesty's decree that human women may once again be invited here after an heir is born."

Curling up in a warm bed sounded heavenly at the moment, but I knew I would just fall back asleep. Lariel would probably let me sleep until this evening, and the last thing I needed to be was groggy *and* sick when I was with Sethian.

I managed a tiny smile. "Talking with all of you over a cup of tea never fails to calm my nerves. If I go back to bed, I'll just worry myself sick again with a bunch of 'what ifs.' Besides, I really want to be able to greet my lord properly in Elvish when I see him tonight, and we all know that my accent is still awful!"

Lariel laughed. "I don't think he will mind it as much as you seem to think."

"Even so, I don't want to embarrass myself," I insisted as we moved as three slowly towards the door, Rinwen a silent shadow at our backs.

I felt the tension in my shoulders start to relax as I listened to my friends chat about a mishap involving spilled water on the floor and a ladle Rinwen had just witnessed in the kitchen that had even me giggling halfhardily after a while. One minefield evaded, but with a sense of bone-deep weariness, I knew better than to think the next one would have such a good outcome.

After all, my life had always been filled with half-empty glasses.

CHAPTER 12

By the time the sky started to darken, I was once again a ball of nerves despite my friends' best efforts to keep me relaxed and laughing all day. Although my nausea had thankfully subsided to a much more manageable level, it was still very much present, a bomb with a tripwire nestled in the pit of my stomach just waiting for me to make the wrong move. As such, I was glad to hand over hair duty to Lariel and Rinwen for once, not even protesting when they wanted to pin my hair back in an elaborate style they said was currently popular within the court in preparation for my evening with Sethian.

I was holding my hand mirror up, staring at my reflection in a bit of fascination as the two women twisted and folded sections of my hair elegantly around several silver hairpins when Sethian abruptly appeared in the mirror behind us as if some kind of ghost. I was so startled that I dropped the mirror, the sound of it hitting the floor preternaturally loud even over the girls' chatter.

My stomach heaved unpleasantly as I turned sharply to look over Lariel's shoulder, half-expecting to see nothing but air, but there the elven king stood in what was probably his full royal regalia of a delicate, almost insubstantial silver crown that seemed composed of little more than light and layered, silver and navy-blue robes that made him look twice as wide. He met my gaze with a slight smile of amusement, the bastard—as though he hadn't even been gone for a *whole freaking month*!

"Visitors usually come through the front door," I found myself saying almost sternly as I tried to calm my suddenly racing heart without letting any of my distress show on my face. I was dangerously close to tripping the wire, and damned if I was going to lose the game *now* after everything I had already been through that day.

No, not a game, I thought in something like despair as I was struck once again by his too-unbelievable-to-be-real beauty just as powerfully as I had been on that first night.

This was the rest of my life.

If anything, Sethian's smile widened at my words. "It seems I caught everyone unawares," he said, nodding to both Lariel and Rinwen, who in turn, bowed deeply and stepped away from me in order to fade into the background. "I thought perhaps we could take a short walk through the garden before dinner."

My heart clenched. Not for the first time, I wondered if Sethian could really read my mind. It was either that, or I was so hopelessly transparent that I might as well have been shouting out my deepest thoughts to him every time I looked at him. Either way, it didn't bode well for me making it through the rest of the day with my humongous secret intact. In fact, it could very well be the reason why he had suggested the walk in the first place—giving me the chance to tell him away from gossiping ears.

My thoughts briefly turned to the conspicuously absent Saeria in sudden suspicion. She had left a bit earlier to, in her words, "oversee" the dinner preparations. At the time, I hadn't thought much of it, figuring she was just trying to help me and my nerves out by making sure at least the dinner part of the evening would go off without a hitch. One less thing for the nervous Royal Wife to worry about. What if she had gone to Sethian, instead, and told him, if not everyone's suspicions about the real reason I was nauseous, then at least their concerns about the cause of my sudden illness?

If everything I had endured up until now turned out to be for nothing, then maybe I should have just gone back to bed and refused to come out of my room at all, never mind what the king wanted.

Even so… "A walk sounds great," I said with as much of a genuine smile as I could muster.

If the king of the elves wanted to fulfill one of my more cheesy fantasies of a "romantic walk," then I wasn't about to say no. Maybe this time we would actually get to really talk about things. By now, my list of questions for him had grown into the thousands. At the very least, talking would help to keep my mind off my queasy stomach, and who knows? Maybe I would actually get a better feel for his true feelings about me, and I would be able to confess that I thought I was pregnant.

Sethian offered me his hand, and I rose with some trepidation, relieved beyond measure that my stomach took pity on me and decided to behave. Also, Sethian's touch always seemed to have a calming effect on me, and thankfully, this time was no different. A rush of warmth washed through my body the moment he clasped my hand tightly, easing my upset stomach until I could barely feel any discomfort at all, and I knew then that he was indeed using his elven magic or whatever it was on me.

However, that fact only served to make me even more suspicious of how much he actually knew about everything. Memories of that strange incident that Sethian had been reluctant to talk about when we had seemed to physically share each other's emotions once again flashed through my head, and I wondered if we were still connected in that way and if Sethian could still sense what I was feeling.

Giving my hand a squeeze, he turned to Lariel and Rinwen and said, "You both may take your leave for the rest of the day. I will call for you in the morning."

And damned if I didn't blush and my pulse start to race when he said that. He may not have meant anything by that, but my attention-starved body suddenly tightened in anticipation.

My friends bowed to him again, then a second time to *me* to my dismay, and swiftly left the room. I now found myself alone with my husband for the first time in a month. Suddenly feeling painfully shy, I started to lower my head, but Sethian would have none of that. He pulled me into a tight embrace and planted a soft, though lingering, kiss onto my slightly-parted lips.

He pulled back and raised a hand to my cheek, gently rubbing his thumb back and forth across my skin.

"You have a little color in your face now," he said with satisfaction. "You were as pale as a silvery moon when I first arrived."

"I didn't sleep well last night," I admitted. The best lies were half-truths...

He tilted my head up and looked at me with a critical eye. "You are unwell," he said after a long pause. It wasn't a question.

It really was a miracle that I didn't flinch. Here it was. The moment of truth. He clearly knew something was up with me. Should I continue this farce, or just admit defeat and let the chips fall where they may?

"I'm okay," I heard myself say as if I were listening to our conversation from another room.

No—I couldn't lose my resolve here, not when I didn't know anything for sure.

When Sethian continued to stare down at me, his expression unchanged, I hastily added, "I was anxious to see you. We haven't really had much of a chance to talk since our wedding night, and I guess—I—got overly worked up about it since yesterday when Rinwen told me you would be coming. There's so much I want to talk with you about—"

The crush of his lips abruptly cut me off, and just like that, every one of my thoughts and worries disintegrated as my head suddenly began to spin as though I were extremely buzzed. His tongue slid almost lazily against mine, coaxing it into a sensuous dance, and my mind fuzzed out even further. I moaned and pressed myself harder against his body, clutching a fistful of his elaborate robes tightly as a feeling very much like relief washed through my entire being.

I was finally where I belonged.

I don't even remember shutting my eyes, just that the darkness I now found myself within had become a little less dark and the air surrounding us slightly cooler. Sethian pulled away with another soft caress of my cheek with his fingers, and I opened my eyes to the exquisite sight of the elven king against a backdrop of several flowering trees of lavender, pink, and cream-colored blossoms and the setting sun.

I knew this scene well; I had imagined it hundreds of times over the past month. He had magicked us to my garden and inadvertently fulfilled another of my cheesy wishes. My chest tightened with emotions I rarely allowed myself to feel at the beauty of the moment, then Sethian spoke, and his words made my heart skip a beat with something other than admiration.

"No one will overhear us here," he said. "Speak as freely as you wish."

Blunt and to the point. Unfortunately, I was still feeling the dizzying aftereffects of his hello kiss, and that frankness only served to completely fluster me. His earlier touch may have eased my nausea, but my nerves were certainly doing a good job of resurrecting that hateful churning in my stomach.

Suddenly unable to face the intensity of his gaze, I buried my face into his chest before I mumbled the Elvish "welcome back" phrase I had been practicing with the girls, stalling for time. It sounded as atrocious as I had feared. No matter how hard I practiced, I just simply could not duplicate the smooth cadence of a language that seemed to be composed of mostly vowels and sighs of breath.

"*I am here,*" came the custom reply in Elvish, definite amusement in his tone.

Yes, but for how long? I thought dejectedly. That thought was enough to clear out the lingering haze blanketing my mind.

I looked up into his dancing eyes with a new determination and said, "Let's walk for a bit. I have some questions…"

Sethian nodded and released me from his arms. Before I could chicken out, I boldly grabbed one of his hands and pulled him after me as I started to walk in the direction of a pond deep within the garden. There were a couple of stone benches situated along the water's edge that would be ideal for the *long* conversation I intended us to have.

Dinner could wait.

CHAPTER 13

"Do you do that often—visit all the different provinces one right after the other?" I asked as we sat side-by-side, not on a marble bench as I had originally intended, but on the slightly-damp grass just a couple of steps from the edge of the pond.

Upon reaching the pond, when I had tried to sit down on the bench, Sethian had squeezed my hand sharply, shaking his head when I had looked back at him quizzically. He had made a face at the ornately-carved bench and had suggested that sitting in the grass before the pond would be much more comfortable.

So far I had kept the conversation on safe subjects, mostly on his everyday duties as king as well as everything he had been doing for the past month. He even seemed to enjoy talking about them, never once giving me the impression that my barrage of questions was becoming tiresome. Although his answers helped me understand more about his standing in the elven realm, it told me very little of the man, himself. We had been talking for at least an elven mark—equivalent to around an hour and a half according to Saeria—and I still hadn't figured out how to ask him the questions I really needed the answers to.

Sethian nodded, his thumb absently stroking the back of my hand. "At least once a year. I like to see the state of my lands and people with my own eyes and not through the mouths of the stewards of those lands as often as possible."

I was still upset from learning that he had returned from making the rounds of his kingdom yesterday. It was a struggle to keep my expression neutral as we talked. He had mentioned it so offhandedly earlier, as if it wasn't a big deal, that I couldn't bring myself to ask him why he had waited until today to see me.

Although he hadn't mentioned specifics, I figured that if he had left soon after the last time we had parted, the entire trip had taken him about three weeks or so, even by elvensteed. The kingdom was a lot bigger than I had imagined.

Lariel had told me that the elves had brought over

horses from the human realm a few thousand years ago and had used their magic to change them into a creature that was almost unrecognizable as such. Her description was of something opaque, fast, and highly intelligent. They were the main mode of transportation within the elven realm.

When I had asked why they didn't just bring a few cars over instead, all three women had heartily laughed as if it was the most ridiculous thing they had heard from me, yet, and had said that those types of metals and materials were incompatible with the natural laws of the elven realm.

Lariel had promised that everyone would take me out riding as soon as Sethian returned and they could ask for permission. Remembering how I was locked within my apartment, the thought of having to ask my husband for *permission* to do *anything* that required the guards to unlock the door was grating, to say the least. Yet another issue I really needed to bring up but had no idea how without sounding accusative.

"But enough about me," Sethian said. "You have yet to tell me how you have fared these past few days while I was away. You did say something about not sleeping..."

"It was just last night," I assured him. "I usually have no problem nodding off as I'm sure Saeria will be happy to tell you. They've been teaching me your language, customs, and history. There are a lot of things they talked about that I would like to see—the cities beyond the castle, the elvensteed, even just the countryside." I hesitated briefly, then continued determinedly, "I would like to see these things together with you."

He blinked in what looked like surprise. "If that is what you wish, then I would very much enjoy showing you around the realm. Perhaps when you are a bit more rested, and your cheeks are not so pale."

Although I was looking directly at his face, I couldn't tell by Sethian's expression whether he was hinting at something more by bringing up my state of being, or just genuinely concerned that I might be coming down with something. Lariel had told me that although elves rarely got sick, viral and bacterial illnesses occasionally popped up here and there. They seemed to think that the possibility was doubly likely for the sole human in their midst, whom they rather matter-of-factly considered much more fragile than an elf in every way.

"I've never ridden a horse before, so you'll have to teach me," I said, steering the conversation away from my health.

It was a small miracle that I could even ignore my health at all right now, but as long as Sethian held my hand and was concerned about keeping me calm and relaxed, I knew that my nausea would be kept at bay.

Sitting here with the elven king had so far been exponentially easier than I had ever thought possible back when I was still redirecting my friends' suspicions while my stomach and head rebelled. I hadn't gotten even close to all the answers I needed before I felt I could confess to my probable pregnancy, but for the first time, I started to think that things might not be so hopeless after all.

Sethian grinned, an expression that gave him a more boyish look that instantly made me want to melt. "Then you will have no problem as an elvensteed is not a horse. Although unable to speak, they understand our language completely. You need only tell them your desires, and they will accommodate you."

"Really?" I said in disbelief. Lariel had not mentioned that part at all! "That's amazing! Oh, but would they understand *me*? Right now I only know a few words and phrases in Elvish…"

"For now, I shall speak for you. I suspect you will be proficient enough in Elvish to direct them yourself within a few moon-cycles."

I looked down at our joined hands in embarrassment. "I wouldn't count on that. I'm not very good at learning languages and even worse at pronouncing them—and don't tell me that garbled mess of a welcome I gave you earlier was anywhere near good enough!

Even the elvensteeds would laugh at my horrendous accent!"

He chuckled, then released my hand and drew me into a tight embrace. He kissed my nose playfully and said, "I think your accent is cute. Perhaps you shouldn't try so hard to correct it."

Hearing an elven king say the word "cute" sounded all kinds of wrong somehow. I let my head fall forward onto his chest and closed my eyes, unsuccessfully trying to will away the heat that had invaded my cheeks.

"It's not fair," I muttered into the silky fabric of his robes. "Why is it that you, Lariel, Saeria, Rinwen, hell, even the guards outside my door, can speak English with virtually no accent *at all*?"

I felt Sethian kiss the top of my head. "It's not the great feat you are imagining," he replied. "We have just had a few centuries more of practice."

"Centuries—you say that as if you're just talking about a few days or something. Just—how old *are* you?"

"By elven standards, I am still fairly young, a little over two thousand years. My father was nearing his ten thousandth year when he died. I have been on the throne for less than five hundred years so you can say that I am a young king as well."

Two thousand, ten thousand...compared to them I was practically an embryo! The life of a human was literally just a blink of an eye for the *Sidhe*. How in the world had I ever thought we could have a more deeply connected relationship when my life was practically a third of the way over? My bones would be dust before Sethian even hit middle age!

I must have stiffened or given him some other sign of my sudden distress because his arms abruptly tightened around my body and he said, “It wasn’t my intention to upset you.”

I shook my head and ruthlessly stamped down the despair that had started to engulf me. Now was definitely not the time for me to start blubbering. Given everything that had happened to me already—the shock of a sudden pregnancy, then having to hide such a violent case of morning sickness from everyone—I would likely cry straight through the night, and then it really would be impossible to keep my secret. Sethian would either guess the reason for my emotional upheaval or send me to a healer who wouldn’t need longer than a few minutes of examination to learn the truth.

I forced myself to look up at him and smile. “You didn’t. It was just shocking to hear,” I said. “To live thousands of years…it’s pretty unimaginable to a human. I can’t even begin to wrap my head around what that would be like. I bet your head is a treasure trove of sights and experiences."

A strange look flashed across Sethian's face before he blinked, and his lips lifted slightly at the corners, transforming his face before I could decipher this new expression. "You like bedtime stories?"

My own smile widened, pretty sure that he was baiting me. "Sometimes." My pulse sped up as I added boldly, "But not tonight."

Then my heart skipped a beat when his eyes instantly sharpened, and his large pupils dilated in unmistakable desire. Maybe I wouldn't have to worry about eating dinner after all...

"We should go," Sethian said softly, but he made no move to stand.

This time I wasn't surprised when the world around me blurred, and we were suddenly sitting on the rug before the already blazing fireplace in Sethian's bedroom. I totally expected him to scoop me up and head for the bed, so when he loosened his hold on me and grabbed my upper arms, I was understandably confused when he merely stood, tugging me up with him, and then stepped away.

"We have the entire night ahead of us," he said, raising a hand to remove his crown. "For now, let us enjoy a meal together. Go on ahead to the dining room while I change out of my formal robes."

I nodded and left without comment. Once I closed his bedroom door behind me, I took in the unfamiliar sitting room before me and realized that this was the first time I had been in any other room in his personal quarters besides his bedroom. The layout and furnishings were similar to mine except being the room of a king, I wasn't surprised that everything from the paintings to the rugs on the floor was much more expertly crafted and beautiful than the ones in my apartment.

Figuring that the layout of his rooms was also similar, I headed to the door on the far left in search of his dining room. The room on the other side was just as large as the sitting room, furnished with a single long, wooden table in the center that could seat up to sixteen people comfortably. Several covered dishes were already spread out and waiting at the head of the table.

My eyes swept the room, half-expecting at least one of the king's staff to be awaiting our arrival, but the room was thankfully empty. A month living in an elven palace, and I still hadn't gotten used to having several of the royal staff hovering around me while I ate with the girls. It was unnerving having all those eyes watching my every move.

I sat down at the end of the row, leaving the head for Sethian, and eyed the covered dishes warily. Even though Sethian was no longer touching me, my earlier nausea had not returned. I knew better than to hope it remained so. I supposed I should have felt grateful that the elven diet involved very little meat, but I wondered if that first bite would be the thing that ultimately triggered the bomb just waiting to explode in my stomach.

I was relieved to see that the kitchen staff had left both a decanter of wine and a pitcher of water. No doubt I had Saeria to thank for that as I had luckily established from the very beginning that I preferred water over wine. I was only an occasional drinker back home, and even though having wine for breakfast, lunch, and dinner was the norm here, that was one elven custom I didn't plan on adopting.

I quickly poured myself a glass of water and sipped at it nervously as I listened for any approaching footsteps. I was definitely beginning to regret not continuing to entice Sethian to forget all about dinner while I'd had the chance.

CHAPTER 14

When Sethian finally appeared a few minutes later dressed in a simple tunic and trews, the first tinges of queasiness were already starting to rise within my body, and I was on the verge of a full-on panic attack. I knew logically that I was making it worse by freaking out about it, but I just couldn't seem to calm down. Sethian couldn't have walked in at a worse moment.

There was no way I could eat now. What was I going to do? I couldn't just give up now and spill everything to him, not when our relationship was still so murky. He had shown interest in spending time with me that actually required us to be dressed, yes, but that hardly said anything about what he thought of me personally.

"You have gone pale again," he remarked as he took his seat at the head of the table, regarding me with a concerned frown.

Thinking frantically, I made a big show of covering my face as if I were embarrassed in order to stall for time. "I was just thinking…" I said, my voice muffled.

"About?" I could see him tilt his head curiously from the openings between my fingers.

About not puking all over the table, I thought a bit hysterically. "I just—"

A loud knock abruptly sounded on the dining room door, making me practically jump out of my skin.

"*My apologies for interrupting your meal, Your Majesty, but I have a message from the queen,*" a male voice called through the door in Elvish. I was pretty surprised that I actually understood almost all his words.

"*Enter,*" Sethian commanded, and a male elf I didn't recognize stepped through the door. He headed straight for Sethian and after glancing at me briefly, bent to whisper his message into the king's ear.

I watched as Sethian's face suddenly became as expressionless as a marble statue's. Whatever the message was, it couldn't have been good. When the messenger straightened, Sethian waved him away without a word.

Once we were alone again, he turned to me with that same unnerving blankness and said, "It seems a matter has come up with Limira that I must attend to right away." Hearing that name was like a slap in the face, and it took every ounce of stubbornness within me to keep the dismay from showing on my face. "Have dinner without me, and retire for the night, as I may not return for some time."

He reached over and softly caressed my cheek. "Perhaps a bit of rest will bring some color back to your cheeks. We shall talk more then."

I was suddenly overwhelmed with a mad desire to grab his arm, to beg him not to leave me. I was utterly shocked at the power behind that desperation, and in the end, that shock was what saved me from doing something so embarrassingly stupid.

Therefore, instead of clinging to him like a limpet, I managed to nod and say, "I hope it's nothing serious."

"It's not," Sethian said with a finality that immediately gave me the opposite impression. However, I knew better than to call him out on it.

"I shall return soon," he said as he rose from the table.

Yeah, but your "soon" may not mean the same as mine, I thought as my eyes followed him across the room and out the door. Would he make me wait another month to see him again? Two?

As soon as I heard the front door open and close, I pushed away from the table and stood. There was no sense in me remaining if I wasn't going to eat. As awful as I was feeling at the moment, and not just physically, I decided that it would probably be best to just go to bed.

Having none of my nightclothes available, I stripped to just my slip and tried to make myself comfortable on Sethian's enormous bed. For a long moment, I lay on my back and stared up at the exposed beams of the ceiling while I tried to will my returning nausea away and my mind raced.

Although the messenger's unexpected arrival had saved me from the corner I had inadvertently backed myself into, it brought with it a problem that was perhaps equally troubling. For all his talk about the queen not caring much for him, she sure seemed to intrude a lot in the few conversations we've had so far—or just flat-out intrude as I thought back to the mortifying incident of her walking in on us while we were having sex.

Maybe she *did* care more about him than Sethian thought, but that really wasn't what had my chest tightening in distress. I realized that Sethian had not said one word regarding his feelings for the queen. For all I knew, he was deeply in love with her and was pining after her just as much as I was starting to yearn for him. After all, he'd had centuries to develop his relationship with her, and I was virtually a stranger to him.

I turned on my side and curled into a fetal position, wrapping my arms around myself in sudden anguish. Who was I kidding? There was no way Sethian could give me what I wanted from him in such a short time. That he rushed off the moment the queen had beckoned told me this clearly. No matter that I was the one who would be the mother of his children, I would always be secondary to his duty to his first wife. I was only a human, after all.

What place did a human have in an elven court?

It was only when I felt the damp trails falling down my cheeks that I realized that I was crying, and I curled up tighter into a ball of misery and silent tears, trying to keep the sobs that were now building in my throat at bay. I didn't want the elves outside the door with their radar ears to hear me and tattle to the king that I had been crying. The last thing I needed right now was to be confronted about yet another thing I couldn't possibly explain nor wanted to even talk about. Telling him about the baby would be hard enough.

With a start, I realized that this was the first time I had even thought the word "baby" since I had ended up on my knees heaving into the aqueduct. It brought home the fact that there was a life growing inside me; this was no longer just about me.

Babies were something I had never given much thought. Motherhood was a far-off concept that hadn't even registered on my radar yet. For the past few years, the only thing I had cared about was finishing my PhD to the point that dating had even fallen to the wayside. Now suddenly I was about to be a mother to a child that I might not understand, and I was terrified.

I covered my mouth as a small sob broke free. It was at that moment I knew that, no matter what, I wouldn't tell Sethian about the baby. No—not for a while. I needed my husband to keep coming to me, to comfort me, to kiss me, to hold me in his arms. I needed him to be my pillar until I could come to terms with the crazy path my life had taken and stand on my own two feet.

I had chosen this for myself, after all. After everything Lariel, Saeria, and Rinwen had told me regarding the distant past when elves had taken human brides, I truly believed that Sethian would have allowed me to return home if I had cried and pleaded with him after that first night. I had chosen the *hope* of finally not being alone over the certainty. I had given up everything I had worked so hard for just for that slim hope.

I now had to lie in the bed I had made and somehow convince my husband that he wanted to be there as well —because *I* was there. The thought only made me cry harder.

I doubted that I would get much sleep that night.

CHAPTER 15

When the knock came at the bedroom door the next morning, I was lying in much the same fetal, self-comforting position as I had started out in, exhausted but too nauseous and upset to sleep. After crying softly for what had felt like hours, I had actually managed to doze off sometime in the middle of the night only to abruptly wake up an indeterminable time later on the verge of puking. I had barely made it to the bathroom in time. After that, I had only been able to lie in bed curled up in misery to wait for morning and presumably Lariel to arrive as sleep had become an impossibility at that point.

I had long since given up on the hope that Sethian would return, which given how awful I felt, wasn't exactly a bad thing. The problem was convincing the part of me that yearned desperately for him.

I forced myself to sit up and lean back against the large, wooden headboard into a semblance of composure before I called out for my visitor to come in. Sure enough, Lariel entered the room with a cheerful smile and a breakfast tray that immediately made me want to scream inside.

"Good morning," she greeted, setting the tray over my lap.

"Morning." I eyed the covered dishes as if they were full of poisonous snakes. I had eaten practically nothing yesterday, so there was no way I would get away with refusing my breakfast today. My chest suddenly tightened painfully as another, more important reason to eat crossed my mind.

Not eating wasn't good for the baby.

"Did you talk with my lord husband this morning?" I asked as I watched her lift the covers off all the various dishes.

I was relieved to see that along with the usual fruits and cheeses I had become accustomed to eating for breakfast, a small loaf of bread was included. If I stuck to having just the bread and tea, then maybe I could get through this meal without raising Lariel's suspicions again.

"A messenger," she replied as she sat on the edge of the bed. "Saeria and Rinwen will be along with a change of clothes shortly. His Majesty wishes for you to remain here in his rooms for the day."

I wondered if Lariel knew that I had slept alone last night. I wanted to ask, wanted to know if she knew where Sethian was right now, but I just picked up the loaf of bread and remained silent. I wasn't really sure if it was proper to ask those types of questions, even if I was the king's wife. Prying into or blabbing about the king's business wasn't something we had ever discussed in my etiquette lessons, and even though I considered the three elven women my friends, they were still part of the king's staff and would be expected to follow courtly protocol.

"You didn't sleep much last night did you?" Lariel suddenly accused, nearly making me choke on the piece of bread I was swallowing. My stomach gave an unpleasant lurch, but thankfully I didn't feel the need to gag.

I coughed and gave her a wry smile. "Do I look that bad this morning?"

"Your cheeks are as white as those sheets. Your eyes are shadowed and also tinged with red." She *tsked*. "I didn't realize that humans had so much trouble with sleep."

"Most don't," I said. "Sometimes I just have a hard time turning my brain off."

Lariel fixed me with a particularly deep stare that made me want to fidget and turn away. It was almost as though she was trying to pry into my mind. With a start, I wondered if she could. So far, the girls had been really vague about the seemingly magical abilities of the *Sidhe* I had witnessed so far. Thinking that it was a taboo subject, I hadn't pressed for answers, but now I wondered if I should have let the matter drop so easily.

"You are still worried that His Majesty will reject you," Lariel said finally.

I looked down at the tray, unable to meet her eyes. "I'll always worry about that. It's not something I can help. I'm a worrywart by nature."

She sighed heavily. "Well, I suppose only time will cure that particular woe. Finish your breakfast and then we shall go to the baths. Hopefully, a nice, warm soak will relax you enough for a nap afterward. Your lessons can wait for another day."

I managed to eat half the bread and a couple of slices of apple without having to make a mad dash for the bathroom, which at that point was a small miracle. Focusing on Lariel's steady stream of light-hearted chatter had certainly helped.

When Saeria and Rinwen showed up, we all headed for the royal baths.

As Lariel had predicted, once enveloped by the pleasantly warm water coupled with the soothing feeling of Lariel's fingers massaging my scalp as she washed my hair, my stomach seemed to settle down enough that it was all I could do to keep from dozing off. A nap was certainly looking more and more possible. Maybe a nice deep sleep was all I needed to better manage my morning sickness.

Yeah and maybe you'll be crowned the elven queen tomorrow, I thought glumly.

Once back in Sethian's rooms, I changed into one of the nightgowns Rinwen had brought me and settled down for a nap with a promise from Lariel to wake me for lunch. I really had to stop skipping meals.

It felt as if I had only been asleep for a few minutes when I abruptly heard someone say "Emily" into my ear.

Hearing my name had me jerking up in bed, looking around wildly in utter confusion and panic while my heart tried to escape my chest. Before my eyes could properly focus, I felt a hand cup my cheek, and the panic seemed to just melt away along the wave of warmth that began to flow into me. I blinked, and Sethian's face blurred into vision. He was looking down at me with a frown and concern in his eyes.

"Sethian!" I blurted, then immediately flushed and looked down, horribly embarrassed at how desperate my voice had sounded.

"I did not mean to startle you," he said, sitting on the bed beside me.

I rubbed the remaining sleep from my eyes and shook my head. "Sorry. I guess I was just really deep asleep. Lariel was supposed to wake me for lunch, but..." Like my room, Sethian's bedroom did not have any windows, so I had no idea how long I had been out.

Sethian's frown deepened. "It's well into the night."

My eyes widened. I must have looked worse than Lariel had let on for her to have allowed me to sleep through *two* meals. My friends were always going on and on about how I never seemed to eat properly, so there was no way they would have let me sleep the day away unless they thought I needed the rest even more.

I anxiously looked more closely at Sethian's expression, wondering if they had been worried enough about my ragged appearance this morning to mention it to him. It was all well and good to blame my insomnia and sickly appearance on my insecurities to my friends, but I couldn't use that excuse here without opening a whole new can of worms that I never intended to open. However, I really didn't know my own husband well enough yet to read anything beyond his obvious concern.

Speaking of concern, I finally realized that I was shockingly nausea-free at the moment. I could only think that this glorious fact was his doing before he had awakened me and wished I could show him how extremely grateful I was for his foresight.

Instead, I nervously smoothed down my hair and said, "I wonder why she didn't wake me up."

"You did not sleep last night after I left, did you?" he asked as if I hadn't spoken.

I stiffened and tried to look away, but he immediately grasped my chin and turned my face back towards him. I reluctantly met his eyes again, afraid that I had made him angry, but they still reflected the same concern. I relaxed minutely.

"Emily?" he said, his tone commanding.

"I—" I took a deep breath and forced myself to continue, "I was worried that something bad had happened. I couldn't get the thought out of my head, and before I knew it, Lariel was knocking at the door with my breakfast." *So won't you tell me what you were doing?* I could only wish to be so straightforward.

I was actually surprised at how smoothly the lie had flowed from my tongue. To my relief, Sethian merely hummed in acceptance, and his grip on my chin turned into a soft caress against my cheek. I closed my eyes and turned my face into his palm.

"If I had known you were going to worry to the point of losing sleep, I would have sent word that all was well sooner," he said quietly.

I opened my eyes and offered him a tiny smile. "I would've still been worried. Sometimes I can't help it. It's in my nature."

He leaned forward and brushed his lips briefly against mine before I could react, as soft and fleeting as rose petals fluttering across my sensitive flesh on their way to the ground, before pulling back slightly until only a millimeter separated our mouths. "Then let me make it up to you." His warm breath ghosted over my lips with every word, making me shiver.

I completely expected to feel his mouth crash against mine with the wild passion of all our previous kisses, so it was almost a shock when those silky lips pressed against mine in what almost felt like a hesitant caress, as though he wasn't sure his attentions would be welcome. I closed my eyes and leaned into the kiss, clutching the front of his tunic tightly with both hands as I opened my mouth to him in encouragement.

His tongue slowly slid against my own in a single, teasing stroke before he pulled back completely from my mouth. I let out a soft sound of protest before I could stop myself and instinctively tried to recapture his retreating lips, but he ducked his head down to my neck and planted a soft kiss along the side before pulling away from me completely.

"Take off your gown for me," he commanded in a voice deeper than normal that seemed to reverberate throughout my entire body, the heated look in his eyes piercing right through me. "I want to see you."

That one sentence had the effect of launching my entire blood volume straight into my face so quickly that I was surprised that my head didn't explode. It was one thing to be nude while we were making love, but the thought of completely exposing myself to him while his eyes deliberately took in every inch of my body brought out my shyness a thousand fold. I had to fight the urge to cross my arms over my chest.

The fact that he could just use his elven magic to make my clothes disappear like before made his command that much more poignant. Was he testing me? Or was I just reading too much into it, and he simply wanted a show today? It wasn't as though I had known him near long enough to have learned even a fraction of his kinks.

I felt awkward and utterly unsexy as I closed my eyes and slowly lifted my nightgown up over my head. The cool air of the bedroom against my bare and heat-inflamed skin drove the fact of my nudity home all the more so that I couldn't even look at him as I haphazardly tossed the garment over the side of the bed. The urge to cover myself was now so strong that I had actually started to lift my arms before I felt Sethian's scorching hands encircle both my forearms and gently, but insistently, push them down to my sides.

"Let me see," he repeated, releasing my arms and pulling away from me again.

His heated tone made me glance up at him, my cheeks now so hot that I was surprised that they weren't glowing. I met his intense gaze for a brief, breathless moment, before lowering my eyes and squirming a bit in embarrassment.

Even though I did not look at him again, I could feel his gaze on me like a physical touch as he took in the entirety of my body. It was as if he was moving his fingertips lightly, teasingly, over my skin, making me yearn for his actual touch but unable to make myself ask for it. My heart was pounding so hard at that point that my chest was beginning to ache. I wondered if Sethian could hear it and if so, if this blatant show of my excitement pleased him.

It seemed like a small eternity before I felt his actual hand on my skin, making me jump then gasp sharply as he slowly moved his palm down the curve of my breast, his thumb lightly caressing my already hardened nipple a single time, before he cupped the soft mound completely and squeezed firmly. A small, satisfied smile stretched his lips when I looked back at him, and I realized that his last action was merely to make me look at him, a part of the sensual game he had begun.

I covered the hand that cupped my breast with my own and moved to my knees, blushing and struggling to hold his gaze as his eyes narrowed slightly with keen interest and increasing lust. I gripped his shoulder and leaned in to lick his bottom lip with a slow, drawn-out swipe. This close I could see his pupils dilate, and the sight gave me a tiny sense of power that I could affect him this much.

My eyes flickered over to one of his ears. I would have to be careful not to touch them this time. I didn't want him to lose control and our lovemaking to end in a rough frenzy like last time—for more reasons than one.

I yelped as I suddenly found myself tumbled onto my back. His still fully-clothed body loomed over me, straddling but not quite touching yet, his weight supported by a forearm on either side of my head. He dipped his head and took my lips hungrily, thrusting his tongue into my mouth aggressively in contrast to the gentle kisses earlier. I opened my mouth wider with a hum of appreciation and sucked his tongue in deeper, sliding my own alongside it until I could no longer differentiate the two.

Blindly, I reached up and grabbed his shoulders, trying to pull him down farther onto my body. There was something immensely satisfying about feeling his weight pressing me down into the mattress, and I desperately wanted to feel that right now. However, it was as if I was tugging on a statue for all I managed to move him. I pulled down harder, but he stubbornly refused to budge.

His lips moved to the skin beneath my chin and sucked hard. The sensation went straight to my groin, making me throb and gasp. I arched up in an attempt to connect with the full length of his body for some much-needed friction.

"Please Sethian..." I pleaded when I felt him immediately push my hips down with a firm hand.

"Not yet," he said against my neck, and I nearly groaned in frustration.

He had barely touched me at all, and my whole body was already tightening and throbbing with a painful arousal that had me writhing beneath him just as fervently as all the other times when he had taken me with little to no foreplay. Hell, just the smell of him was like an aphrodisiac, an indescribable musk that defined the very essence of what it meant to be male and powerful.

Sethian moved his hand from my hip over to my groin, his fingers sliding through my already damp pubic hair to the very center of my pleasure where he began to slowly, maddeningly massage my clit with two fingers in a light, barely there stroke. His mouth moved down from my neck to latch onto one of my aching nipples. I entangled the fingers of one hand in his hair along the crown, absently tugging in time to the circular motions of his fingers teasing me towards completion while I crammed the other into my mouth and bit down hard in order to keep from screaming.

Being masturbated by Sethian felt inordinately different than pleasuring myself. The utter lack of control over the rising tide of my approaching orgasm had somehow amplified that pleasurable tension by at least a factor of three. For all I knew, his intentions could be to bring me to the brink of ecstasy and then at the last second leave me hanging and begging him to let me come just to tease me. I never knew that uncertainty could be so stimulating…

I cried out and nearly yanked his hair out by the roots when I abruptly felt him bite down on my nipple with enough force that the sensation crossed the pleasure threshold into pain. I shuddered as his tongue immediately began to caress the sting away, and his hand between my legs began to rub my sex more quickly and aggressively. I gripped the sheets tightly in my hands and arched into both sensations, his name spilling from my lips over and over as if that alone would push me closer to the climax I was now so desperate to achieve.

Sethian pulled on my nipple with his teeth as a parting tease that broke my litany of his name and made me squeal before moving his head down my body. Then suddenly his hand was gone from between my legs, and I groaned in utter dismay at the loss of stimulation just as I was nearing the peak.

I arched up, trying to find something, *anything* to rub myself against to relieve the maddening throbbing and pressure in my groin, but Sethian once again firmly pushed my hips down. He proceeded to spread my legs a little before I could voice my displeasure, and then I nearly swallowed my tongue when I felt the first wet, utterly *fantastic* swipe of his tongue across my clit.

I had always thought that I would be too embarrassed to ever allow anyone to perform cunnilingus on me, but it had never occurred to me that the very act would short-circuit my brain to the point where I couldn't have formed a thought to save my life, much less felt anything like shame. My whole existence had shrunk down to only the feel of that tongue vigorously caressing the most intimate part of me until my toes were curling into the sheets and I was pushing myself into his mouth, literally begging him to give me release before I went insane with overstimulation.

Then my entire being seemed to explode with an ecstasy that turned my already hazy vision completely white and tore Sethian's name from my throat in a drawn-out scream that was also a half-sob. Even still, Sethian kept up his relentless oral stimulation as my body shuddered and was racked with spasm after spasm of pleasure.

An eternity later, Sethian lifted his head, and my whole body just sank bonelessly into the mattress, exhausted and totally wrecked, but still tingling like mad. Breathing heavily, I looked down the length of my body at him with half-closed eyes that felt as though they were weighted down with boulders and was not really surprised to see that he was no longer wearing anything but a sexy smile.

Apparently, it was his turn now.

CHAPTER 16

L*ariel deserves my eternal gratitude,* I thought as Sethian crawled between my legs and moved up my body as fluidly as a panther advancing on its prey, making me shiver as his warm silkiness slid over my sweaty and still-hypersensitive skin. If she had not decided to let me sleep the day away, I doubted I would have still been conscious. To have missed such an erotic sight would have been a travesty.

I held out my arms and embraced him as soon as he was within reach, somehow finding the energy to lift my head off the bed to kiss him. I felt him smile against my lips before he opened his mouth to reciprocate. For a long moment, we merely sucked on each other's lips and tongue, and I finally got to feel that satisfying heaviness of his body when he settled on top of me.

I squeezed my thighs more tightly against his sides, wanting to feel him against as much of my body as possible, but I didn't try to rub myself against the cock that was currently a firm, hot bar against my groin. Before I jumpstarted that particular engine, I needed time to recuperate from that mind-melting orgasm, or else I feared that my body and mind would give out before he was satisfied. Engaging Sethian in a bit of enthusiastic tonsil-tickling was definitely the perfect way to accomplish this, especially when he was in such a —giving mood. I could lie here in his arms feeling him suck the breath from me forever.

It was Sethian who finally began our sensuous dance, rolling his hips in a slow, deep grind against my groin that immediately had my sex throbbing with need again. I released his mouth with an appreciative moan and arched my head back, offering him my neck to be devoured. His tongue painted a wet line from my chin to the hollow of my throat and back up to the junction of my neck and shoulder before I felt his teeth against my skin.

I drew in a sharp breath in anticipation, but the expected sting of pleasure/pain didn't come. Instead, he slowly scraped his teeth lightly along my shoulder, making me twitch in reaction to the different intensities of his increasing thrusts and the barely there rasp of his teeth. I kept expecting him to bite down when I once again felt the moistness of his lips at my neck. He alternated between those teasing scrapes of his teeth and the occasional tug as he sucked firmly on my skin. However, the bite never came, and that uncertainty, like before, served to only heighten my arousal.

My hands slide down his back, loving the silky feel of his skin beneath my fingertips, and followed the curve of his ass to grab each mound tightly. I dug my fingers into the firm muscles, encouraging his hips to move faster just as his mouth moved in for another kiss. He made a small sound of appreciation when I flexed my fingers again, so I couldn't help but try to make him do it again.

I arched up into his thrusts, trying to match his rhythm in order to increase the friction, but he abruptly stilled his hips and pulled away from the kiss. For a split-second, I froze, scared that I had done something wrong, hurt him somehow; then he grinned down at me, and I could breathe again.

"Sethian?" I said, letting my uncertainty bleed into his name.

His grin melted into a gentle smile that seemed to temper some of the lust in his eyes. He bent down and gave me a soft kiss.

"You will have me climax before my cock can taste

what my tongue has already savored," he scolded playfully.

Hearing him say the word "cock" was so jolting and out of place that the rest of his lewd comment went right over my head. It was almost like hearing your grandma cuss for the first time. There was just something so inherently *wrong* about such a crude word coming from someone who could very easily be mistaken for an angel if he only had wings.

Luckily, Sethian's next kiss saved me from both embarrassment and having to reply. I wrapped my arms around him in something like desperation and pulled him closer, hoping that we were done talking for the night. Although my ardor had cooled somewhat thanks to his out-from-left-field remark, my yearning for his touch was as strong as ever.

After kissing me breathless again, he bent his head to whisper in my ear, "Turn on your side."

I shivered at that low tone and immediately moved to obey once he had lifted himself off my body. He grabbed my uppermost leg behind the knee and pushed it up until my knee was touching my chest.

"Hold this here," he commanded, and once again, I rushed to comply.

Opening myself to him like this felt inordinately naughty even though I knew there wasn't anything particularly special about the position, but to someone who had only lost their virginity a month ago, any position other than missionary felt kinky. I was eager to see what he had in mind, and he didn't make me wait long to find out.

I watched with hooded eyes and heat in my cheeks as Sethian settled on his knees halfway behind my ass and straddling my other leg. He then positioned himself at my opening, his cock rubbing teasingly against the length of my vagina a few times until it was slick with my juices. His eyes met mine as he did this, piercing and just plain hot.

Then without warning, his entire member entered me in one powerful thrust, making me almost lose my grip on my knee as I jerked and let out a surprised moan. One hand clutched the top of my hip while the other fondled my clit as he slid himself in and out of me in deep, undulating strokes that seemed to reach more deeply inside me than ever before.

My nails dug into the skin of the leg I held while my other hand had begun to mindlessly tug at my own hair in time to his thrusts. The room quickly became filled with the sounds of my moans and the slap of flesh hitting flesh as Sethian pushed into my passage with increasing speed.

I almost screamed in frustration when I felt him slow

just when I was nearly at the pinnacle, but his change of pace was only so he could sink into the bed behind me until we were more or less spooning. As his hips resumed their vigorous pace and the hand rubbing my clit began to jerk me with more determination, Sethian curled his left arm beneath my body and began caressing and pinching my boobs as well until I was practically going out of my mind with overstimulation.

A split-second before I started to orgasm, I felt Sethian bite down hard on my right shoulder, the shock of *finally* feeling the pain I had been unconsciously anticipating since I first felt his teeth scrape along my skin made me come so hard that I couldn't even draw enough breath to scream. My passage clamped down tightly around his cock, making him moan and sink his teeth even deeper into my flesh. He then pushed into me with one final, heavy thrust and spilled his seed deep within me.

Panting, I released my leg, letting it stretch out on top of my other. Sethian immediately swung his own leg over it, entangling our limbs and pulling me back more snuggly against his body. I was keenly aware of his member deep within me, pulsating and somehow still hard despite his climax, but he made no move to withdraw it from my body.

I squirmed a bit as the wound he had bitten into my

shoulder began to throb. I wondered if it, too, would be mysteriously healed by morning like that bite wound on my breast, then decided that it didn't matter.

The only thing that did matter was that Sethian was with me, he was holding me, and it didn't look as though he planned to leave anytime soon.

CHAPTER 17

It was somewhat disturbing how at peace and safe I felt wrapped tightly in Sethian's arms with his body solid and warm against my back. This is something I had never experienced back home, and for it to elicit such strong feelings of security for me when Sethian and I were still practically strangers was something I just couldn't wrap my head around. With nothing to compare it to, even our previous couplings as I had either passed out during the act or soon after, there was no way to know if this was just something everyone normally felt when cuddling with a partner after sex.

We had not spoken once afterward, not even when he had finally withdrawn his cock from my body and had once again settled me back against him for what I presumed was sleep, but no matter how sated and drowsy I had felt, I just couldn't shut down my racing thoughts enough to drift off. Judging by the quiet, even breaths I felt at the back of my neck, Sethian was already well into sleep.

I had a strong urge to look at his sleeping face, wondering if sleep had softened that intimidating air of power he always seemed to carry, but I didn't want to risk waking him and losing my current cocoon of warmth. I could only hope that I would get countless other chances to watch him sleep in the future.

For the next few moments, I closed my eyes and simply listened to him breathe, trying not to think about anything at all, least of all the secret I stubbornly insisted on keeping and the problems doing so would likely cause. I just wanted to enjoy this moment where for the first time since my mother had passed away, I felt cherished.

When Sethian suddenly shifted behind me, I didn't react, thinking he had done so in his sleep.

"So—do you want to tell me why you still have not told me that you are carrying our child within you?" he then said so abruptly into my ear that I swore my heart stopped beating for a couple of seconds.

He *knew.*

My eyes instantly welled up with tears as a wave of anguish thundered through my entire being. It all made sense now. Of course his attentiveness tonight would have a reason. I had screwed up majorly, allowed myself to believe that the kind of relationship I wished with him was within the realm of possibility after all. Now the hammer was about to fall, and I was completely unprepared for it.

I curled in on myself and clamped my mouth shut tightly to hold back the sobs that were threatening to burst from my throat, but I was unable to keep the tears from falling. Unfortunately, once the waterworks had started, it was as if I had opened a floodgate, the tears pouring from my eyes in hot streams of hurt and fear that I had no hopes of stymieing. I'm sure my out-of-whack hormones weren't helping matters much, either.

What would become of us now?

"It's all right. You must not think that I am angry with you. You can tell me," he coaxed gently, but I barely heard him, already lost too deeply in the mourning of my shattered dreams.

When I remained silent, Sethian tried to turn my face to him, making a distressed sound deep in his throat when his hand encountered the wetness on my face, but I refused to budge. I didn't want to show him such a pathetic face, and I especially didn't want him to be kind or to feel guilty because of his strong sense of duty. In a way, that was even worse than if he had been indifferent from the beginning.

I wanted him to love me.

"I am *not* angry," he repeated firmly, wiping at the tears that were still streaming down my cheek. "You were terrified at the thought of having a child before. If you are still just as conflicted, then it's completely understandable. There is no shame in that."

Those words meant to comfort only served to make me cry harder, to the point where I could no longer keep my sobs behind my teeth. He really was too kind for my piece of mind.

He let me cry myself out without another word, stroking my back soothingly and planting soft kisses on the back of my neck and shoulder while I trembled uncontrollably, and to my shame, I drank up that comfort like a woman dying of thirst in a desert. It was this that finally allowed me to pull myself together enough to speak.

"I didn't want to lose this." My whispered confession sounded as loud as a shout in the silence of the bedroom.

I felt Sethian still completely, his hand freezing on my upper arm mid-stroke.

"'This'?" he asked finally after a tense moment of silence. His confusion was so palpable that I could practically taste it in the air.

I sniffled and swallowed thickly against the huge knot that was still lodged in my throat. The damage had already been done, so I supposed anything else I said wouldn't make much difference either way. It was time to lay out all my cards, no matter how embarrassing or painful.

"You brought me here because you wanted a child," I began in a small voice.

I was glad that I was facing away from him or else I don't think I could have gotten out more than a couple words before chickening out. It was hard enough to meet his gaze normally without the added difficulties of telling him my deepest fears about our relationship.

"Although you say that I'm your wife," I pressed on, "I've only been able to see you on the days that I've been fertile. I understand that you have duties way more important than me, but I had at least hoped that you would spend some evenings with me, maybe even share a conversation with me over a meal or two. Even though our marriage was as far from conventional as you could get, I've accepted that fact, but at the same time had hoped that it could eventually *mean* something more than just an act of convenience for the sake of your laws of succession.

"I didn't want my pregnancy to signal the end of even those visits. I thought, maybe if we could spend more time together, then maybe you would come to enjoy my company enough to keep coming back regardless of not needing to try for a baby anymore. Life is short for a human, so I really don't want to spend the most important parts of it existing in a constant limbo of waiting and yearning for just a few moments here and there of real living."

There it was, words I could never take back, and I held my breath, terrified of his reaction. The rest of my life depended on this one moment, and I prayed desperately that I wouldn't have to regret the power over my fate I had so willingly, stupidly, given him on that first night.

"Emily—please look at me."

The tone of his voice was strange, something I couldn't readily identify, so it was with a large dose of apprehension that I scrubbed the remaining tears from my eyes and slowly rolled my body to finally face him. The look in his eyes was every bit as intense, piercing, and utterly unreadable as I had feared, and it took every last ounce of my courage to not look away in panic.

Then Sethian suddenly leaned forward, and for a moment, I couldn't understand what he was doing until I felt the soft press of his lips against mine and everything instantly stuttered to a stop. A fleeting caress, then he was pulling back before I could unfreeze my mind enough to react.

"I'm sorry," he said, the absolute sincerity in his voice hitting me like a knife to the chest. The *last* thing I had expected was an apology. "To make you feel such abandonment and uncertainty—it was unbelievably thoughtless of me to forget that humans do not experience the flow of time in the same manner as the *Sidhe*. Yet, it is downright unforgivable of me to have forgotten to tell you a very crucial detail of the process that has allowed you to enter and remain in the elven realm. I have done a very cruel thing to you in allowing you to believe something that is no longer true, and even a thousand years of apologies will not be enough."

I—don't understand—" I began, but he cut me off with a finger against my lips.

"You were greatly changed when you were brought here. In truth, your physical body now has more in common with an elven body than a human's—and that includes an elf's longevity. One year, fifty years, or five hundred. They are but a blink of an eye within the existence you now have before you."

For a long moment, I was too shocked to do anything but stare back at him in utter disbelief. To live for thousands of years just like an elf…the idea was as alien to me as the concept of aging must be to Sethian. How could a living being even have the natural ability to change something so fundamental about another?

"I—I—how can that even be possible?" I stuttered.

Sethian shrugged. "Transmutation is not an ability that I possess, so it is not something I can explain with any authority. My abilities, as you have already witnessed, deal with the manipulation of the fabric of space as well as the energies associated with healing. Only a handful of my people possess the ability to transmute, it is so rare."

He began to absently thread his fingers through my hair as he spoke, and the sensation relaxed me enough that I was able to calm down significantly. I had gone into this conversation expecting to have my world crushed beyond repair, but instead, Sethian had opened up a whole new one. I had been so emotionally rung out in the last hour or so that I didn't know what to think or feel anymore.

However, he wasn't finished yet. "What was done to

you is not something that is often done, and never on a whim. Only the most skilled mage is ever allowed to perform a transmutation on the living. The mage that performed your transmutation is one who has lived for nearly six thousand years, old enough to have performed the transmutations of the human brides during the last Plague of Infertility."

Sethian suddenly cupped my face in both hands. "I would never have given permission otherwise. Never think that you mean nothing to me. The passion you have stirred within me in just the short time you have been here is incomparable to what I feel when I am bedding Limira. With her, it is an act as mechanical as walking. There is no passion, no joy, just rutting in the name of our royal duty to continue the royal bloodline."

I made a face before I could stop myself. The last thing I wanted to hear about was my *husband's* sexcapades with the queen, never mind that she was his wife as well.

"Is that where you were last night?" I asked, proud that I managed to keep the jealousy I was feeling from my tone.

He frowned, and I suddenly kicked myself. Crap! Had I just overstepped my bounds? But dammit, I really wanted to know the answer. I had just spent the past two days in a constant state of hell because I knew so little about what he did beyond these walls that it had driven me to desperate acts of stupidity, so didn't I deserve some kind of answer now?

"Limira has been distraught since I took you as my wife," he said, and the tone of his voice when he said the queen's name made me realize that it wasn't me that he was currently upset with. "After meeting you in the royal baths and seeing us together in my bed, she suddenly demanded that we try once again for a child." He shrugged and continued rather matter-of-factly, "It is her right as queen, no matter that the entire exercise was useless. If she has not conceived in a thousand years, then the chances of it happening now are fairly nonexistent. Although I already knew you were pregnant when I received her summons yesterday, I gave her one last night out of respect for our years together and the sadness of her fate."

There was no way I could continue to feel jealous after hearing all that. If it were me, I would have been desperate to conceive, too. Knowing the history of various royal families back in my world, she was probably under tremendous pressure from her family. Whether human or *Sidhe*, the continuation of bloodlines was always important.

Not wanting to think about the elven queen anymore, I quickly asked before Sethian could continue,

"How did you know I was pregnant anyway? Did Lariel tell you? They were all pretty suspicious from the very beginning."

"No, nothing like that," he replied. "From the moment I appeared in your bedroom yesterday, our child's soul spoke to me."

"What!" I cried, half-rising on my elbows in my shock and nearly causing us to bump heads.

"It is not as extraordinary as you may think," he insisted, chuckling at what was probably a very dumb look on my face. "All elven women can hear their child's voice soon after conception, but according to the old texts, the changed humans were different. It seems only when the elven child had developed the ability to form clear thoughts that they were able to connect mentally with their human mothers."

"That's—that's—amazing!" I exclaimed lamely, unable to find the right words to describe the sense of wonder I was feeling.

Sethian smiled. "Unlike humans, elven babies do not cry. The connection is necessary for communication. It is not so much words, but a sense of intent or emotion. That is why I am also able to hear our child. Had we any other children, they would be able to hear their sibling's voice as well. It is our genetic ties that allow this."

It was becoming abundantly clear that I was still

laughingly ignorant about the *Sidhe*. A few days ago, I had thought that I was finally starting to grasp my new adoptive culture, and had said as much to the girls. Now I'm surprised that they hadn't laughed in my face.

"If you knew from the start, then why did you let me go on thinking that you had no clue about me being pregnant?" I said, trying not to sound resentful.

"I wanted to give you the pleasure of telling me this joyous news, but…even when we were alone in the garden and you still had not told me, I thought that perhaps you had a specific place and time in mind. It seems I completely misread you and the situation. Forgive me."

I shook my head and snuggled up to him with a sigh. "I should've never tried to keep all my fears to myself. Maybe if I had just confided my fears about the pregnancy to Lariel, or Saeria and Rinwen, then *a lot* of misery could have been avoided. Before you did whatever you did to me to make me feel better, the morning sickness was practically torture!"

He *tutted* and then ran a hand over my belly. The look in his eyes was suddenly so nakedly joyous that I felt the prick of tears in my own.

"I never, *never* thought that a child would be conceived this quickly," he said with the largest smile I had ever seen anyone wear. "According to the old histories, it had taken several decades for the first human woman to conceive an elven child. That this has happened is truly extraordinary!" Then abruptly, his smile dimmed. "On the other hand, for your sake, I am sorry that this has happened as quickly as it has. It would have been best if it had happened after you had been settled into this new life for a bit longer. As I said before, it is understandable if you are frightened."

"Yeah, I'm scared," I admitted, trying to smile bravely, "but—what first-time mother isn't? Luckily, I still have another eight months or so to get used to the idea. I'll be fine."

And I would be fine. Sethian may not love me just yet, but at least some of his words had rekindled my hope that it could happen, especially now that I apparently had thousands of years to persuade him. I felt lightheaded just thinking about the oceans of time I had ahead of me.

"Once your pregnancy is physically evident, I shall present you to the whole of the elven court." He paused, and the look in his eyes became deadly serious. I suddenly found myself looking into the eyes of, not Sethian, but the elven king.

"Your pregnancy will change *everything*."

I blinked in surprise at the sudden shift in his demeanor. His people had been longing for the birth of an elven child for over five hundred years, hadn't they? My friends were constantly telling me how excited a lot of the elven women were about the prospect of children filling their homes again.

So why did Sethian sound so worried?

CHAPTER 18

As my sleeping mind drifted towards full consciousness, I slowly became aware of an unfamiliar firmness and warmth at my back. For a long, confusing moment, I couldn't figure out what it could be. I pressed back against it then stiffened when I immediately felt an answering kiss to the back of my neck and an arm tighten around my waist. I panicked for ten whole seconds, struggling to remember why someone was in bed with me before snippets of last night finally began to surface within my frantic thoughts.

After Sethian's cryptic remark, he had urged me to sleep, and I must have nodded right off because I could remember little after that. I never expected to wake up still intertwined within his arms—and I had no idea how to act in this kind of situation. Should I say "good morning"? Turn around and give him a good morning kiss instead?

I felt Sethian's hand start to slowly caress my belly, and I sucked in a startled breath. Wait! Did he want to…?

"Another three to four moon-cycles or so and this will be rounded enough to present you to the court," Sethian murmured into my ear, and I was suddenly glad he couldn't see my face because it was probably as red as a cherry.

Had this last month changed me so much that my mind automatically ended up in the gutter with every little thing he did, no matter how innocent?

"What—does that mean exactly?" I asked, deciding that the time for greetings had long passed.

"For you, it is a change in status," Sethian replied. "It signifies your official entry into the elven court as the Royal Wife. For the court, it is an official announcement and proof about the forthcoming birth of a potential heir."

My ladies-in-waiting had already given me a rudimentary idea of the political and social structure of the elven court, a system of titled nobles that all claimed relation to at least one of the ten noble founding families of the realm. Lariel had claimed that the founding of the realm was quite an exciting origin story, but had insisted that I needed to learn much more about present-day elven society before I could fully understand everything the history would entail.

To someone like me who always had the need to know and understand every tiny detail about everything, having something as potentially earth-shattering as that dangled before me was practically torture. To think that I would now actually become a part of the amazing elven history I had already learned. It was a bit…overwhelming…

"I hope you don't expect me to give a speech or address the court or something," I said in a small voice.

I still had nightmares about the speech class I had been forced to take as an undergraduate. Having to stand before a class of five hundred of my peers and deliver a speech without stuttering had been bad enough, but having to do so in front of a room full of hundreds of elven nobles—which would probably include the queen—would be agony. My fear of public speaking was the one weakness my PhD advisor had constantly badgered me about fixing that I had placed in the "I'll do it later" category. Now my procrastination may have just come back to bite me in the ass.

"No, nothing like that," Sethian said, and had I been standing, I would have probably collapsed in relief.

"Once you are announced, you will merely have to cross the length of the throne room to first, present yourself before me as I sit on the throne. I shall then address you before the eyes and ears of the entirety of the court as my 'Royal Wife who now carries the potential heir to the throne.' Next, you will take the seat a step below and to the right of me in order to accept words from each courtier in turn. I'm afraid it's a rather long and tedious affair, but one that tradition mandates."

As far as I was concerned, I would sit there all week like a curiosity to be gawked at without one word of complaint as long as it meant I didn't have to say anything—especially in Elvish.

"I've sat through worse," I assured him.

He shifted behind me, then I felt his hand leave my belly and grasp my chin, turning my face back towards him. He brushed his lips against mine briefly for that good morning kiss I had wanted to give him earlier before pulling away from me altogether and sitting up. I couldn't help but feel disappointed at losing the warmth and comfort of his body, but he was the king. I couldn't expect him to lounge around in bed with me all day.

I sat up as well, pulling the sheets up with me to hide my nudity. It would probably be a long time before I would ever feel comfortable enough to just lay it all bare in front of him when we weren't having sex or about to have sex.

"Let me see you."

I could feel my traitorous cheeks start to heat up as the memory of Sethian's commanding words from last night echoed throughout my mind, but I ruthlessly stopped those thoughts in their track before the blush could get any worse. The last thing I wanted right now was Sethian asking embarrassing questions.

Sethian leaned towards me, for another kiss I thought, but he merely cupped my cheek and said, "Your coloring is looking better this morning, but I want you to rest for the rest of the morning, all the same. Once I remove myself from your presence, your sickness may very well return. I will send for a healer, as well as your ladies, to attend you while the servants fetch your things from your rooms."

"My things?" I echoed in confusion.

He nodded. "From now on, you will remain here with me in the royal suite."

It was all perfectly logical, but his words still stunned me. With the way he had initially explained the living arrangements between the queen, me, and him, I had thought that I would continue to live separately from him indefinitely, or more correctly, I had never actually allowed myself to hope that things could ever be different.

This was exactly what I had wanted, but I still had to ask, "Won't the queen be upset?"

"Our child is now second in rank only to me unless the birth proves otherwise. She will voice no protest," he replied firmly.

His answer was less than reassuring. "The baby outranks the queen?"

"For now, yes. It will remain so only if you give me a son, an heir to the throne. If it is a daughter, then the newly born princess will rank just beneath the queen."

The intricacies of a monarchy really were just one big headache. I could already see the various problems that would spring up if I gave birth to a girl.

"Can you tell?" I asked. "The sex of the baby before it's born, I mean? You said you could 'hear' the baby's soul, so…"

Sethian shook his head. "Whether male or female, a child's soul feels the same." He smiled and bent down to kiss me briefly on the forehead. "You must not fret over it. I suspect we will have many children over the years, so this first child need not be an heir. That a *Sidhe* child will be born at all is joyous enough."

My brain stuttered to a stop at the word "children." The reality of having *one* soon was scary enough. That he talked about having multiple children as though it was just par for the course was something I wasn't prepared to deal with yet, especially when I really hadn't come to terms with *this* pregnancy.

"Do I need to keep my pregnancy to myself until you announce it publically?" I asked.

"You may tell your ladies, but I believe, for now, the news should go no farther. Until my people can see with their own eyes the truth of your pregnancy, spreading the news now will only cause unrest. The last Plague of Infertility was several thousand years ago. Thus, there are few alive today who remember a time when human brides walked among us. You, as well as they, will need time to adjust to this coming change. As I said before, I never expected a child would come so soon no matter how much I wished for it."

Hearing all of that, I suddenly wondered if his recent trip across the realm had involved more than just checking up on the state of his lands as he had told me earlier. I suspected he was purposely vague in his explanations in order not to worry me, but I just couldn't shake the feeling that his bringing me here had caused a lot more strife within the elven court than just a little voiced unease.

After all, the queen had looked at me as if I literally was the mongrel she had named me. It wouldn't be a stretch at all to say that there were likely others, and not just those in the nobility, who wouldn't hesitate to call me the same. Then there was the unavoidable fact that my baby would be a half-breed. Knowing how sensitive these types of caste-minded societies could be about the mixing of blood, would they even accept the son of a human as heir?

Suddenly the locks on the door and the armed guards weren't so irritating anymore. At that moment, I realized exactly how incredibly stupid I had been. All this time, I had been agonizing over the wrong thing. I had let Sethian and my friends' complete acceptance of my humanity blind me to the fact that there were always those who railed against a change in the status quo. More than my husband would have to accept me if I ever expected to find happiness here.

"Emily?"

I started and focused once again on Sethian's now frowning face. Crap! How long had I zoned out?

"Sorry, I was just—thinking about what you just said," I said sheepishly, deciding that some of the truth was needed here.

"You mean 'worrying,'" he chided, and it took a humongous effort to keep from squirming beneath his gaze.

"No, just *thinking*," I said a bit more forcefully, hoping that my insistence would make him drop it.

I half-expected to see his frown deepen, but his expression changed into something I couldn't quite understand. The intensity and seriousness of his stare remained the same, and although he was no longer frowning, his lips were set in a fairly neutral line. Nevertheless, for some reason, he gave the impression that he was really laughing at me even though there wasn't an ounce of amusement present physically in his demeanor. It was really unnerving.

After staring at me for a few more nerve-wracking seconds, his lips finally twitched up into a half-smile, and I was thankfully able to breathe normally again. He took one of my hands that had been unknowingly clutching the sheets around my waist tightly and gave it a squeeze.

"I shall send the healer to see you after the midday meal, so make certain to rest well before then," Sethian said.

Because the healer will no doubt report immediately back to you, I thought wryly. I really hoped that he didn't expect me to spend the next eight months "resting" in bed. I would die of boredom.

I nodded anyway, content to follow his instructions, if only for today. I was still blissfully free from yesterday's terrible nausea, and without Sethian here to remedy me, I wasn't about to do anything that may cause it to return.

Sethian smiled and squeezed my hand one last time before he slid off the bed and strode across the room to his closet, offering a nice, long parting shot of his nude backside that had my face heating up with arousal rather than embarrassment. It definitely made up for the slight disappointment of not receiving a parting kiss.

I took advantage of his absence to snatch my discarded nightgown from the ground and quickly slipped it on. In a few minutes, I would be telling Lariel, Saeria, and Rinwen about the baby, and the last thing I wanted to be was nude when all the inevitable hugging occurred.

CHAPTER 19

"I knew it," Lariel said in lieu of a greeting as she hurried into the bedroom, Saeria and Rinwen, carrying what was probably my breakfast tray, on her heels.

I winced inside at her accusative tone. I had thought the plan was for me to spill the beans on my pregnancy, but…

I rose up a bit onto my elbows from my prone position on the bed and asked, "Knew what?"

"His Majesty just informed us that a healer would be in to see you after the midday meal and to make sure that you did nothing but rest until then," she replied. She stood at the side of the bed and peered down at my face critically. "I *knew* you were sicker than you wanted us to believe. Why would you even want to keep something like that to yourself?"

I let myself fall back onto the bed, internally sighing with relief. They still didn't know, and now I wouldn't have to explain why I had kept the pregnancy from them. I could tell them on my own terms.

"The healer isn't coming here because I'm sick." I paused and then amended, "Well, I *was* pretty nauseous yesterday, but it wasn't because I had caught a bug or because of my nerves."

I looked from Lariel and Rinwen and smiled sheepishly. "It seems both of you were right to be suspicious. My lord husband confirmed it for me last night. I'm going to have a baby."

Although I didn't expect any of them to squeal like a tween at a boy-band concert or something as equally undignified, I did expect exclamations of delight or the usual congratulations at the very least. That's why when Lariel suddenly burst into tears, I didn't know what to think or how to react. She didn't sob noisily or even move to cover her face with her hands. They were silent tears that fell slowly down her cheeks as she looked down at me with eyes so full of happiness that they practically glowed, as though I had given her the greatest gift in the world.

I reached a hand up to her, wanting to stop her tears

but having no clue what to do. "Lariel..." I said uncertainly, feeling my chest tighten almost painfully with a maelstrom of emotions.

She smiled prettily at me and shook her head. "I'm sorry. This is unseemly, I know."

She sat down next to me on the bed and took my hands into both of hers as gently and carefully as if they were made of glass. I finally got a good look at the strangely silent sisters standing side-by-side over Lariel's shoulder.

Rinwen's usually pale face was flushed red, and her expression was so ecstatic it seemed she was a breath away from bursting, her eyes shimmering with blatant happiness as she looked at me with a wide grin. It almost looked as though she was on the verge of tears, herself. Saeria was both smiling and absently wringing her hands as if she was anxious to jump forward, to touch me or to hug me, I don't know, but as the sisters always seemed to follow Lariel's lead, she would probably stay rooted to that spot while the younger elf was still gushing over me unless I called her over.

I freed one of my hands and beckoned them over. "Come, sit with me. Just put the tray on the desk over there, Rinwen. I'd like to talk for a bit before I eat."

"You were so certain that you had not conceived—did you not hear the child's soul?" Saeria asked once everyone had arranged themselves comfortably around me along both edges of the bed.

I shook my head. "Seth-my lord says that human women can't hear it until later on in the pregnancy."

"I can just imagine your shock when the king told you," Lariel said.

"I had no idea he would be able to hear the baby like that. In hindsight, I should have asked more questions about elven children. I never considered that things would be so different."

"It seems we all should have asked more questions about each other," Saeria said. "Having a mental connection with our families is just so fundamental that I never once considered that it would not be so for you and your child, especially since you already have such a strong connection to His Majesty."

"Huh? Connection?" I tried to sit up, but Lariel's hands were immediately on my shoulders, pushing me back down again. "Wait a minute! What do you mean?"

Saeria and Rinwen shared a *look* before Saeria answered, "So you don't hear His Majesty's soul either?"

I was about to shake my head no, but then the memory surfaced again of that strange incident when I had momentarily felt what Sethian was feeling. Is that what everyone meant when they said they "heard" a person's soul? Some kind of super empathy?

"I think I might have once, on the second day I was here, but sometimes I've gotten the feeling that—"

I abruptly stopped, unsure for what seemed as though the thousandth time if it was something I should even talk about. I wanted to scream and yank at my hair in frustration. I *really* hated all this royal court etiquette crap, having to second-guess myself every time I opened my mouth.

All monarchies should be abolished, I thought crossly. "Never mind," I said aloud. "It was probably just my imagination, anyway."

"No, the connection definitely exists," Saeria insisted. "His Majesty already knew you were feeling out of sorts before he saw you two evenings ago when I spoke to him on my way to the royal suite."

I looked at Saeria sharply. It seems I was right to worry that she had been talking to Sethian while off running her errands that night. I would definitely have to watch what I said around all three of them from now on. Not that it would make a whole lot of difference, I suddenly realized. If Sethian knew what I felt even when he wasn't anywhere near me...

I closed my eyes with a groan. We seriously needed to talk about the soul reading thing a lot more the next time I saw him because apparently, I needed to teach him a little something called boundaries.

"Maybe I can't hear his soul or whatever very well because I'm still pretty much human even with all the changes my lord said that mage did to me."

"Perhaps," Rinwen agreed, the sound of her soft voice startling me a little. She had been so quiet during our discussion that I had forgotten she was there. "The accounts of the human brides in the old texts are vague at best, so I doubt anything was ever written on the matter. That being said, I think I should go to the archives after the healer attends you anyway and ask the archivist to find as many documents or books that reference the human brides of old. We may find something important that our earlier histories have missed."

"I wish I could read them, too," I said wistfully.

There was very little I could read from both the bookshelves in my bedroom or the library back in the apartment. Although Lariel had been trying to teach me the seemingly endless amount of elven glyphs, it would be a long time before I would be able to read with any proficiency given my dismal foreign language skills.

"One day I expect you will be reading our histories to your child," Lariel said firmly.

My chest tightened at the mental image her words conjured up of me sitting on one of the overstuffed reading chairs in the library with a small, blond boy in my lap and a thick book in his much as I had done with my father before he had died.

"But you three will need to teach him or her Elvish," I said, my voice thick with emotion. "God knows my horrendous accent doesn't need to be passed on."

All three women laughed. "Your accent will get better, as well," Lariel said.

The sound of the front door opening abruptly resonated in the background and everyone stilled.

"It's still too early for the healer," Lariel said with a frown towards the closed bedroom door.

"It's probably just my lord husband," I said. "I mean, who else would the guards just let waltz into the king's rooms unannounced?"

A second later I nearly jumped out of my skin when the door to the bedroom flew open, and there in the threshold as if the universe was giving me the ultimate finger stood my worst nightmare glaring at us from a face as beautiful as a porcelain doll's.

"Leave us," the elven queen commanded sharply. "I wish to speak with the Royal Wife alone."

CHAPTER 20

I mutely watched Lariel's back, stiff with unease, disappear as she closed the bedroom door behind her with a feeling akin to panic. Once again, I mentally cursed the courtly protocol that prevented not only my friends but also me from disobeying a direct order from the queen without severe consequence. Sethian had said that our unborn child currently outranked the queen, but that fact in no way meant that I did, too. Until he presented me to the elven court officially as the Royal Wife, I didn't even exist in their eyes.

I hastily sat up and scooted back against the headboard. If I had to talk to the queen, I sure as hell wasn't going to do it flat on my back. I expected her to come over to the bed, maybe even order me to get up and demand that I prostrate myself before her or something equally demeaning. When she did neither and just continued to stare expressionlessly at me from across the room, that's when I realized that I really had no idea what kind of person she was other than the bits and pieces I had gleaned from the rare times Sethian or my friends had mentioned her over the past month.

There was no way that she was here to congratulate me on my pregnancy, but maybe she did want to offer a kind of truce between us for Sethian's sake.

"I trust that you warned your ladies-in-waiting not to speak of the child?" she abruptly asked.

I didn't, but I nodded anyway since I had every intention of doing it later once this very uncomfortable visit was over. This definitely wasn't how I thought she would begin the conversation.

"It's a disgrace, you see," she continued, sounding quite matter-of-fact, "a disgrace to our people letting a *human* birth the next heir who will rule us all one day. Our king and a good many of our people may see you humans as our race's salvation as the people of old once did, but I am not the only one who believes it would be better for our people to just fade into the pages of our long history than to couple with lesser life-forms."

The more she spoke, the more my back stiffened. Every ounce of good will I had been prepared to offer her for the sake of civility drained out with each ugly word. Then to add insult to injury, she suddenly laughed at what was probably the look of disdain on my face that I just couldn't hide.

"Is that so?" I forced out past the huge lump of rising anger in my throat.

"Truth is always hard to hear," she said with a look that almost looked like pity had someone else been wearing it. "I am speaking to you of this as much for your sake as ours. What the king is doing is unnatural, and it was this very unnatural act of mating with humans that is ultimately the cause of our women's sterility."

"What do you mean?" I asked reluctantly, utterly sure that I didn't want to hear anymore but knowing I couldn't afford not to.

At this point, I was pretty sure the queen was trying to rattle me for whatever messed up reason, but it was for that very reason that the things she was about to tell me would be the truth—or at least the truth as she saw it.

The smile she flashed me was bitter. "Sethian would never tell you this, but our healers believe that our genome was irrevocably tainted sometime in the ancient past when a few of our male ancestors for whatever unfathomable reason mated and had offspring with humans. The *Sidhe* have never been a very fertile race, and when it was discovered that these half-blood children were extraordinarily fertile, they were sought out by all the noble families. Thus, the human taint was spread far and wide through several generations before the first of our women began to be born barren."

"How can you be so sure that the human genes were the cause?" I asked. "How can you be sure it's not just a case of correlation rather than causation?"

The queen sniffed. "Our present-day healers are not so primitive as your human doctors. When examined, all the barren women had one thing in common. Their genome had reached a threshold in which at least ten percent of it was comprised of human genes."

"But—with that logic, wouldn't a first-generation child of a pure elf and a pure human also be born barren?" I said pointedly. "That obviously didn't happen since you said that there was a lot of interbreeding with these half-breed children over a long period of time."

For a moment, the queen looked slightly taken aback, as though she didn't expect a "mongrel" like me to really understand her explanation.

Then she scowled, and with the air of the long-suffering, she replied, "That is because it is a problem that can only present itself after a long period of time. Human genes are not easily passed to my people, and the few that do, with the exception of those that determine virility, are recessive, thus remaining mostly dormant. However, once the human taint is introduced, it can never be reduced, but it *can* accumulate, doubly so within our daughters. Eventually, it is this human poison that disrupts a *Sidhe* woman's very essence, an essence vital in the process of conception. Without it, our partner's seed will never reach its destination.

"Many a healer and mage have tried to remove the humanity from within us over the millennia, but they have yet to find a way to do so without it killing us. However, they believe that, in time, a solution *will* be found."

I couldn't for the life of me figure out why she was telling me all this. What exactly was she hoping to gain? Was she trying to make me feel guilty about her inability to have a baby out of spite? Did she want me to apologize? I would do it if only to reduce the amount of these kinds of confrontations that I would have to deal with in the future.

However, the queen was still talking, so I kept any forthcoming apologies behind my teeth for the moment.

"It has long been suspected that Sethian's mother was a human transmuted to look completely like an elf and the realm fed the lie that the king had decided to take a second wife from among the *Lithvir Sidhe* royal family when the queen chosen for him from my own people failed to produce a child after several thousand years. It was a very unconventional decision as the *Lithviri* rarely interact with our two peoples, much less intermarry.

"The king went to great lengths to make certain that her blood was never examined, and when she died, he tended to her body himself and held her wake only a few marks later rather than wait the traditional complete moon-cycle. It was also strange that although she was supposedly a member of the Nalldir royal family, not one *Lithvir Sidhe* attended her wake."

The queen paused, and the smile that stretched her lips was unnerving, as though she knew she was about to drive in the knife. "She conceived within their first year of marriage, though Sethian was to be their only child. Now that you have conceived just as quickly, the suspicion is even more plausible. You have proved more perceptive than I had initially thought possible, so I believe you have noticed that the king's features are very different compared to the *Sidhe* men around him. The ancient texts mention this as a characteristic of a true half-blood."

I reluctantly nodded. His face did look a little less alien than all the other elves I had seen.

"For a half-blood to conceive a child with a human—could that child even be considered a *Sidhe?* You must understand that the people will never accept such a creature to sit on the elven throne."

"It seems the only way 'the people' would even know that my baby was different than they expected was if *you* told them your suspicions about Sethian's parentage," I said coldly. "Suspicions, I might add, that you can't even prove."

The queen's eyes narrowed. "The elven realm is no place for a human. You cannot possibly understand the turmoil you will cause once your pregnancy becomes public. The very act will open the gates for more of your kind to flood this realm to introduce more tainted children to those who are too desperate to care. The healers of my people are so close to finally finding the method of safely removing the human genes from our genome. Are you so selfish to deny all the women of this realm a chance to have a child of their blood?"

Her words hit me like a well-aimed slap to the face. No matter that she had chosen to deliver them in the bluntest way possible, it didn't take away the uncomfortable fact that there was some truth in them.

"What is it you want me to do by telling me all this?" I demanded, suddenly feeling as tired as I had yesterday and unwilling to play this game with her any longer.

The look of triumph in her eyes that she couldn't quite hide had me instantly regretting my words. "What is right. Return to your own realm, on this very day before the king returns to these rooms."

I sucked in a sharp, startled breath. "Even if I wanted to, which I absolutely *don't* just so we're clear, I can't exist completely in the human realm anymore because of the changes to my body, right?"

"My family has a mage with the ability to return you to your previous form. The king will be told that you miscarried, that you came to me heartsick and asking for help to leave the realm, unable to bear the thought of facing him."

For a long moment, I stared at her, frozen in utter disbelief of her audacity. It didn't take a genius to figure out what having such an extreme transformation to my entire body would do to a baby at such a fragile stage of development. That she would even propose something so horrible as calmly as if we were discussing a change of clothes was just so…so…

"Get out!" I snarled. To hell with court etiquette! There was no way I was going to let her get away with even *thinking* something so despicable. "I don't care if you *are* the queen. If you're not out of this room in two seconds, I'll scream for the guards! I may not outrank you, but my baby *does*. If it's for the heir's welfare, then I'm sure no one will object to my throwing you out of here, least of all Sethian! How *dare* you even *suggest* something that would hurt *my* baby!"

The queen suddenly stepped towards the bed and grabbed my upper arm before I could flinch away. "Hurt? I am trying to *help* you, you foolish child!" she hissed, squeezing my arm tightly. "There are many things the king has failed to tell you out of his own selfish desire for a child. He knows very well the trouble this half-blood child will bring to the stability of the elven court. Why do you think that he keeps you locked away and guarded as closely as the royal coffers? You have no idea of the forces that are currently moving around you. Soon you will be begging to be sent home!"

"Your pregnancy will change everything*."*

I wrenched my arm from her grip, Sethian's words from last night echoing ominously in my mind. "I hardly call two guards on the door extensive protection. Forget your games of intrigue and just tell it to me clearly because right now all I see is a desperate woman trying to scare me into doing something unbelievably stupid."

I knew I should stop, that I was probably going too far. There was no telling what this powerful woman could do to me, but once my anger had been unleashed, it was impossible to hold my tongue, especially when I had no real desire to.

If looks could kill, I would have been dead *and* mutilated a million times over. Yes, the line had definitely been crossed—on both sides.

"If insults are my thanks for trying to help a human then this will definitively be the last time," the queen spat as she turned on her heel and stalked towards the door, wrenching it open. "Take a knife to the throat of one of those Maelenas sisters, and you will see that you truly know *nothing*."

The door slammed so violently behind her that I thought the walls around it would crack.

The queen was right about one thing. The last few minutes proved that I really did know absolutely nothing about the elven realm, but now that my eyes had been opened wide, I was determined to change that fact, starting with a little question to Saeria and Rinwen concerning knives…

The moment I heard the door to the front entrance slam equally as hard as the bedroom's, the bedroom door swung open, admitting three very-worried-looking elven women.

"I'm okay," I was quick to assure them as they hurried over to my side again. "The queen just didn't like what I had to say, is all."

"I don't think I have ever seen her show that much emotion," Lariel said, tilting her head at me with an implied question.

I sagged against the headboard wearily. Talking with the queen had been as draining as a long, uphill hike. "Let's just say that she just gave me a crash course in elven politics and was unhappy when I didn't want to play along." I turned from Lariel to the sisters. "She also hinted to something interesting about you two."

When both Saeria and Rinwen stiffened, it was as good as an admission. Encouraged, I pressed on, "Did my lord husband assign you both to me as bodyguards as well as my ladies-in-waiting?"

They exchanged a look before Saeria sighed, looking resigned. "His Majesty is going to be very angry when he learns the queen told you this. He had been quite emphatic that you were to never know."

"He probably just didn't want to worry me," I reasoned as Lariel stuffed a couple of my pillows behind my back. "The queen was trying to make a point about my ignorance or else I don't think she would have brought the matter up at all."

"No matter the reason, it was still forbidden to tell you," Saeria said.

I shrugged. "It's not like I mind." I looked at them curiously. "Are you hiding a bunch of knives or daggers on you?" Their dresses looked so thin and airy that I couldn't see how they could conceal anything as large as a dagger.

Rinwen sat on the edge of the bed and held out her hand. "Watch," she instructed.

Then her entire hand glowed a bright, white light, and a second later, a rather large, jewel-hilted dagger with a black, shiny blade that looked like obsidian appeared in her hand.

"Wow, so you can manipulate space just like the king," I said, impressed.

"No, nothing like His Majesty," Rinwen replied. "My power is very limited. This dagger is the largest object I can phase into another dimension. Saeria can conceal objects as large as a long sword. Our family's strengths lie in protection and combat rather than what you would call elven magic. Our father is the head of His Highness's royal guard. Our mother is quite the archer and huntress."

Come to think of it, this is the first time either one of them had mentioned their parents. They had often brought up their older brother and an occasional cousin or uncle, but it had never crossed my mind to ask about their parents. Lariel's family served as either tailors or scribes in the palace, so I guess I had just assumed that Saeria and Rinwen's family did something similar.

"I would very much like to meet both of your families sometime," I said. "Oh, but my lord husband wants us to keep my pregnancy to ourselves for now, so it would probably have to wait until after he presents me to the court and announces it publically."

Lariel nodded. "That would be best."

"Speaking of, that was another thing the queen came here to discuss with me," I said, watching their expressions closely, "how the court will react to the news of my pregnancy."

The fact that their expressions didn't change at all was quite telling.

"Did you know?" I asked. "About your ancestors having children with humans being the cause of your infertility?"

I don't know what changed, but suddenly Lariel no longer looked even remotely like a teenaged girl, her true age making itself known through the eyes that stared back at me with the weight of centuries. "We did, but it does not matter," she replied quietly, solemnly. "What use is there blaming anyone for something that was impossible to foresee? All we can do now is move forward. Before you arrived, we couldn't even do that. Now, we have the chance to grow again, maybe not exactly as the beings we once were, but still *Sidhe* all the same."

If only Limira could have heard all of that, I thought, my lips stretching into a smile. "I think so, too."

CHAPTER 21

I knew he was behind me before I felt his arms encircle my waist, alerted by a strange thickening of the air around me. I turned away from the vast ocean I had been admiring, its waters reflecting a bright orange as the sun slowly sank below the horizon, and smiled just as brightly up at Sethian as I leaned back into his embrace. He would probably scold me for being out of bed, but after lying in bed all day, I had started to get a bit of cabin fever.

I had flat-out told my friends that I was getting up to watch the sun set out here on the king's balcony as I had often done on my own over the past month. Our balconies luckily faced the same direction, so the same gorgeous ocean view was available to me here. It had become somewhat of a comfort to see that the sun still looked the same here in the elven realm.

"You know what I am going to say, don't you?" Sethian said, the amusement in his eyes taking the sting out of his words.

"Fresh air is good for me, too," I said firmly, turning completely around inside the circle of his arms. I wanted to see his face better while we spoke. "Besides, even the healer said it was fine for me to get up. She also did something like you did to ease my nausea when my morning sickness started to come back, something more permanent, she claimed."

He nodded. "Yara tended to the last of our pregnant women centuries ago."

"No wonder she seemed so—enthusiastic." When the woman had placed her hands on my abdomen, they had shaken, she had been so excited, but it was nothing to the joy she had expressed when she announced that she could feel the baby's "essence" and that it was vibrant and strong.

At one uncomfortable point, I had thought for sure that the healer was about to start crying just like Lariel had. It had made me wonder if she had never been able to have children of her own. Not that I would have dared asked.

"I hear that the healer was not your only visitor today," he said, his eyes daring me to deny it.

The guards, damn them, must have blabbed to him since none of the girls had left my side for longer than a few minutes all afternoon. The fact that the queen hadn't seemed worried at all about me ratting her out to Sethian really worried *me,* so I hadn't really decided whether or not I was going to say anything to him about the awful things she had tried to get me to agree to. There had to be a reason for her fearlessness, and I wondered if she actually *wanted* Sethian to know she had done these things—as a warning, to hurt him, the list of possible motives was endless.

I had suddenly found myself playing a game full of potentially dangerous pitfalls without knowing the rules, and I was scared.

"You must have ears in all the walls," I mildly accused.

"Whatever Limira came here to say to you must have really upset you if you do not wish to speak to me about it."

I sighed and pressed my face into his chest. "She was really upset herself when she came to talk to me, so I'm not sure I should say anything about it at all. It couldn't have been easy for her to hear about my pregnancy."

I felt Sethian suddenly stiffen. "Did she berate you

because you are human?" he demanded, his voice tinged with anger.

I looked up at him and was a little shocked at the level of anger that smoldered in his eyes. They were practically glowing with it, and the effect was more than a little unnerving. It made me wonder if they had argued about me concerning the very issues the queen had ruthlessly shoved in my face earlier.

"Actually, she seemed more concerned with you," I said hesitantly. It was probably a very bad idea to bring up the question of his mother's true identity right now when he was already so angry, but for the sake of our baby, I needed to know the truth before he or she was born. "She mentioned your mother, that a lot of people suspected that she was like me, a human who had been transmuted. Only—your father went one step farther and had the mage change her to look completely like an elf and then lied about her being a member of the Nalldir royal family."

Sethian's arms tightened around my waist in reaction to my words, but his expression remained angry and unchanged. "Yes, I have heard that particular tale many times. Limira is hardly the first person to think me a half-blood because of my facial features, and she certainly won't be the last. What she probably failed to mention is that it is not unheard of for an elven child to exhibit a purely human trait. For me, it is the wider dimensions of my face, for others, it has been brown eyes or a more rounded ear tip. After all, we all possess at least a few human genes."

"She made it seem like half-bloods were looked down on by a lot of people." His eyes seemed to darken with every word I spoke. I swallowed nervously and forced myself to go on, "She was worried that the people wouldn't accept our baby as heir because he might just be more human than elf."

For one long, seemingly eternal moment, I forgot to breathe as Sethian's eyes literally flashed brightly with what looked like rage. However, before my mind could really start to freak out about just how scary he now looked, he shut his eyes tightly and took a slow, deep breath in an obvious attempt to calm down.

"No—I shall not play this game with her," he said quietly, the anger gone from his voice. He took another deep breath and opened his eyes, looking down at me with an expression that was less angry and more grim. "Do not let what she has told you upset you any longer. Although what she has told you concerning the prejudices among the *Sidhe* in regards to humans is true enough, she has inflated the views of a very small portion of my people and hers completely out of proportion. They are deep-seated prejudices these individuals have held for longer than I have been alive and have nothing to do with your appearance here in the realm. The vast majority of the realm will accept our child as their future king with open arms and much joy. Your ladies-in-waiting reflect this attitude well."

I knew very well that he was just telling me what I wanted to hear, that the issue was nowhere near so simple. Had that been the case, he wouldn't have gotten so angry at the mere mention of it. However, after the emotional upheaval the queen had put me through earlier, I was just too worn out to pursue it any further right now.

"Yes, they were pretty ecstatic when I told them I was pregnant. I think it'll be very hard for them to keep the news to themselves until you announce it. Saeria and Rinwen have been telling me for days how anxious some of their relatives are for the chance to have children of their own. I imagine they thought they would have to wait decades."

"For some of them, it may in fact be decades. The process of bringing human brides to the realm can be a long, complicated affair, and conceiving a child, even more so."

Sethian loosened his arms around me and pulled away just enough to grab one of my hands. "Come. I ordered dinner be brought to us before heading to the suite. I suspect you have several days of illness to make up for."

I WAS PICKING up the nightgown one of the girls had left folded at the foot of the bed when I abruptly felt Sethian walk up behind me and rest a hand on my upper arm. I paused and turned to look back at him over my shoulder quizzically.

"Leave it," he said. "Tonight I wish to feel the bareness of your skin all night. Undress for me?"

That he had made it a request this time rather than a command was somehow more embarrassing. I could feel the fire in my cheeks before I could even turn my head back towards the bed. I had been feeling somewhat bummed out all evening since he hadn't kissed me once, not even on my forehead, and now he suddenly wanted me to strip without any kind of foreplay!

Feeling as awkward as I had the first time, I slowly pulled down the left sleeve of my dress off my shoulder, my mind going a mile-a-minute. I had no idea how to make taking off my clothes look sexy, but you were supposed to slide everything off slowly, weren't you?

I pulled my arm free of the sleeve, getting my elbow caught in it along the way which was definitely *not* sexy, and started on my right. By now, it was all I could do to keep myself from hyperventilating, and I knew if I had not started this with my back turned to him, my head would have either exploded or I would have been unable to begin, period.

My right arm was now out, and I started on unlacing the bodice. This part I knew I should turn around for, the revealing of one of the "main courses" in the feast for his eyes, but I just couldn't make myself do it. I would definitely make the world's worst exhibitionist, and I was certain that, at this point, Sethian was getting more than a little irritated with my performance so far if the dead silence coming from behind me was any indication.

With my bodice unlaced, it became a simple matter of pulling the material apart and then either pulling the dress over my head or letting it fall to the ground. Knowing that hell would freeze over before I could make pulling the dress over my head into something erotic and appealing, I opted for the latter.

As I clutched the edges of the material that were opened on either side of my boobs and prepared to allow them to spill out, I had a sudden epiphany. Maybe if I looked ridiculous enough, he would never ask me to do this again. I just had to turn around and convince him what a bad idea this had been.

Taking a deep breath, made much more difficult by the huge knot of nervousness in my throat, I slowly turned around. At first, I couldn't meet his eyes, looking at a point just over his shoulder when I took the plunge and pushed the material slowly down to my waist. You could have heard a pin drop in that room—well, in the space of time between each of my ragged breaths, I mean. The silence stretched on, to the point where my breaths were starting to sound a little panicky, and I just couldn't stand it any longer. I had to look at him.

I don't know what I really expected to see when I looked at his face. Irritation? Amusement? Bewilderment? Stunned at how stupid I looked? That's why when my eyes met green eyes that were almost—spellbound as they stared at my semi-nude body, I was the one left stunned.

Sethian watched with that same intense interest for a few more seconds before he reached over with both hands and yanked the dress the rest of the way down over my hips until it fell to a heap at my feet. He then stepped back as I stood frozen, his eyes slowly running down the entire length of my body and then just as slowly back up again. It was almost as if he was licking me with his eyeballs the way my groin suddenly began to throb with arousal.

He reached out a hand again, and my stomach

clenched in anticipation of his touch. However, instead of caressing a breast or even tweaking a nipple as I had expected, his hand touched my breast bone lightly, as though afraid that my skin would shatter.

"So lovely," he said almost to himself. He ran the pads of his fingertips lightly across my chest, then moved his hands up to cup the side of my face. "It's as though your skin is glowing from within now that you are with child."

He tilted my chin up and finally delivered the kiss I had been waiting for all evening. It was soft, and gentle, but did not go beyond a brief, pleasurable caress of the lips.

"Although I enjoyed your efforts to please me just now, immensely, I did not mean to imply that we would make love tonight when I asked you to undress. I wish you to rest for tonight. The feel of your skin against my own will be pleasure enough for the moment."

If the floor suddenly opened up under me right now and swallowed me whole, I would have been grateful to the fates for saving me from the utter mortification I was feeling at the moment. Why, *why* did I keep turning every innocent thing from Sethian's mouth into something dirty lately? I wasn't so sure that I could blame my messed up hormones on sexing up my thoughts, either.

Sethian released my chin and gestured for me to get

into bed. I was beneath the blankets in record time, curled up on my side and my face buried into my pillow in a lame effort to hide from the world. I wondered if my face would ever lose its red tint of humiliation tonight.

A few minutes later, I felt the mattress dip as Sethian slipped into bed beside me, as naked as I was, but I did not turn to face him until I felt his hand on my shoulder.

"Lie on your back and draw the blankets down to your waist," he instructed.

Curious as to what he was up to, despite myself, I rolled onto my back as asked and looked up at him questionably. Sethian flashed me a smile before arranging himself on his side next to me and then laying his head carefully between my bare breasts.

"This way I can hear you both," he explained once he was settled.

His words made something in my chest tighten almost painfully. That he wanted to hear my heart as well was just…

I tentatively threaded my fingers through his hair and felt him sigh in pleasure against my skin. I had to say, this certainly was a pleasant way to end such a disquieting day.

CHAPTER 22

The way Sethian was currently scrutinizing my bare stomach this morning was a clear sign that the day I had been secretly dreading had finally come. I was now nearly five months along in the pregnancy, and my belly had grown to the point that my pregnancy was obvious.

"Today is the first day of spring," Sethian said with a grin. "I can think of no more appropriate day than this to announce the imminent birth of the first elven child in over five centuries."

"Then maybe now you will *finally* take me into Talloth like you promised," I scolded in an attempt to hide the fact that my anxiety levels had just shot through the roof.

"My people will probably wish to see you as well

once the announcement is made," he replied amicably. "Tomorrow, we shall make a day of it."

I blinked at him in surprise, not expecting him to give in so readily. Yes, he had promised, but as the days turned into months and I still hadn't been allowed to go anywhere outside the palace other than my garden, I had begun to think that it would never happen.

"Now, I will leave you to your ladies to prepare. Make certain to wear a gown that accents your waist. I want there to be no question as to the authenticity of your pregnancy."

A few elven-marks later, I found myself standing outside the enormous double doors leading into the throne room on the verge of a panic attack. My friends had dressed and groomed me within an inch of my life, making me feel like a princess in a pageant—or more accurately, a princess *doll* in a pageant. I had never seen three women looking more gleeful than when they had been stuffing me into this convoluted piece of white cloth they called a dress I was currently wearing. I swear there had been at least a thousand ties *and* buttons that needed to be done up in the right order and/or configuration or it would not fit as intended. I never in a million years would have been able to put it on by myself.

The least said about my hairstyle the better as far as I

was concerned. I was sure that my scalp was going to ache for weeks after all the pins and clips were removed.

It was utterly unsettling how much I had looked like an elf after they were done with me. Had I had the pointed ears and blonde hair, I don't think anyone would have known I was actually human. Maybe that had always been their intention, to make it easier for the court to accept a human in their midst and thus easier on *me,* but to see myself unexpectedly looking so vastly different *yet again* was more than a little upsetting.

I could tell that some of the guards that lined the walls on either side of the doors and along both sides of the wide corridor leading up to the entrance were staring at me, or rather my protruding belly, hard. The back of my neck practically itched with the feel of all those eyes fixed on me. It made me feel like a strange animal being paraded before a gawking crowd. To some in this crowd, the animal analogy might not be an analogy at all, I suddenly realized with some dismay.

When the herald finally announced me, I grimaced at the long list of pretentious titles attached to my very mundane name.

"Emily Ford, now of the Royal House of Elerren, Probationary Royal Wife of His Majesty Sethian of the Royal House of Elerren, King of the Second Realm!"

Even with Lariel, Saeria, and Rinwen at my back, I

felt horribly exposed the moment I stepped through those double doors and walked up the ridiculously long, center aisle that led up to the dais where Sethian sat on his throne looking every inch the regal and powerful elven king. The queen sat on the throne-seat to his left, her posture stiff and formal. The dais was too far away for me to see her face properly, but I swear I could feel her eyes trying to bore holes into my forehead.

To keep myself from hyperventilating, I fixed my eyes on Sethian and did not move my gaze from his face as I slowly walked what felt like miles towards the two monarchs. Even when I heard the soft murmurs, the gasps of shock, and felt the stares of the nobles standing on either side of me, I refused to look at them. I didn't want to know how many of those eyes held looks of disgust or even malice.

Once I reached the dais, my three friends bowed behind me and then split off to the left to stand in a single-file line just out of direct sight of the king and queen. I bowed to both monarchs in turn, as well. The queen might as well have been a statue for all she even acknowledged me or even *moved* for that matter. Sethian beckoned me closer with a flick of his wrist, and I started to climb the steps up to the king's level.

Once I stood before him, I bowed again and waited with my hands folded over my stomach. Only then did

Sethian stand and reach out a hand to me. He had explained to me that a Royal Wife could only be acknowledged within elven society as such if the king publically offered her his hand in front of the whole of the elven court. The deal was sealed when the Royal Wife-to-be accepted that hand publically. It was strange to me that something so simplistic had the power to make or break a person's life in this particular society.

I immediately placed my hand in his, and he clenched it tightly. "Let this be our bond," he said firmly, his voice echoing throughout the large chamber.

"Let this be our bond," I echoed, my voice sounding weak and unsure in comparison.

I was just glad that the words hadn't gotten stuck in my throat. It had been one of my main worries, but focusing completely on Sethian and refusing to look at anyone else had ultimately been my salvation.

Sethian lowered our hands but did not release me, instead, threading our fingers together more securely. Now came the part I dreaded the most. I slowly pivoted to stand beside Sethian to face the whole of the elven court for the first time. I tried not to look too closely at all the various expressions, but I saw them regardless. The excitement on some of the women's faces, the scrutinizing looks on others...a flash of disgust, a look of anger, a look of sympathy, though that last one was not directed at me but in the direction of the queen.

Sethian turned slightly to me and placed his free hand on the curve of my belly. "In a little over four moon-cycle's time, the plague of sadness that has ravaged our lands will finally see its first hope. Within the Royal Wife's womb lies the next potential heir to the throne of the Second Realm. With my child's birth, a new generation of *Sidhe* will come forth!"

The room abruptly erupted in a roar of voices, swallowing the last echoes of Sethian's last words. It was generally a sound of joy, there were even a few tears, but I couldn't help noticing the one noble here and there that remained silent while their neighbors celebrated. Some had their eyes fixed on me; others were looking at some of the other nobles around them with disdain. It wasn't just the men. I caught more than one woman looking at our joined hands with open disgust. I was actually a little shocked at how blatant these elves were being in their contempt.

It was a little galling to see how right the queen had been in her warnings, but I wasn't about to discount those warnings just because they came from someone I didn't like. It made me wonder if that had been her intent all along.

CHAPTER 23

I placed one hand on the stone ledge and gazed out towards the far horizon while my other hand rubbed my belly absently. Not for the first time, I wondered what my friend and roommate, Anna, was doing now. I could only imagine how much she had probably freaked out when she had realized that I was actually missing. It would have been only a matter of time before she had decided to go through my room and had discovered that not only was my car still parked outside the apartment but my purse with my driver's license, wallet, cell phone, and car keys inside was still sitting on my desk where I had left it.

Was she still living in the same apartment we had shared? The lease would have ended a month after I had disappeared. Had she renewed it in the hopes that I would either return or be found? So many unanswered questions...questions that would forever remain unanswered on both sides.

My chest tightened painfully as guilt surged up within me. Anna had been there for me during my grief after my mother had died as well as during my frequent bouts of self-doubt as I pursued my PhD, and this is how I had repaid her—a lifetime of wondering if her friend's body was rotting in a ditch somewhere.

Without warning, something dense hit me square in the back, making me violently jerk forward against the balcony ledge. For a split-second, I had no idea what had just happened until the sick feeling of falling registered in my mind, and I frantically reached my hands out blindly in a desperate attempt to grab onto something, *anything*! My arm slipped through one of the marble rungs that ran vertically across the entire length of the balcony. My hand immediately clutched at it and hung on for dear life as my arm very nearly wrenched out of its socket when I jerked to an abrupt stop, my hip slamming painfully against the unforgiving stone wall of the castle.

"Help me!" I screamed as I frantically tried to reach my other hand up to grab onto another one of the rungs and only succeeding in making my grip on the other more tenuous. "Lariel! Saeria!"

My arm was screaming with pain at the shoulder socket, and my feet could find no crevices within the castle's outer walls in order to dig my toes into. Then something seemed to grab onto one of my legs and pull down harshly, and I shrieked fit to wake the dead when I nearly lost my grip.

"Emily!" I heard Saeria suddenly cry out in horror from above.

She immediately fell to her knees and grabbed the arm above the elbow that I had wrapped around the rung with both hands just as I was losing my hold. She jerked up on my arm, trying to heave me up and through the gap between two rungs, but she could not raise me more than a couple of inches, as though my body weighed a ton.

Her hands gripping my arm like a vice, Saeria moved from her knees to her bottom and braced herself with the soles of both feet against a couple of the rungs just as I saw Lariel drop down to her knees and reach down to me with a look of utter terror in her eyes. "Rinwen!" Saeria called. "Summon the guards, quickly! We cannot pull her up on our own! Emily, reach your other hand up to Lariel!"

I immediately tried to lift my free arm higher towards Lariel's outstretched hand, but just as my fingers brushed her palm, my arm suddenly felt as if someone had strapped a hundred pound weight to it and dropped helplessly to my side again.

"I can't!" I cried, my voice high-pitched with fear and panic. "Something's pulling hard on both my arm and one of my legs!"

As if on cue, I abruptly lurched downwards with a shriek of pain as my leg was pulled hard enough that I feared it had been dislocated at the hip. There was an enormous pressure surrounding my calf, as though a huge hand was squeezing it tightly. I tried to reach for Lariel's hand again, but the invisible weight on my arm was too much. I didn't dare use more force, afraid that I would accidentally jerk out of Saeria's hold.

Then suddenly, impossibly, the air shimmered and warped behind Lariel and Saeria like a heat wave in the distance, and Sethian faded into existence. The second he spotted me, his expression melted into a look so horrified that I knew I would never forget it for the rest of my life. He brushed the younger girl away without a word as he fell to his knees and thrust his arms through the rungs to grab my arm over Saeria's hands. Our eyes met, and my whole body seemed to freeze.

"Don't let go," he told Saeria in a tight voice.

Then the rungs of the balcony above me began to fade and change, and my knees abruptly slammed painfully down onto something hard as one of the couches in Sethian's suite faded into view. I grunted in pain as I started to fall forward, but then Sethian's chest was suddenly there, his arms reaching out to catch me before I could fall more than a few inches.

I couldn't help it. All the fear and panic came rushing out in an overwhelming avalanche of emotion, and I burst into tears just as he gathered me up into his arms.

I almost died! I almost died! Oh my God, I almost died!

That terrifying realization ran through my head like a mantra stuck on infinite repeat as I clutched the front of Sethian's robes so tightly that my fingers ached and sobbed noisily into his chest. I don't know how long I remained in that state, but when my sobs finally began to die down and the world outside my head came into focus again, I became conscious of the fact that I was sitting sideways across Sethian's lap. One of his arms was wrapped snuggly around my body and his other hand gently stroking through my hair. He, in turn, was sitting on one of the couches. I had been so far gone that I hadn't even felt him lift me up and carry me over.

I drew in a slow, shaky breath in an effort to stifle the last of my sobs and snuggled even closer to his body. I would have been fine to remain as we were for the rest of my life, to not have to deal with what had just happened, but as always, reality had a bad habit of intruding.

A loud knock sounded at the front door, and I practically jumped out of my skin with a cry of alarm. I felt Sethian stiffen beneath me but then Lariel's familiar voice called through the door, and he instantly relaxed. He began to rub my back soothingly.

"Enter," Sethian called, and the front door swung open to admit both Lariel and Yara, my healer.

I immediately lifted my head from Sethian's chest and began scrubbing at my eyes vigorously, embarrassed to be seen in the aftermaths of my emotional breakdown, even by my friend and a woman I had grown to trust implicitly over the past three months.

Both women came into the room only a few steps and bowed to Sethian while the guard that had admitted them closed the door behind them. The room was so silent that I easily heard the guards bolting the door heavily from the other side.

"Hold on to me," Sethian said suddenly, turning my attention back to him.

I hastily put my arms around his neck as he gathered me more securely in his arms and stood.

"She will be more comfortable in the bedroom while you examine her," he directed at Yara before proceeding to carry me, bridle-style, to the bedroom.

Sethian carefully laid me down onto the bed without bothering to draw down the blankets. I winced when I started to straighten my legs and a sharp pain flared up in both my hip and my knees. Now that I was no longer sobbing, I realized just how much my body was hurting.

"Where does it hurt?" Sethian asked, his brows furrowed in concern.

"Almost everywhere," I replied truthfully, "but the worst places are my left hip and both knees. I remember hitting both pretty hard." I rubbed a hand over my swollen belly. "I was lucky," I said softly, my throat tightening when I felt a little flutter of movement inside and another onslaught of tears threatened to rise. "I didn't hit my stomach at all, not even when I went over the edge of—"

Sethian placed a finger against my mouth and shook his head. I flushed, realizing that what had just happened wasn't something I should be discussing in front of the healer.

He lifted up the skirt of my dress, and I gasped loudly when I saw the huge blood-red bruise that had already formed along my hip and extended halfway down the side of my upper leg. The look on Sethian's face was almost murderous as his eyes moved from my hip down the length of my legs. A couple of reddish bruises had also begun to form on both knee caps, but nowhere near as alarming in appearance as the one on my hip.

"I shall deal with these injuries," he said, turning to look at Yara. "It is the child I wish you to examine."

That's right. I had completely forgotten that he had mentioned healing as one of his abilities. I hadn't really thought about what that meant, so I had no idea what to expect. I lay still and watched quietly as he gently ran a hand over the bruise on my hip while Yara placed both of hers onto my stomach as she always did when examining me.

I had always been able to sense that Yara was doing *something*, as though I was somehow being touched on the inside of my abdomen. However, whatever Sethian was doing was definitely causing some kind of change because, for the first few seconds, my hip lit up sharply with a pain very much like the pain I had suffered when that elven mage had transmuted my body into its current form. I let out a startled whimper but managed to keep from moving as the pain swiftly lessened. The ugly red blotch on my skin began to noticeably fade along with the pain until the skin returned to its normal color and all I could feel was a pleasant warmth.

Sethian looked up at me, concern swirling in his eyes, and I flashed him a watery smile. "I'm fine," I assured him.

He nodded and moved down to tend to the bruises on my knees. I braced myself for the coming pain.

"All is well," Yara announced a few minutes later just as Sethian was finishing up my second knee. "The child was not physically harmed at all by the accident. I have calmed her energies, so there should be no lasting trauma to either."

I closed my eyes in relief. "Thank God," I whispered.

Yara removed her hands from my stomach and drew the skirt of my dress down again. I opened my eyes in enough time to see her bow again to Sethian.

"Shall I remain here to watch over her for the night, Your Majesty?" she asked.

Sethian shook his head. "I shall call for you if there is a need."

She bowed again without protest and turned to me one last time. "Rest—at least for a couple days just to be safe. I do not want you walking around unless absolutely necessary."

I sighed but nodded. So much for that trip into Talloth tomorrow that I really had been looking forward to. I swear the universe really was conspiring against me.

"You may take your leave," Sethian said formally, and after squeezing my hand affectionately, Yara quietly left the room.

Now that we were alone, I expected Sethian to immediately start grilling me on what had happened, but instead of the Spanish Inquisition, I was met with dead silence and a hard stare.

I wet my lips uneasily and said, "Sethian?"

Only then did he seem to shake himself and look back at me with a more normal expression. "They can wait," he said enigmatically.

Puzzled, I watched him swiftly round the bed and then climb onto the mattress beside me. He pulled a couple of pillows from beneath the coverlet and used them to prop himself up against the headboard. Then he held out his arms to me.

"Come. I need to feel you against me. I need to hear our child's soul."

I didn't need to be told twice.

I settled myself between his legs, sitting with my back pressed up against his chest. His arms immediately snaked around my middle until both hands rested on my baby bump.

For a long moment, we just sat together in silence, his nose buried into the crook of my neck where he would occasionally inhale deeply as if savoring my scent, before he said simply, "Tell me."

"Something or someone pushed me from behind while I was standing near the edge," I said with utter certainty.

Whatever hit me in the back could be explained

away by a piece of falling stone that had suddenly broken off from the castle walls above or other such debris—if it hadn't been for that invisible force that had tried its damnedest to pull my leg off before Saeria and Lariel could pull me back up, and I said as much.

I felt him go positively rigid beneath me.

"Have you ever felt something like that before?" he asked in a voice so devoid of emotion that it was chilling.

I shook my head, suddenly unable to talk around the huge lump of anxiety that had formed in my throat as I felt his presence swell around me until it had become a physical thing that was slowly weighing me down from all sides. He must have sensed my sudden distress because the suffocating pressure around me immediately lessened, and his hands started to rub soothing circles over my belly.

"I shall find the one responsible, I promise you," Sethian said, each word dripping with a potent anger.

Once again, I could only nod my head. Although his anger scared me, I took some comfort in his obvious outrage.

"How did you know I was in trouble, anyway?" I asked once I could make my tongue work again.

"I heard your cry of fear."

"So you were already nearby? Thank God for coincidences."

I felt him shake his head. "No. I heard it here." I followed his hand with my eyes as he lifted it to tap the side of his head. "And here." He placed that same hand over my heart.

I looked back at him incredulously. "How is that possible? I'm not an elf. I can't do incredible things like that!"

"Is it so strange to think that when you cried out with your voice with such strong emotion, your soul cried out as well? One needs only the ability to listen. After all, you have 'heard' the voice of my soul once before."

"Huh? Oh…that's right…" He was referring to the Incident, the one that he *still* hadn't explained. The one I would have to bring up later because right now I had a more important question.

I turned a little in his arms so that I could see his face better. His expression was grim. "Do you know why someone would want to try to—to try to k-kill me?" I asked tentatively.

The queen's face flashed through my mind, but it was a choice so obvious that I immediately dismissed it. Besides, it wasn't that long ago that she had warned me in a roundabout way that something like this could happen. Although she probably wasn't the culprit, that hint alone said that she knew a lot more than she was telling either Sethian or me.

Sethian's lips tightened as his anger resurfaced. "Unfortunately, there are more reasons than I can name, any just as likely as the other," he replied. "There are some that had hoped my coupling with you would fail, that after a hundred years or so without an heir being conceived, my claim to the throne would become invalid by reason of sterility."

"Then—this isn't about me being human? Someone wants your throne? Someone in the queen's family maybe?"

As soon as those last words left my mouth, I wished desperately that I could take them back. I hadn't meant to accuse her at all given my obvious bias against her from the beginning, but I was still severely shaken by my near-death experience; the pause button between my brain and my mouth was apparently still broken.

However, instead of an increase of anger, Sethian's expression merely became much graver.

"Perhaps yes to all of that," he said. "Today you saw some of that contempt firsthand when a few from the court looked upon you. It is resentment born from feelings of failure. How can we need the genes of humans to insure that the next generation is fertile, especially when it was those same human genes that caused the sterility in the first place?

"On the other hand, there are more things afoot than the desire to erase an imagined shame. Limira's people have always coveted the power my family wields. A king will never bear their family's name. Their desire for the throne has been something of an open secret for millennia, a deadly game our families have played against each other since my ancestor won the right to rule over our people tens of thousands of years ago.

"Of course, the House of Vanvir aren't the only ones who covet my throne. I am certain members of my own House were equally troubled by your extremely swift pregnancy. Had I been confirmed sterile, then the next in line to the throne would have been given the chance to either conceive a child with Limira, or even a human wife, in order to cement his claim to be king."

He suddenly leaned forward and brushed his lips briefly against mine before pulling back and flashing me a tight smile. "I imagine whoever was behind the attempt on your life is now desperately hoping that the child is not male because, as you humans say, hell will freeze over before anyone will ever get near enough to you again to try."

CHAPTER 24

That I was now living in a gilded cage was an understatement.

The day after my attempted murder, Sethian had assigned what amounted to a small army to stand guard at every possible point around the royal suite and my personal garden. Visits to said garden had been reduced by Sethian's order to only once every few days, and never on the same day. What I had loved the most about my previous walks in the garden was the openness and sense of freedom that it had given me after being cooped up within the castle walls for long periods of time. That air of freedom no longer existed as the moment I so much as stuck a toe outside, I was immediately surrounded by no less than twenty elven guards, making me feel even more claustrophobic than when I was indoors.

At least I still had sitting out on the balcony to look forward to, but even my access to that had been, understandably, severely restricted. Unless Sethian, himself, accompanied me, those doors were kept tightly locked.

These days, I often felt like one of those clichéd princesses that were locked up in a tower for whatever reason served the plot. To someone like me who had spent practically every night of her life gazing up at the stars, being cooped up indoors was practically torture.

That trip to Talloth? At this point, I've pretty much given up on seeing it anytime soon. Sethian had tried to assuage my disappointment by assuring me that after the baby was born, we would all be taking a trip across the realm to introduce the new royal child to the elven people once the baby was a few "moon-cycles" old. However, I had tried not to get too excited or even to think about the trip very much because the way my luck had been going for the past few months, something catastrophic was sure to happen the day before we were to leave, thus forcing Sethian to cancel the trip.

Today was one of my "garden" days, and even though my back had been killing me all morning, I was determined not to miss my walk outside. Well, waddle really, as I now resembled a beached whale. My stomach had grown so large in these last couple of months that I was afraid that I was going to have twins, no matter that Sethian had constantly assured me that he could only hear one soul. The thought of giving birth to one baby was already scary enough. Having to go through it twice within minutes was a terror that was unfathomable.

I had only been walking for less than half an elven-mark when a sharp pain abruptly shot from my back, then radiated through my abdomen, causing me to stumble and fall heavily to my knees onto the thankfully soft grass.

"Emily!" Lariel cried, instantly falling down to her knees as well beside me, placing a hand worriedly on my shoulder. "Are you all right? Did you hurt yourself?"

Another sharp pain closely followed the first, and for a couple of seconds, I was unable to answer her as I doubled over. By then, Rinwen had also dropped down to her knees beside me, and the circle of guards had moved in more closely.

What the heck? Everyone had always said that contractions didn't come this closely together until a woman was pretty close to delivery. Maybe that lower back pain I had been feeling since the middle of last night hadn't been so benign after all. Of all places—why did this have to happen to me *now*?

"I think I'm in labor," I finally managed to gasp.

Both Lariel and Rinwen's hands instantly jerked away from my body as if they had suddenly been burned. Then both women rose to their feet and hastily backed away from me, the guards following their lead just as quickly. What in the world was going on?

I moved as if to get up, and Lariel immediately said, "Emily, don't try to get up! Just please sit down right there for now." She turned to the other woman. "Rinwen, please go find His Majesty."

"Lariel, why did everyone step away from me all of a sudden?" I asked in bewilderment as I did as she had instructed and let myself sort of topple over from my knees to my backside.

"His Majesty didn't tell you?" she asked in surprise.

Once again, I seemed to be missing something major. "Tell me *what*?"

"It is forbidden for anyone other than the father of the child to touch a woman once she has gone into labor. The birthing process opens your soul and the child's soul up in a rather unique way in order to forge the familial bond between mother, father, and child. Even the physical touch of an outsider can contaminate that sacred bond, and that *must* be avoided at all costs."

I cradled my stomach in my hands, wincing as another contraction hit. If that was the case, and I had indeed been in labor since last night, then I just screwed up royally as all three of my friends had touched me at least once while helping me bathe and dress this morning.

Lariel made a sympathetic noise. "Just a little while longer and His Majesty will be here to take you to the royal birthing room."

At least Sethian had told me about that particular room one night when I had grilled him about where I would be having the baby, though I had not been allowed to see it beforehand. When I had asked why, his answer had just been confusing, something about "disrupting the energies of the room" whatever that meant. When I had pressed for more details, he had just shrugged and said it wasn't something he could really explain, that the room had been created by the mages of old using archaic forms of magic now lost to the pages of history to ensure the power of the royal family.

That had made me a little nervous. I had wondered what exactly those mysterious "energies" within that room would do to the baby, if anything. Sethian's answer of "what needs to be done" was less than reassuring. I was coming to understand that there were many aspects of the elven culture that I would never understand, or more correctly, *couldn't* understand, simply because I was human.

The fact that I still couldn't "hear" my baby's soul had

driven this point home better than anything else. It was something that I had been really worrying about over the past few days as the possibility of going into labor had gone from "sometime in the near future" to "maybe in the next few seconds."

How would I even know if the baby was hungry or distressed or sick or *anything* if elven babies didn't cry and I was the first human mother in their history that was mentally and emotionally deaf to her child? Sethian had told me not to worry so much about it, that it would definitely happen at birth. He had seemed so genuinely confident about it happening that it should have reassured me, but the fear just wouldn't leave me. Now that the moment of truth had arrived, I was more scared about finding out whether or not Sethian was right than of the pain of actually giving birth. Before I had started freaking out about my possible defectiveness, I had thought that nothing could be scarier than childbirth.

Another contraction hit, and I doubled over with a moan. Although that one had been slightly more painful, there had definitely been a longer interval between it and my last contraction. The frequency of the previous two had probably been a fluke, thank goodness.

I was also grateful that my water had yet to break. I would rather be somewhere less public when that happened. I glanced over at the guards, some of which were staring at me with way too much interest. Yes, somewhere less public and hopefully with less of an audience.

A few moments later when the air began to shimmer and warp in front of me, it was all I could do to keep from crying in relief. Even before Sethian had completely faded into view, I was already reaching for him. Although a bit caught off-guard, he easily caught me under my armpits and lifted me to my feet as though I weighed nothing.

My face must have shown my fear clearly because he immediately pulled me into a tight embrace and said, "It's all right. Soon the unpleasant parts will all be over, and you will have our child in your arms." I could hear the excitement and pure joy in his voice.

He looked over at Lariel and Saeria. "Have all the necessary items prepared for when we return to my rooms. I suspect you will not see us until this evening."

"Yes, Your Majesty," they replied in perfect tandem.

I flashed them a tremulous smile before the scenery around me began to change, and a tall, gold-plated door that I had never seen before, reminiscent of a vault to a treasure room in some late-night adventure movie, faded into view before us.

CHAPTER 25

That Sethian unlocked such an intimidating door with a large, though ordinary-looking golden key rather than with some form of elven magic seemed a little strange to me given the mystical bent that surrounded this particular room. However, the moment Sethian ushered me across the threshold, it felt very much like the time I had accidentally gotten too close to an activated Tesla coil during a lab at the university. The room positively thrummed with power in a way that sent every warning bell in my subconscious screeching.

Then another contraction hit, and the uncanniness of the room became the least of my worries as the strength of that sudden pain almost had me collapsing to the ground in a ball of agony.

"Wait! I can't—" I moaned as Sethian continued to urge me forward. If the pain was already this bad, I couldn't imagine how I would be able to endure it when it inevitably got worse closer to delivery.

Sethian began rubbing my back as I bent over with my arms wrapped tightly around my belly. "Just breathe slowly," he said. "We are almost to the pool. You will feel much more comfortable once we are inside the water."

Right, the water. I had been a little surprised when Sethian had stated that all elven births were water births.

After a few more seconds, the contraction subsided, and I was able to breathe more easily. I straightened, and said, "I'm okay now."

I was able to focus on the room again while he left my side for a moment to pull the heavy door closed. The room was completely composed of marble from ceiling to floor. In the center was a large, circular pool about forty to fifty feet in diameter that was sunken into the floor. It was filled to the rim with water so clear that it almost appeared to be empty. The space reminded me of a futuristic version of an old Roman bathhouse without the columns.

Along the edge of the pool was a large pile of towels and next to that, looking completely out of place, a small, leather-handled dagger. That was it. No flasks of medicines or bowls of herbs that I had half-expected. Sethian had told me he would be personally seeing to my pain with his healing abilities, so I suppose painkillers were really not needed here.

A loud series of clicks suddenly resounded throughout the room, and I instinctually turned towards the sound in enough time to see Sethian turn the last of the door's four locks.

"Shouldn't we wait until Yara gets here before you lock us in?" I asked, rubbing my stomach anxiously.

"Yara?" he echoed in confusion. Then he shook his head. "I never did explain, did I?" he said as he wrapped an arm around my waist and guided me towards the pool. "It is forbidden for anyone other than a child's father to be present for a birth. An outsider's presence would interfere with the familial bond that is newly being formed."

"Lariel did mention something like that, but…" *But what if something goes wrong?*

"A healer is not necessary for a successful birth," Sethian said as if reading my mind. "It is very rare for a *Sidhe* woman to have complications during the delivery."

"But I'm human," I couldn't help adding. "We have complications all the time."

"Yes, but you are having an elven child," he said as if that answered everything.

Then another contraction hit, and I lost the chance to question him more as I focused completely on breathing slowly through the cramping pain. Before the painful spasm had ended, Sethian busied himself with unlacing and removing my dress. I kicked off my slippers, and he carefully guided me into the warm, barely-waist-deep water. There was a seat made of marble in the very center that reminded me of an open-ended toilet seat on three legs, and I sat down somewhat awkwardly onto it at his urging. I concentrated on keeping my breathing even while he undressed.

A huge wave of warmth suddenly began gushing out of me, and startled, I looked down to see that the once pristine water was now slightly cloudy around me.

"My water just broke!" I exclaimed, and then I was unable to speak again for a long moment as my body was rocked with a contraction twice as strong as the last one.

When it was finally over and I raised my head with a grimace, I saw that Sethian was already in the pool and wading out to me. Once he reached me, he positioned himself behind me, to my surprise, and knelt down. Wasn't he supposed to deliver the baby? Why in the world had he knelt down back there?

"Lean back against me for a moment," he said before I could voice any of my questions.

I did as I was told, and Sethian immediately wrapped his arms around my waist, his hands positioned flat on either side of my belly.

"Close your eyes and relax," he murmured in my ear. "I am going to ease your pain now, though it will not disappear completely. You will still feel each contraction as a mild twinge. For now, just concentrate on connecting with the baby's soul just as I have instructed you rather than on the frequency of those twinges. The time between now and a mark before the birth is the most important time of the whole process. This is when we both shall bind mentally and spiritually with our child."

I nodded and closed my eyes, trying my hardest to relax against Sethian's chest as the weird chair I was sitting on wasn't very comfortable. I concentrated on sensing emotions that I knew I did not feel just as Sethian had taught me, but without really understanding what it would be like to "hear" the baby, I couldn't be certain that I wasn't missing something already.

For the next six hours or so this is what we did. As the seventh approached and Sethian informed me that I still had not dilated completely, I was counting my blessings that Sethian was a healer because I don't think I would have been able to handle such excruciating pain for so long without losing my mind. As it was, I was already exhausted.

So far, the only emotions I had been able to sense were definitely Sethian's, as he was having a hard time containing his excitement and occasionally, impatience. During this time, he had only spoken to me a few times, and mostly just to ask if I was comfortable and if I had heard the baby "speak." No and no on both issues, but I had kept the first one to myself as it involved the chair and there was probably nothing he could do about it. He still didn't seem worried about my failure to hear the baby's soul, so I decided not to worry about it either at this point.

As it was getting fairly close to the actual birth, I was more concerned with how awful the actual birth would be and whether or not I would be able to push the baby out at all than something that was completely out of my control.

Another half hour and I was starting to wonder if it was possible to overdose on Sethian's healing magic as my head had started to spin and everything took on a blurry, surreal look.

That's when I felt it, a rush of bewilderment and fear that was not my own. Was that…?

"The baby's...scared," I said a bit deliriously.

Sethian rubbed a hand across my stomach. "Ah, your minds have finally bonded," he said with satisfaction. "It won't be long now, I think."

"Wait, you mean it's because of the baby that everything's gone all loopy?" I slurred.

"Yes," he replied, rubbing my shoulders. "You perceive the world partially as the world the baby perceives. It is skewing your sense of reality."

About fifteen minutes later, I was finally pushing, and Sethian was half embracing my body and half reaching between my legs in preparation for the baby's appearance. A couple of pushes later, the baby was partially out, and I was crying and certain that I would be unable to push again.

However, at Sethian's coaxing, I managed one last big push, and I felt the baby's body slide out completely amidst a cloud of red and a huge surge of adrenaline. I collapsed back against Sethian's chest, exhausted to the point of passing out, but I struggled to keep my consciousness with everything I had in me. I had to see the baby. I *had* to—

As Sethian had warned, there was no cry as he lifted the baby from the water, just a series of small gasps followed by a larger, startled gasp behind me as I looked at my child—no, my *son*—for the first time. Only then did I understand Sethian's reaction.

Tiny, pointed ears poked out cutely from within a mass of wet, *black* hair.

CHAPTER 26

A *son. I have a son,* I thought, still a little shell-shocked about the idea as I stared at the tiny bundle in my arms who silently stared back at me with the most brilliant green eyes I had ever seen. He was beautiful, so beautiful, and I couldn't get enough of just looking at him.

Sethian sat beside me on our bed where he had propped me up with a multitude of pillows so I could hold the baby properly, perhaps equally as shell-shocked as I was, but for an entirely different reason. He was looking down at our son as if he couldn't quite believe that he was real.

"You're *sure* that this has only happened once before?" I asked for the umpteenth time, still kind of freaked out about the whole thing.

He shook his head. "As I said, I have only *heard* of one other instance. Whether or not it is actually true is anyone's guess as there is no physical documentation to support any of it."

"Sethian, will you please just tell me what you think this means?" I pleaded.

He reached out a hand and ran the pads of his fingers caressingly down my cheek. "It's not something bad no matter what the reason, so you can ease your mind," he said. "Either his black hair is the result of him exhibiting a human trait as I explained before, or—"

"—he's just like the elf from that myth you mentioned," I finished for him, "the one you *still* won't properly explain to me."

He sighed. "I should have never brought it up at all. Most today do not believe that such a being as Hirion ever existed, that the circumstances that led to his extraordinary abilities and unconventional appearance are just too unbelievable to be anything but fiction. I have read some of your human literature over the centuries, and the works that are the most comparable are the stories of Merlin or the demigods of Greek and Roman myth, at least in regards to the extraordinary abilities they were born with."

He paused and suddenly grinned, probably because I

likely had a stupid look on my face as I stared back at him in mute disbelief. I looked down at our son, looking small and cute and innocent and nothing like the mythical people he had just mentioned.

"You're joking. The last thing anyone would ever accuse me of being is something like a demigod, and unless there's something really important you forgot to mention about yourself to me, you aren't one either."

He nodded. "As I said, it is only a comparison of myths with similar themes. Just as a demigod was a child of two worlds, Hirion was said to have been born with the perfect balance of elven and human traits rather than just inheriting the few human genes like every other half-blood. As a result, he was able to wield the power of both races, giving him access to a power that had never been seen before nor since in all our long history.

"The realm we now live within is not the first. The origins of my people lie within a realm that no longer exists. It was said that Hirion carved from the very fabric of a chaotic dimension normally beyond the reach of our own a mythical Third Realm by his power alone, a land of immortality, great beauty, and magic, and took half the then elven population with him."

"But," I interjected, "humans don't have the kind of

power that elves do. Our abilities lie in innovation, not magic."

"No," he agreed, "but the potential is there all the same. Otherwise, you would never have connected mentally with our son, nor would have any of the human brides of old with their children. Perhaps it is a matter of evolution—the next step—or humans simply just need to be shown the way by another. The moment our son reached out to you for comfort when he was frightened and confused during the birth was the moment that you were finally able to hear his soul, was it not?"

"You're saying it's because of something he did, not something that happens naturally?"

"Yes and no," he replied maddeningly.

I made a face. "That doesn't help, Sethian."

He chuckled. "Bear with me, my Emily. These are questions an elf does not normally have to answer, much less spend much thought on. Our bonds to each other, as well as our manipulations of the natural energies of the world, are things that are as ingrained and instinctual to the *Sidhe* as breathing is to a human. A human does not have to be taught how to take that first breath at birth; they just *know*. Thus, our son reached out to you with his mind and in essence, joined with yours as easily as though he had merely reached out a hand to clasp your own. If you wish a deeper explanation, then that is a question you will have to pose to the scholars who study such things."

Now that I was becoming fairly proficient in basic Elvish despite my inability to correctly pronounce a lot of the more tongue-twisting words, I would definitely seek them out as long as Sethian allowed them to visit me in the royal suite. I doubted the archives were a good place to take a newborn for any extended length of time. The baby—

I cut myself off mid-thought and frowned over at Sethian. "Do we really have to wait seven days before naming him?" I asked. "It feels kind of awkward to keep calling him 'my son' or 'my baby.' We humans usually have a name picked out long before the baby is even born."

He nodded. "It is important that we learn his natural personality from the beginning in order to select a name that suits him the most. For instance, my name means 'the one who forces a new path.'"

"Yes, I would say that name suits you perfectly," I said dryly. Bringing me to the elven realm without so much as a "may I?" and taking a human bride despite the many protests from the elven court reflected the essence of that meaning very well. “Fine, we’ll wait, but I hope you at least have something in mind.”

Even before the birth, I had decided to let Sethian pick the name without any input from me. I had gleaned enough from my conversations with my friends to understand that names were very important in the elven culture, and I was nowhere near understanding all the nuances involved.

“I do,” he replied, smiling at me as if I had just said something incredibly funny, which I usually interpreted as “said something stupid.”

“Good. Then we’ll leave that discussion for another time. Now, you were saying about the balance…?” I said, steering us back on topic.

“Ah, yes. According to the tale, there was much speculation of how this balance came to be. Some said that the human mother was not human at all but of a race of beings from beyond even the human realm.”

“Is that even plausible?” I asked with interest.

“There are many realms,” he replied enigmatically, and I could have strangled him when he didn’t elaborate.

“One of these days, maybe you’ll actually answer one of my questions completely,” I grumbled.

“A few centuries from now you will better appreciate leaving some things for later discussion,” he said.

As always, whenever he threw a wrench that big into the conversation, I had no idea how to reply, leaving me feeling a bit unsettled. It seemed it was happening more and more often lately, but maybe it was because ever since someone had tried to push me off the balcony, he had been spending more time just sitting and talking with me.

The baby picked that moment to wiggle a bit, giving me the perfect excuse to turn my attention away from Sethian to him. I couldn't believe how well he was already able to focus on my face, as though he was months and not hours old. When I looked into his eyes, I could practically see the wheels turning within. It had been a bit disquieting at first, but now I couldn't get enough of just looking at him, wondering what he was thinking, if anything.

I couldn't resist bending down and kissing him on the forehead. The moment my lips touched his incredibly soft skin, I felt a tiny surge of an emotion that made me think of how pleasant it felt to feel the cool wind on my face while sitting out on the balcony.

"I think I just felt one of his emotions," I said in something like awe. "It made me remember a time when I had felt the same. Is that what it's been like for you all this time when you said you could hear his soul?"

"Yes," he said, sounding strangely hesitant.

I immediately looked over to him, but the expression on his face hadn't changed. "What is it?" I asked anyway.

"What we were talking about before, about the reason for Hirion being born with such incredible abilities, about how such a perfect balance came to be..."

I could feel myself stiffen in response to the gravity I heard in his voice. "Just tell me," I said firmly.

Suddenly I felt a wave of foreboding crash through me so powerful that my entire soul, as well as my body, shuddered in reaction.

"W-What did you just *do*?" I stuttered.

"I just accepted the truth," Sethian said.

"Huh?" I said intellectually.

He reached over with his free hand and gently cupped the side of my face. The expression in his eyes was something that I had only seen once before, and just as it had that time, the shock of it hit me like a bolt of lightning to the heart.

"There was another version of Hirion's tale that offered a very different answer as to how the balance had come to be. It was said that his *Sidhe* father and human mother had bonded as soulmates at the same moment that he was conceived, something I never thought could happen—" The smile Sethian gave me was beautiful and simple. "—until it did."

I opened my mouth, to say what, I had no idea, but

the implications of Sethian's declaration left me stunned and unable to utter a sound. Tears welled up in my eyes as I suddenly understood the emotion I saw in his eyes. It was impossible. Things like this never happened to someone like me. I was suddenly terrified that this moment wasn't real, that I had passed out during the birth and was dreaming this whole conversation.

Sethian leaned forward and brushed his lips tenderly against mine, soft and fleeting. A rush of pure affection instantly flooded my being, causing the tears to begin falling down my cheeks. There was no more doubt. That strong connection we had seemed to form the second time we had made love still existed, and judging from the clarity of the emotions I could now sense from him, it had probably never faded at all.

He pulled back and rubbed a thumb beneath my eyes, wiping the tears away. "There is nothing to fear," he said. "I am truly here. This moment is real. Just as I never thought I would be able to gaze upon my child like this, I believed I would never find this kind of love with another and did not allow myself to see our bond for what it was until our son opened my eyes. Forgive me."

Love… Just hearing him say that one word, the word I had desperately wanted to hear him say for all these long months made a quiet sob burst forth from my throat. It wasn't a straight out "I love you," but it had been a declaration all the same. I needed only to feel the affection that had flooded my soul and see the love in his eyes to know it wasn't just wishful thinking.

A soft sound of exclamation from below had me instantly looking down at my son. His little arms were waving back and forth as if in either agitation or excitement. The moment my attention was entirely focused on him, a feeling of extreme interest washed over me, overriding Sethian's own feelings of affection.

Not wanting him to see me cry, I made a huge effort to pull myself together and smiled down at him brightly. He blinked and the feeling he was projecting changed to the one I had felt from him earlier, the one that made me think of the wind on my face.

"He likes your smile," Sethian said, the sound of his voice drawing the baby's eyes to him.

Sethian reached over and lovingly caressed our son's head. The intensity of the baby's emotions instantly doubled, making me feel a bit light-headed and dazed.

That strong surge of emotion triggered the memory of the dizzying and near overwhelming rush of energy I had felt while giving birth, of the moment my son was completely free of my body. At the time, I had thought it was a result of my own emotions going haywire about the event itself, the realization that I had just brought a life into the world that most first-time mothers probably experience.

Thinking back to everything Sethian had told me about that mythical elf, Hirion, and the fact that I still knew very little about elven magic, it made me wonder if I had been wrong. What if what I had felt hadn't come from me at all, but from him?

"Sethian," I said hesitantly, "when he was born, I felt a huge surge of what I thought at the time was an adrenaline rush. Now, feeling the baby's emotions like this, how strong they are, I just realized how incredibly ignorant I am when it comes to an elf's power. It never occurred to me to ask about things like whether or not your abilities are present at birth, or do they come later at puberty or adulthood?"

"An elf's power awakens at birth," he replied. "That initial surge of power is strong enough that it can be felt for many spans. Our son's awakening was particularly strong. It released enough energy that I have no doubt it was felt by everyone in Talloth and perhaps even beyond."

"Then everyone knows I've given birth," I said slowly, hugging the baby closer to my chest.

I suddenly had a new appreciation for the lack of windows in the bedroom. Ever since someone had tried to kill me, I had been worrying about whether or not they would target the baby after failing to prevent the birth in the first place.

Sethian's eyes sharpened at my reaction, and he nodded approvingly. "Yes, and you are correct to think that the game has changed once again. We must both be doubly vigilant now."

CHAPTER 27

As we neared the king's entrance to the throne room, my levels of anxiety rose exponentially as I remembered vividly the discomfort of having to endure what had felt like an eternity of stares and/or glares from the entire elven court during my presentation as Sethian's pregnant Royal Wife. The whispering alone was enough to drive one mad. I could only imagine their reaction when they realized my son resembled an elf from myth.

I felt Sethian tighten his arm around mine, and I glanced over at him sheepishly. No doubt I was sending some interesting emotions his way. Ever since he had acknowledged that we were soul-bound, the block his uncertainty had unconsciously placed between us had been removed permanently, and now our emotions always flowed between us like a two-way river. I still had not quite gotten used to feeling someone else's emotions and wondered if it was even something you *could* get used to.

"This is our son's naming ceremony," Sethian said. "Just focus on that, and all the rest will become mere noise in the distance."

I smiled thinly and nodded. He was right. I was *finally* going to learn my son's name, and that's all that mattered. I was still a little miffed that I hadn't managed to get him to cave and tell me the name beforehand, no matter how much I had begged. I had learned over the last seven days just how stubborn my husband could be.

With my beautiful son cradled securely in my right arm and a husband whom I now knew loved me linked with the other, I really had no room to complain, anyway. A year ago, I could have never imagined my life ending up this well. That was probably why I really dreaded stepping into the throne room. The nobles would be bad enough, but the fact that the queen would be there as well left me feeling cold and angry, and if I were completely honest, more than a little helpless.

I did *not* want the woman who so casually insisted that I do something that would have surely caused me to miscarry to even *look* at my son. She had no right, but just because she was the queen, she had every right.

Adding insult to injury, I still couldn't even tell Sethian about what she had wanted me to do because I had no idea what her game was or if she really had been trying to help me in her own twisted way. For all I knew, her hands could be as tied as mine and my anger misplaced, so for the time being, I had to face her with a neutral expression and pretend that I wasn't dying to punch that china doll face until it cracked.

It was probably for the best that I would be little more than a prop throughout the ceremony. It would take more than birthing their future king for the majority of the elven court to accept me as one of them, but after nearly dying for the sake of their political games, I wasn't very keen on being included as a member of the court at all. I was happy to just step back into the shadows and allow Sethian to handle the political side of our lives. I had total confidence that he would keep our son safe.

Four guards stood in pairs on either side of the double doors that opened up onto the dais. They noticeably stood more stiffly as we approached and then bowed to both of us as we came to a stop before the door. I saw a couple of the guards glance with unbridled interest at the bundle in my arms, but I had covered the baby's head so only his face was visible. He had been asleep when we left the royal suite, but now he was wide awake, his eyes darting around and taking in all the new sights. I could feel his interest seeping in through my anxiety.

Sethian nodded at the guards, and the inside two each opened a door. I heard the herald announce us, and a few seconds later, we were through the door and facing the multitudes of courtiers. The atmosphere in the chamber felt completely different this time. Instead of curiosity or just-barely concealed hostility, the air was alive with excitement. However, it was completely disconcerting on how every eye immediately zeroed in on me, making my skin crawl.

As we walked to the center of the dais to stand before Sethian's throne, I glanced at the queen's throne where Limira had already risen to her feet to face us, her face a mask of perfect neutrality, though unsurprisingly, her gaze was fixed on the baby.

Sethian unlinked our arms, and I handed our son to him, glad to have something else to focus on briefly other than that sea of eyes or the queen. After uncovering his head, the elven king turned to face his subjects with the baby held out vertically before him with a hand supporting his head and the other his bottom and gave them their first good look at their new prince.

The low buzz of conversation abruptly stopped in what sounded like one loud, collective gasp, followed by a silence so profound that I could feel it down to the very marrow of my bones. Nobody moved; nobody *breathed.* It was as though reality, itself, had frozen while teetering on the edge of a precipice.

Seemingly unperturbed, though the slight feeling of concern I was picking up from him said otherwise, Sethian announced in Elvish in a booming voice, *"Behold my son, Prince Thaylan of the royal House of Elerren, heir to the throne of the Second Realm!"*

His voice echoed loudly throughout the room, but all I could hear was my son's name.

Thaylan…

My heart thumped loudly in my ears in excitement, once, then twice, three times, and then the room roared with the sound of a thousand voices that made the very glass on the windows tremble. Shouts of disbelief, cries of confusion, and accusations of trickery, all of this hit me with the force of a wrecking ball.

Then the queen was suddenly beside Sethian, staring down at Thaylan as though she couldn't quite believe what she was seeing. She reached a hand out as if to touch his face, and suddenly enraged, I started to move towards them, intent on stopping her. I only managed a single step before a surge of utter agitation raged into my being, and a clear wave of pure power suddenly erupted out from the baby, making me stagger as it pushed me backward and knocked the queen completely flat on her back.

Cries of surprise and pain sounded out from the direction of the courtiers, and as I regained my footing, I turned and saw everyone to a man sprawled out on the ground in every position imaginable, some moaning, some still shouting, and others not moving at all. I reached Sethian just as he turned to me, his eyes wide and his face pale with shock.

"Thaylan! Is Thaylan okay!" I demanded, reaching for him.

Sethian nodded somewhat dazedly and let me take the baby from his arms. Thaylan was clearly upset, his face scrunched up just like a crying infant's, but the only sounds from his throat were those little noises of exclamation that he would make every once in a while as though he was trying to talk but frustrated that nothing would emerge. That was probably why holding him felt as if I had gotten dangerously close to a live wire. His tiny body thrummed with energy, making my arms start to feel a little numb. I immediately sat down onto the steps of the dais and used my lap to support his back, afraid I would abruptly lose all the feeling in my arms and drop him.

"Good. Stay there while I tend to the queen and my

people," Sethian said after giving both of us a once-over, his voice strained.

Both Sethian and my friends had warned me that something like this could probably happen, that some elven children might use an inborn ability without warning, but judging from the completely stunned look on Sethian's face, Thaylan wasn't supposed to be able to do something like *this*.

I rocked him gently in my arms and smiled down at him in an effort to calm him, but from the waves of unhappiness that his emotions were shouting at me and the way he was kicking his legs and flailing his arms, it was clear that he was in no mood to be comforted. If he were a human baby, he would have been screeching fit to wake the dead. I'm not sure if it was the queen, the roar of the crowd, or even some negative emotion I had inadvertently sent him when I had seen that the queen was about to touch him that had set him off, but maybe it was better to take him out of the throne room until things settled down.

Sethian was currently at the queen's side, helping her to sit up and asking if she was injured. I started to call out to him, but all I managed to get out was the first syllable of his name before the throne room rapidly faded from view and a startled breath later, I was sitting in the center of our bed. Thaylan started to thrash about more vigorously, and I felt a rush of excitement from him, probably because he had just spotted his bassinette beside the bed.

"I guess no one will ever question whether Sethian's really your father with a power like that," I told him, smiling weakly as I continued to rock him.

If the elven king had been hoping for our son to shake up the court today, he certainly got more than he had probably bargained for. I didn't have to be a political expert to know that knocking your future subjects on their asses wasn't the best way to win hearts.

Suddenly, the door flew open, and Sethian came running in, his crown lying skewed on his head, followed closely by Lariel, Saeria, and Rinwen. "Thank the High Powers I found you!" Sethian exclaimed, relief flowing from him like a bleeding wound. "When I saw you two disappear, I did not know what to think!"

"It seems Thaylan just wanted to come home," I said with a helpless shrug. "I don't think he liked the noise."

"'Noise' is putting it mildly," Sethian replied with a sigh, running his hand through his hair and catching his fingers in his crown. He frowned and opted to just remove it rather than try to move it back into place.

"It sounds as though we missed a rather grand spectacle," Lariel said hesitantly.

"Yes, you could say the baby had quite the temper

tantrum," I said with a slightly hysterical laugh. I was probably still in shock.

I guess hearing familiar voices and being in a familiar place again were enough to finally settle Thaylan down because the energy emanating from his body completely died down, leaving my arms to tingle madly as if they had gone to sleep. His face had also lost that pinched look, and his eyes were currently fixed on his father—or rather, the light from the oil lamp glinting off the crown in his hands.

"We left a pretty big mess back there," I said to Sethian. "The baby's calmed down now, so if you need to get back, I think we'll be fine here with everyone."

His hands clenched the crown. He started to say something, then shook his head and gave me a *look*. I nodded. We would have much to discuss later when the room wasn't so crowded and no more nobles were moaning on the floor in the throne room. Sethian bent over and kissed both of us on the brow before phasing out of the room.

"So our little prince has been named, Thaylan," Lariel said, sitting on the bed beside us. "'The one who sees all.' Auspicious."

No, threatening, I thought with an inward groan. What was Sethian thinking giving him a name like that? The name had a pleasing ring to it, but if that's what it meant, it really did come off as a not-so-subtle warning, especially after what had just happened in the throne room.

Of course, I told none of them this as I smiled and said, "I certainly hope so."

CHAPTER 28

"I don't think I have ever seen anyone so excited for a journey as you," Lariel remarked as I stuffed a few last minute things for Thaylan into a pack that I would be keeping with me inside the carriage tomorrow.

Sethian had assured me that his staff would see to the rest of our packing, and I was grateful. I had never gone on a trip that lasted over a few days, much less a couple of months. I wouldn't have known where to start.

I was both relieved and a little disappointed that we wouldn't be riding the elvensteed but instead pulled by them inside a carriage. Although Sethian had taken me to see them once before, with Thaylan in tow, I had only been able to pet them. At this early stage of an elven child's life, the child rarely left the side of his or her mother as the first few years were important to the strengthening of their familial bonds. It was more than just cultural.

Learning to ride would have to come later when Thaylan was old enough to take the lessons with me. I had to constantly remind myself that there was no hurry, that a few years was nothing in this new lifespan I had been given.

"Remember, I've been living in the elven realm for over a year now, and this is the first time I've ever left the palace grounds," I said. "I've been dying to see Talloth. Hell, I've been dying just to see the realm, itself, to see how it differs from my world. Getting to go to a bunch of cities, too, is just icing on the cake."

"It will be a refreshing change of scenery," Saeria agreed.

"That's why I told you, all of you, that you should take a few days off every once in a while," I said pointedly. "Even if you don't want to take a year off from serving here like you're *supposed to,* everyone needs a little time to themselves to recharge."

"We shall take our year after your children are grown," Lariel said with a grin.

"The last time I looked, I only have one," I retorted.

I glanced at the bed where Thaylan was currently

playing with an assortment of colorful wooden blocks of various shapes and sizes with Rinwen. And by playing, I meant he was levitating a few of them around her body in a rapid whirlwind while a giggling Rinwen tried to keep from getting pummeled.

The first time I had seen him do this I nearly had a heart attack, but the elven women had been delighted. Thaylan had launched one at me, expecting me to catch it or levitate it like him, but it had hit me square in the nose hard enough to make it bleed. The confused look on his face would have been adorable had I not been choking on blood.

Lariel's grin widened. "That will change soon, I think."

I felt heat rise in my cheeks despite myself. Not for the first time, I wondered if they could hear us making love at night. When Sethian was here, my friends stayed in the servant wing attached to the Royal Suite, which was only a few rooms away. I could get pretty loud sometimes, to my eternal embarrassment.

"If by soon, you mean in about ten years, then sure, a sibling for Thaylan would be great."

I could only imagine the chaos that would erupt if I had two gifted children hurdling blocks and lord knows what else at each other. Not to mention phasing in and out of existence. That alone would probably have me completely gray by the time he turned one. Luckily, the farthest he had gone was wherever Sethian happened to be in the palace. Maybe it was because of the familial bond, but he always seemed to know exactly where Sethian was at any given time and would just pop over to see him whenever he felt like it. The maddening part was that there was absolutely nothing I could do to stop him from doing this, being the mundane human that I was.

Unfortunately, Sethian seemed to find the whole thing extremely amusing. When I had pointed out rather crossly that Thaylan could end up on the other side of the realm, he had assured me that the ability to manipulate space was limited, and he doubted Thaylan could even manage to phase to somewhere outside the palace. I wasn't as confident.

"I would hope sooner, but ten years is also fine," Lariel said with a nod.

I just shook my head. Sometimes my sarcasm just went right over their heads, and it was easier to just let it go rather than try to explain.

"You should probably put the little one to bed soon," Saeria said. "Didn't His Majesty say that we would be leaving at first light tomorrow?"

"Or as soon as he gets back from Nallos, whichever is sooner. It had something to do with a land dispute between a couple of pretty important nobles that couldn't wait until after the trip, so I don't really expect him back by dawn, either."

I went over to the bed and sat next to Thaylan. "Hey, sweetie, it's time for bed," I said, pointing to his bassinette once I had captured his attention.

"No!" he said clearly in English, making me sigh.

Some days it was in Elvish. Whether human or elf, I guess some things were just universal.

THE FIRST THING I became aware of was the feeling of something moist on the back of my neck. I shifted and tried to turn my head, but a hand immediately pushed my face back towards my pillow.

"Sethian?" I said somewhat groggily.

Was it morning already? I felt as though I had only been asleep for a few minutes.

"*Mmph,*" he replied against my skin as he moved his kisses from the back of my neck to my collarbone, pulling the collar of my nightgown away to give his mouth more access to my skin.

I gasped as he sucked rather hard on my pulse point, the sensation bordering on pain. Although waking me up like this was nothing new for us, I was surprised that he even had the stamina to make love after riding what must have been all night to get here if it was indeed morning. Well, at the slower pace of riding in a sort of caravan, we would be on the road for the next two days before we reached Talloth, so I suppose I understood his desire to get in one last tumble before we left.

I felt Sethian press tightly against my back, his erection already digging into my lower spine. Maybe it was the grogginess, but his kisses this time seemed to make my head swim more than usual until I felt not only lightheaded but euphoric.

He hadn't bothered to turn on one of the oil lamps, so when he rose up above me and rolled me onto my back, all I could see of him in the darkness was the outline of his body and the lighter shade of darkness that was his hair as it spilled over his shoulders and tickled my nose. I was a little surprised that he was already completely nude, but then his mouth crashed onto mine. Whatever thoughts had been going through my mind scattered until the only things I could focus on were his hot mouth trying to suck the life out of me and his hands aggressively fondling my breasts through my gown and tugging a bit impatiently at the thin material.

A smell of something like cedar permeated my senses through my haze of pleasure. I had enough mind left to wonder where it was coming from. From Sethian? The scent was so strong that it was possible, but elves didn't wear anything like colognes or perfumes. They didn't have to, as their natural musk always reminded me of something elemental or meteorological. Sethian had always smelled of fresh linens and clean air, of something powerful and masculine, and right now I didn't smell any of that at all. Maybe that's why this new scent was bothering me so much now. It made me feel that I was suddenly with a different person.

With a tremendous effort, I pulled my mouth away from his and gasped out, "Sethian…wait…that smell…what…"

That was all I managed to get out before his mouth covered mine again more roughly than before, and I immediately lost my train of thought as my head began to swim again. He was certainly more aggressive than usual this morning—or night—or whatever. Did something happen that made him need to release some pent up energy?

Then that smell hit my nostrils again, and my head cleared a bit as a strong sense of annoyance shot through me. Was that my emotion or his? Maybe he could smell it too, and it was bothering him just as much as it was bothering me.

I pulled my mouth away for a second time and started to push at his shoulders to get his attention—and in that instant, I finally got a good look at his face. Even in the darkness, the outline was narrow and alien and definitely *not* Sethian's!

With a horrified shout, I shot one of my palms hard into his nose. He flinched back violently, grunting in both surprise and pain, and in that moment of confusion, I was able to get both hands between my chest and his and shove up as hard as I could. I only managed to move him partially off me, his lower body still pinning my legs.

"Saeria! Rinwen! Help me!" I screamed as I struggled to roll off the bed in order to get to Thaylan before my attacker could recover from my blow.

Although it had been my aim, it was still a shock when I abruptly fell off the edge and slammed onto the hard, marble floor, shoulder first. Then I wasted more precious seconds trying to orient myself enough to climb to my feet and stumble over to the baby.

I was just picking a now awake and upset Thaylan up when I was aggressively grabbed around my waist from behind. I shrieked and tried to shake him off while at the same time hugging Thaylan closer to my chest. A split-second later the bedroom door crashed open and light from the room beyond illuminated both the bedroom and Saeria in the doorway just as Thaylan shouted "Mama!" in fear.

Then suddenly the crushing arms around my waist were gone, and the vision of Saeria with Rinwen at her back, daggers raised and threatening, rushing towards us faded out of view. They were replaced by a row of tightly packed trees under a night sky that was just starting to lighten and the cold marble under my feet by cool, damp grass. Behind me, the *clomp, clomp, clomp* of what sounded like hoof beats had me whirling around and hugging Thaylan to me more tightly even as his emotions shrieked with confusion and fear that was so powerful, my legs nearly gave out on me as they thundered through me and threatened to completely overwhelm my mind.

I gritted my teeth and fought to find some semblance of balance within me. I could fall apart later when we were safe and the horror of what had just happened to me fully sank in. Right now I had to be strong for my son.

I was standing about ten feet from a cobblestone road, and I could just make out the shape of at least five elvensteed as they barreled down the road towards us. At the verge of collapse, I started to turn in order to hightail it to the shadows of the trees before we were spotted by God-only-knows-who, but Thaylan abruptly shouted a word that had me freezing mid-step.

"*Father*!" he cried out again in Elvish, reaching out over my shoulder towards the oncoming riders.

"You're kidding me…" I whispered in disbelief.

Squinting into the distance, it was still too dark to see anything except the outline of the riders, but if my son said one of them was Sethian, that was good enough for me. He had never been wrong—not yet, anyway. I moved closer to the edge of the road, rubbing at Thaylan's back, hoping to calm at least some of his still-lingering fear.

"Yes, your father is coming," I crooned to him, praying that wouldn't turn out to be a lie. How pathetic was I that I had needed my six-month-old son to save us from a would-be rapist, and I knew I would have to rely on his power again if by some million-to-one chance he was wrong about the riders.

Suddenly, one of the elvensteed broke off from the others, and both rider and animal nearly blurred into something unrecognizable as they shot towards us at an incredible speed. A new wave of fear that did not originate from me washed over me, and this time I did stagger a bit. The emotion was easily twice as strong as Thaylan's had been and negated the maelstrom of emotions I had been feeling all on my own as well as those I was receiving from the baby. However, this time

I welcomed that outside emotion because the essence of it was *very* familiar.

"Sethian!" I cried in relief, not able to hold back at that point.

As that name was swallowed up into the pre-dawn air, Thaylan became even more agitated, wiggling in my arms with everything he had in him and seemingly trying to crawl over my shoulder so that it was all I could do to hold on to him. Then the steed was only a few yards away, and I could finally see Sethian's face clearly as he vaulted from his saddle before they had even come to a full stop.

Then before I could blink, my face was suddenly being cradled between his hands and Thaylan was twisting around to grab at Sethian's tunic, calling out *"Father! Father!"* over and over again in an excited tone.

It took every last ounce of my fragile control to not start crying right then and there.

"What in the name of the High Powers are you two doing *here*!" he demanded, his eyes frantically roving over both of us, likely looking for injuries. "And in your nightclothes, no less!"

"Thaylan," was all I managed as I choked back a sob. Just the feel of his hands on my cheeks made the painful knot in my chest start to loosen.

"Thaylan phased you..." he echoed in disbelief. "This

is at least a couple of spans from the palace grounds. Even *I* could not bend space between two points so far apart!"

I would have said "I told you so" had I not been so damned glad to see him.

"He was scared," I said. "We both were! Sethian, someone attacked me in my sleep! He fuzzed out my mind with elven magic and tried to make me think it was you! He tried to—"

My throat closed on the words, and I couldn't finish. The tears I had been trying so hard to keep from rising now began to spill freely from my eyes, and this time, I didn't try to stop them.

Without warning, a wall of rage slammed into me, and everything instantly went black. The next thing I knew, one of Sethian's arms was wrapped around my waist bearing the entirety of my weight, and the other was now carrying Thaylan, who clutched at the front of his father's tunic and was staring at me with wide eyes. Not even an echo of that powerful rage was left within me.

Sethian's eyes swam with guilt as he said, "Are you all right now?"

I clung to his middle and closed my eyes. "I think I need to sit down for a moment."

He immediately helped me lower myself to the

ground, urging me to lean against him as he sat cross-legged beside me and wrapped a comforting arm around my waist, Thaylan securely nestled in his lap. For now, he seemed content to just snuggle against Sethian's chest. I hoped he would fall asleep.

Sethian planted a tender kiss on my forehead and said, "I'm sorry for that. I am in control of myself now, so please continue."

The sound of hoof beats and men shouting reached my ears before I could open my mouth to reply. I looked behind me and saw the other four riders I had glimpsed before plus an additional six in the process of dismounting and rushing towards us. Sethian immediately held up a hand, and every one of them stopped dead in their tracks as though they had suddenly met with a barrier only they could see.

"Return to your steed and wait," Sethian commanded them. "I wish to speak with my wife, alone. We shall return to you, shortly."

Without a word, they all bowed and moved to obey. Knowing how well elves could hear, I wasn't at all certain that they would be out of earshot so was hesitant to say anything more about what had just happened back in the bedroom. However, I found myself watching the world around me fade out for the second time that night, only to phase back to a point that looked virtually identical to the place we had left. I glanced back towards the road, but Sethian's guards were nowhere to be seen.

"No one will hear us speak here," he assured me. "Tell me."

I closed my eyes again and buried my face into his shoulder. I knew we should probably be racing back to the palace ASAP, but I needed this time with Sethian to wash away the feelings of violation that were beginning to surge back to the surface now that the initial crisis was over. My attacker hadn't gotten far, but he had gotten far enough.

Also, I felt guilty for leaving Saeria and Rinwen to deal with the bastard alone, but I was more worried about them freaking out about our disappearance than the chance that they would be hurt. They had shown me on more than one occasion just how deadly they could be.

"I couldn't *hear* you," I said, knowing he would understand what I meant. That was probably what had ultimately saved me. Not even an elven enthrallment could fake a soul bond. "Even when he had my mind totally under his control, the fact that I could feel no emotion emanating from him, that he didn't smell like you, broke the enthrallment, I think. The only reason I was able to push him off me was because I completely blindsided him."

Even though Sethian had deliberately blocked any emotions from reaching me, and likely Thaylan as well, at the moment, he was so enraged that some of that rage managed to leak through. I could feel his whole body quivering with the effort of keeping it contained.

"Go on," he urged when I hesitated, his voice eerily calm.

"I screamed for Saeria and Rinwen then went straight for Thaylan. The bastard grabbed me just as I was picking him up. I tried to shake him off, but he was just too strong. That's when Saeria crashed through the door, but by then Thaylan was so freaked out that he took us to the one place where he knew we would be safe."

"It seems my royal guards will have much to answer for when we return," Sethian said blackly, his arm tightening around my middle.

CHAPTER 29

I never thought in a million years that I would actually see a medieval-style dungeon outside of a movie set being put to its real use rather than as just a tourist attraction. It was just as dark, dank, and smelly as I imagined it would be, the smell of waste and unwashed bodies assaulting my nose from the moment the guards had opened the door to admit us at the bottom of the longest staircase I had ever had the misfortune to descend.

Beside me, Sethian was still bristling with unhappiness that I was even there at all, but in this one thing, I had not backed down. I wanted—no *needed*—to hear with my own ears why the elf had chosen to assault me because I didn't trust that Sethian would tell me the whole truth in an effort to spare me more pain.

We stepped into a wide corridor made, or maybe even carved, out of a dark gray natural stone that could have been granite or some other stone found only within the elven realm. With my arm looped tightly with his, Sethian led me down a long row of thick, wooden doors that were swung wide open to reveal, I was glad to note, the empty, fully-enclosed cells beyond and came to a stop before the one on the end.

I instinctually stepped closer to Sethian as one of the three guards that had accompanied us unlocked the cell door and entered first. I was relieved when I saw that the cell was pretty well illuminated by several oil lamps hanging from the walls that had probably been pre-lit just for the king's visit.

Even though I should have expected it, it was still a shock to see my attacker chained by his wrists and ankles back against the far wall. I guess the whole setup just seemed a little too barbaric for a people as refined as the *Sidhe*.

Sethian's expression was cold and utterly without mercy as he confronted the man that had done such an unspeakable thing to me for the first time. "Speak in the tongue of my wife so that she may understand your every word," Sethian commanded. "I would first hear the reason why you assaulted my wife and defiled my home. We shall discuss your method of entry afterward."

I expected him to turn his head, to refuse to talk, maybe even to sneer defiantly, but he looked his king straight in the eye and said without any hesitation, "I did what I had to do. Nothing more, nothing less, and I shall not apologize for it."

There wasn't even a hint of shame or fear in his expression. His voice was also eerily relaxed, completely out of place for a man currently accused of assaulting a member of the royal family. Was he an assassin? Did one of the king's enemies hire him to do this to me in order to send Sethian some kind of twisted message?

Sethian's eyes seemed to ignite in the face of such nonchalant defiance. "I fail to see how committing the worst kind of sacrilege against the royal House of Elerren could be to your gain."

"There is nothing that I would not do for my Esdil, even go so far as to mate with a *human*," was his confusing reply.

"Esdil?" Sethian inquired with a frown.

Instead of answering, his eyes turned from the king to me. They were now accusing, angry, as if *I* was the one who had committed a great wrong against him by preventing him from succeeding. Just looking at him made my stomach turn. However, I didn't look away, not wanting to give him the satisfaction of knowing that his very presence disturbed me.

He turned his attention back to Sethian. "I did what I had to do," he repeated. "Soon, another will, as well."

After that maddening declaration, no matter how Sethian threatened him, he did not utter another word.

Needless to say, we never did make it to Talloth that day, and not for a long time after.

CHAPTER 30

INTERLUDE

Looking at myself in my hand mirror, it was hard to believe that I had been living in the elven realm for thirteen years now. My features were the same now as they were the day I first looked into this mirror and saw a semi-stranger staring back. Had I been in the human realm, I would have been nearing middle age. Now, except for a few hiccups now and then, it was as though I was living the best years of my life over and over again.

I didn't wait ten years to give Thaylan a sibling as I had once sarcastically told Lariel. He was four when his brother Anir was born. A year after that, my daughter, Rinya, arrived. The last had been my youngest daughter, Arra, four years ago. After four children, it had become apparent that Thaylan really was a special little boy as the rest of the children were born as blond as their father and nowhere near as powerful.

As it turned out, Thaylan's ability to phase to different places just like Sethian had only been the tip of the iceberg, a fact that had no doubt shaved off a few hundred years from my lifespan before he had grown old enough to understand that he shouldn't go around creating and leaving what amounted to mini-portals in walls, floors, and furniture for his poor unsuspecting mother to fall into.

By age six, he had mastered the ability to permanently alter the space around him. It had been a year before either Sethian or I had realized that the little booger had carved out an entire, separate room the size of our sitting room from a dimension none but him could touch. It was a place where he and his little brother could run around and play with his portals without having to worry about their mother scolding them about "the dangers of messing around with reality."

By this time, I had integrated so deeply into the elven realm and life as a member of the royal family that my old life back in the human world no longer seemed real. Now, except for official ceremonies, I always appeared in public on Sethian's arm, his clearly favored wife, which had raised more than a few aristocratic brows in the beginning.

The queen as well had been less than impressed with this new development, but over the years we had finally managed to find a compromise of sorts where we basically pretended that the other did not exist—on the surface, at least. I still could not quite shake the suspicion that she was up to something, so I had finally caved and shared my concerns with my friends, asking them to keep their eyes and ears open for me without alerting Sethian to my fears.

However, it was really because of Thaylan, more than Sethian's influence, that I had been accepted into elven society as well as I had. Even those who clearly despised the fact that a human dared walked among them as though she were a *Sidhe* didn't dare say or do anything publically to express that disgust because of their fear of Thaylan's power, never mind that he was still only a kid. Thaylan's affection for me was obvious to anyone who had eyes, so to disrespect me, the adored mother of their future king, was essentially akin to political suicide.

He had also proven to be a problem for some on another front. Over the years, people had begun to realize that Thaylan resembled the mythical elf, Hirion, in more than just his unique looks. Although not clairvoyant, he had an uncanny ability to sense when someone was up to no good, whether it was his younger brother playing a prank on him or something more sinister like a plot against my life—and there had been a fair few of those in the early years.

I felt a chill go up my spine as I remembered the last, a scene four years ago that I would unlikely forget, even after a thousand years. It was the day our enemies had truly learned to fear my son.

"MY HUMAN BRIDE-TO-BE wishes to speak with you, milady, before she makes her final decision."

I had heard this request twice before in the past two years, but I was a little surprised to hear it from the noble before me. He had been among the ten families that had just been given permission by Sethian to seek out a human bride a moon-cycle ago. That he had found a bride so quickly was astonishing. There were some from the very first group that had set out seven years ago that still hadn't had any luck.

I glanced at Saeria, and she shrugged. "We can go now if you like."

When we arrived at the point between worlds he had been frequenting, I could tell immediately that this was going to be another bust without the blonde woman who was sitting in a daze in the middle of the field having to even say a word. This was what a lot of the nobles didn't understand. Here under a Sidhe's *full enchantment, a woman would agree to anything because to her, this was only a dream world. However, almost every time the women returned to the human realm and their minds became clear again, they freaked out about what had happened and would never return.*

Seeing this dazed woman, it now made sense how he had found somebody so quickly. He really hadn't. There was no way she would pass Sethian's final test to gain permission for the change in this kind of state. Still, I had promised the noble I would talk to her, and I would.

I was so busy observing the woman that I didn't notice that the noble had stopped at the threshold of the "door" we had used to enter this space.

Without warning, he lunged at me. I don't know if he had intended to grab me or push me into the space beyond the barrier between both realms where God-only-knows what terrible thing would have happened to me, but the moment both hands came within an arm-span of me, they disappeared up to his wrists in an instant. There had been no flash of light, no sound, or not even a sign that his hands had met with some kind of resistance. They were just—gone.

I stared in a kind of horrified shock as he fell, screaming, to his knees, stretching out his arms to reveal two perfectly healed stumps where his hands had been only seconds ago.

They looked like amputations that had happened years ago, the skin only slightly darkened along the end of the stumps and none of it bloodied or even reddened with inflammation.

However, even though the stumps looked completely healed, the elf continued to scream and scream while the poor human woman he had probably forcibly brought into the Inbetween as his red herring rocked back and forth with her arms wrapped firmly around her knees. She had woken up from the elven enchantment straight into what had probably seemed like a nightmare.

UNDERSTANDABLY UPSET ABOUT all the attempts on my life, Thaylan had somehow used his spatial manipulation abilities along with the natural familial bond we had between us to erect a barrier around me that he had said would prevent anyone with ill intent from harming me physically. When I had pressed him for more details, he had just shrugged and said that his gifts were instinctual, and it wasn't something he could really explain.

Even though we had tried to keep what had happened that day a secret, word had still somehow spread, but instead of causing the problems for Thaylan that Sethian had feared, it had instead been the solution to mine. No one has tried to come after me physically since.

Now, despite my misgivings, Sethian, the children, and even Thaylan, himself, have the same protection, but that was the maximum amount of barriers he could maintain without draining his personal reserves of energy too much.

But now Thaylan was gone, off studying with a renowned, four-thousand-year-old mage from the *Lithvir Sidhe* for a year, and I knew that Sethian was secretly worried that the attempts on my life would start again. Not only that but this time, there were also a handful of human brides now living in the realm that could also be targeted. None of them had conceived yet, so I prayed that some anti-human fanatic didn't get it into his or her head to get rid of the "problem" before it became a problem.

I also worried for Thaylan, afraid that while he was far away from the protection of the king's mantle and the eyes of the elven court with its convoluted system of social checks and balances that someone would try to assassinate him as well.

No, there *was* one thing that was different about my reflection. The eyes that stared back at me this time were just a bit heavier with the weight of the ages I still had before me.

CHAPTER 31

"I don't care if it *is* your duty. You. Are. Not. Going!" I said firmly as I pushed Sethian equally as firmly back down to the mattress as he tried to sit up for the third time since we had woken up this morning.

"It is not a matter I can just pass off onto the queen," he insisted stubbornly, but at least he didn't try to rise again, "*especially* since it is Limira."

Or more correctly, he just didn't have the strength to make an attempt.

"It is just a little weakness. As long as I am seated, I shall be fine."

I sighed in exasperation and shook my head. "After thirteen years, this is the first time I have ever seen you sick. You *Sidhe* are always going on and on about how you rarely get sick, so the fact that you suddenly woke up this morning in a cold sweat and feeling as weak as a kitten is definitely cause for alarm. I've already sent Lariel to fetch a healer. Those traveling dignitaries can just wait a little longer. Besides, aren't you the one who is always telling me that time means very little to an elf?"

"Time has nothing to do with this. Certain protocols must be followed; you know this."

"So says the man that is constantly thumbing his nose at those same protocols," I countered.

The dismay that washed over his face was almost comical. "I shall see the healer. That is all I shall promise."

I nodded, though there was no real satisfaction in having won the argument. He couldn't see himself. He couldn't see how gray his complexion was or how his brow was glistening with sweat even though his skin felt as cold as ice to the touch. No, the reason I was being so stubborn about him staying in bed was that I was worried as hell. I was supposed to be the only one that got sick around here. Powerful beings like the elven king were supposed to be invulnerable.

"Where are the children?" Sethian asked.

"I sent them to the archives with Rinwen for their morning lessons today," I replied. "I didn't want them getting sick, too, if whatever you have is contagious. If that's the case, it's already too late for me. Whatever you have, you've probably had it for longer than just the last couple of days, and we've exchanged spit more times than I can count during that time. I've noticed for a while now that you've been looking more tired than usual. In hindsight, I should've been more suspicious, but I thought it was because of all those trips to Talloth you've had to make lately."

"As did I," he said with a sigh.

When the healer arrived a few minutes later, he took one look at Sethian and dove immediately into his examination without a word. After what seemed like an eternity, he finally drew back the hands that had been pressed against Sethian's chest and opened his eyes. The expression within them was less than reassuring.

"Forgive me, Your Majesty," he said, "but I would like to bring in a couple of my associates to examine you as well. What I am seeing—well, I fear it has me at a loss."

"What do you mean?" I demanded before Sethian could even open his mouth.

"His life-force is severely disrupted as it would be with any illness," the healer explained. "The problem is that I searched his entire system over and over, and I simply cannot find what is causing the disruption." He turned to Sethian again. "Your energy levels fell inexplicably even as I examined you! Except for the depletion, I can find nothing amiss at all!"

"Can you bring them now?" I asked anxiously.

He nodded. "Of course."

Once the healer had gone, I went to sit on the bed beside Sethian. "What do you make of that?" I asked.

"That perhaps you were right to be as concerned as you are," he said grudgingly. He closed his eyes for a moment, a frown of concentration wrinkling the skin of his brow momentarily before he opened them and continued, "Now that he has pointed it out, I can clearly see the disruption in my life-force he spoke of."

"If it isn't viral or bacterial, couldn't just plain fatigue cause a drop in your energy levels?" I asked.

He shook his head. Even that simple gesture seemed to require a tremendous effort. "Not like this, and especially not this quickly."

"What are the odds that you picked up some new, unknown sickness?"

"Yesterday, I would have said next to zero, but after seeing this…" He shrugged.

"Maybe I should have one of the healers take a look at me, too, when they come," I said, now more alarmed than ever.

"That would be best," he agreed, closing his eyes wearily.

I took his hand and gave it a squeeze. "Rest for a moment," I urged.

He must have been feeling really awful at that point because he just nodded without even a token protest.

By the time four more healers returned with Sethian's chief healer, Sethian had fallen into a deep sleep. Agreeing that he should not be awoken, they each carefully examined Sethian in turn, and each emerged from their healer's trance with the same frustrating answer. There was definitely something wrong with Sethian—any fool with eyes could see that—but other than his rapidly depleting energy, every other aspect of his physical body was functioning normally.

An examination of my life-force thankfully did not show any anomalies, but they suggested minimal contact all the same until they could get to the bottom of it. I immediately sent the children to stay with Lariel in my old suite while Saeria and Rinwen remained behind to aid the healers and me.

By evening, it had become apparent that Sethian was no longer just sleeping but had fallen into a coma-like state despite the healers' best efforts to restore his lost energies. A mage was brought in at that point to examine Sethian's depleting energy reserves in the hopes that seeing the problem from a different perspective might yield a better understanding of the anomaly, itself. It was then that the healers finally realized that what they had been trying to diagnose and fight was not an illness at all.

That day, I learned the frightening truth that curses were only too real.

When the commotion first started somewhere beyond our bedroom, my heart clenched with instant dread, and I involuntarily squeezed Sethian's lifeless hand more tightly and hugged Arra, who was currently sitting in my lap, closer to my chest. Was it another assassin? It had been so long since the last. Had we grown too complacent, so much so that they saw the distraction of Sethian's illness as a golden opportunity to exploit that complacency?

The two healers bending over Sethian visibly stiffened. The one on Sethian's left opened his eyes, breaking his healing trance, and turned towards the noise with a frown. He started to take a step towards the door. I opened my mouth to shout a warning, but before I could utter a word, the door crashed open with all the force of a battering ram. A swarm of guards, their swords drawn, began spilling into the room without so much as a "by your leave."

Arra screeched and swiveled in my lap, wrapping her

arms around my neck and burying her face in my hair in fear. As I tightened my arms around her, my eyes anxiously scanned the faces, looking for the men who had been on guard duty for the royal suite since last night, but none of them were present, none of them even looked vaguely familiar. I gathered my daughter more securely and started to stand from the chair beside the bed where I had been keeping constant vigil ever since Sethian had fallen into his coma-like state, but then the final person that walked through the door behind the men froze me on the spot.

For one seemingly eternal moment, our eyes met, and the triumph I saw within those normally cold, green eyes made all the blood instantly drain from my face. I remembered seeing that look only once before—and it had immediately been followed by the suggestion of a plan that would have killed Thaylan before he had even been born.

"Take her," the queen ordered, sounding as casual as if she were only saying hello.

It had been inevitable really from the moment Sethian had fallen unconscious yesterday. With the king incapacitated and the heir out of reach, the seat of power automatically fell to the queen until either of the previous two could take up the mantle again. She could have me forcibly banished back to the human realm, killed, tortured, and not one person could lift a finger to help me without being accused of treason and having the same done to them.

Her endgame had finally been revealed, and it was quite the master stroke.

Knowing that resisting would likely end with a sword in the gut, a child traumatized for life, and a very satisfied queen, I softly whispered into Arra's ear to get on the bed with Sethian. I then took his hand again and gave it one last squeeze as I stood, willing him to feel my love, my desperation for him to fight the curse that was slowly draining the life from him. I could only pray that he was somehow able to hear what was happening here, that his resulting anger would fuel his soul and keep him in the world of the living long enough for Thaylan to return to take back the power of the throne from Limira. To save his siblings from falling under her thumb because I didn't really expect to live past the day.

My eyes stayed on my family's faces, one slack and one pinched with fear, as I felt hands grab both my arms roughly from behind and pull me away from the bed, forcing me to release Sethian's hand before we could be wrenched apart.

Then suddenly one of the healers was marching forward, and he grabbed one of my shoulders until I momentarily found myself in a strange kind of tug-of-war between him and the guards at my back.

"With all due respect, Your Majesty," the healer said before the guards could raise their swords, "whatever quarrel you have with the Royal Wife must be set aside for the time being for the sake of His Majesty. We have finally managed to slow down the effects of the curse a bit, and I fear depriving him of her presence will deplete his essence more quickly."

"It is already too late for the king," the queen said harshly, "and I shall not allow his murderer the satisfaction of witnessing his final breaths no matter the reason! To allow him to die with dignity is the only gift I can give him now!"

"What?" I blurted, turning to look back at the queen in utter shock. She wasn't seriously going to—just what was her game this time?

She smiled at me nastily. "A witness has come forth, one who overheard a *very* interesting conversation with a *Lithviri* mage and a small, hooded woman who spoke with a very strange accent. The mage in question was captured as he was fleeing the palace with the aid of Lariel of the family Elerdir. I have just returned from interrogating both of them, and while your lady-in-waiting has stubbornly refused to speak, the mage was much more forthcoming after a little persuasion from a few of my personal guards. However, your servant *will* talk. Of that, I have no doubt."

You lying bitch! I snarled in my mind, though outwardly, I struggled to keep my expression from changing. I would be damned before I gave her the satisfaction of seeing me lose control in front of my daughter.

"I didn't think even *you* would have the guts to just flat-out lie," I said, staring at her challengingly. "Lariel was just in this very room dropping off my daughter a few moments ago. These healers can attest to that. I hardly think you had the time for an interrogation between then and now."

"The coin of power within the royal court is very tempting, especially when the one paying has blood ties to the heir and the heir is blinded to his mother's perfidy by affection," the queen continued as if I hadn't even spoken.

"Mama!"

"Stay with your father, Arra," I told her as calmly as I could, which didn't amount to much as I was likely inadvertently drowning her with my inner turmoil.

"Do not worry. The half-blood will be—dealt with appropriately," the queen sneered.

And that's when I lost it.

A red haze seemed to fill my eyes as I tore out of the

grips of the two elves that held my arms and lunged for the queen's throat. I just managed to get my hands around her neck when the back of my head abruptly exploded with pain a split-second before everything went black.

CHAPTER 32

A rush of panic thundered through my awareness, and I shot up from the rough surface I had been lying on to a seated position, my heart trying its damnedest to break out of my chest. I looked around wildly, confused about where I was and why I felt as if I was currently having a full-blown panic attack, then winced when that frantic movement set off an explosion of pain in my head. It was dark, so dark that the only thing I could make out was the outline of a door because of the very faint light coming in through the thin crack between what looked like a stone floor and the bottom of the door.

I raised my hands to cradle my head and moaned as it continued to throb. I tried to take slow, deep breaths in an effort to stem the panic that had permeated my entire being, and that's when I felt Thaylan's essence and realized that the panic I was feeling was his.

Thaylan *never* panicked…

"Thaylan!" I called out into the dark, but my increasing confusion and now rising fear was met with only silence.

The excruciating pain in my head was making it extremely difficult to think. So I was alone here, wherever here was. I drew in another deep breath, and this time I noticed that the air was muggy and had a faint odor of mold and old sweat. It was a familiar combination, somehow. Where—

"Shit!" I cursed loudly, dropping my hands and scrambling to my feet.

I stumbled over to the door, praying that I was wrong as I frantically felt for a door handle and was instead rewarded with a palm full of splinters. Biting back a sob, I backed up until my back hit the stone wall behind me and let myself slide down to the floor again.

How in the world had I ended up in the palace *dungeon*?

It was the queen. It *had* to be the queen. No one else other than Sethian would have had the authority to lock me up here, and as far as I could remember, the only "crime" I had been guilty of was nagging Sethian to stay in bed because he had really looked like crap...

And just like that, the image of my hands wrapped around the queen's throat and those hateful eyes widened with shock flashed within my mind. It was followed by the memory of sitting at Sethian's side helplessly watching the life drain out of him with every shallow breath while his healers fought to prolong his life long enough for Thaylan to reach the palace.

Even with the incredible distances he could reach with his phasing ability, the *Lithvir Sidhe* lands were on the other side of the world, and not even Thaylan could move that kind of distance in a single jump. Nor could his personal energy reserves support the number of spatial manipulations it would take to reach the palace without resting several marks between each. The healers had given Sethian a day at the most, and that was about the amount of time it would take his son to reach him.

It was no wonder that Thaylan was so panicked!

At that moment, I felt like the most worthless person in existence. Tears of self-loathing began to flow down my cheeks. While Sethian lay dying and the queen was doing God-only-knew-what to my children and friends, I was stuck here in the dark waiting for the ax to fall—literally. I clenched my hands tightly into fists at the image that thought conjured up, of the queen smiling smugly as she ordered the downward stroke of a sword in an old-style beheading.

No—there *was* something I could do. Fury, like I had never felt in my life, erupted within me, washing away the anguish as I scrubbed angrily at my tears. I really would be worthless if I just sat here crying without trying to do *something*.

There was no way I would be able to get out of here, but maybe I could use our familial bond to send a warning about the queen to Thaylan. At the moment, he had no idea about the nest of vipers he was about to walk into, and despite all the fuss about the incredible power he wielded, he was still just a twelve-year-old boy about to face the cunning of a snake thousands of years his senior. I didn't have even an ounce of Thaylan's empathic abilities, and I knew that he was probably still too far away for my puny efforts to reach, but maybe if I kept shouting out to him in my heart, he would eventually be able to sense me.

It was the only weapon I had, and I only prayed that it would be enough.

I HAD no idea how long I had been mentally shouting into the void, but it was only when I suddenly heard voices outside my cell door that I came back to myself and realized I was on the verge of collapsing from exhaustion. I smacked both my palms against my cheeks hard in an effort to clear my head and managed to drag myself to my feet just as I heard someone turning a key in the lock. Damned if I would meet whoever was on the other side of the door sitting down.

For a split-second, I considered charging the first person that walked through the door and in almost the same thought dismissed it as incredibly stupid. It would probably be a guard, and what were the odds that someone like me would be able to get more than half a step past a heavily trained guard without a whole lot of hurt? I doubted my title of Royal Wife held any weight at all anymore, and I would end up with another goose egg or worse on my head. For all I knew, these guards were in the pocket of the queen or anti-human zealots just itching for any excuse to permanently remove the source of the current "taint" that had begun to permeate the elven realm.

"Unless you want a sword in your gut, back away from the door and stand against the back wall," an unfamiliar male voice called through the door.

I did as instructed with an air of resentment, and a few seconds later, the door creaked open. Even though the light in the corridor was poor, I still flinched away violently when it hit my eyes. Squinting against the illumination, I watched as a couple of guards stepped across the threshold, swords in hand but thankfully pointed down at the ground, followed unsurprisingly by the queen, a lit oil lamp hanging from one hand.

The expression of extreme smugness on her face looked so uncannily like the one she had worn in the image I had conjured of her during my imagined beheading that for a moment, I felt slightly unbalanced.

"Leave us," Limira ordered the guards. When both of them hesitated, she added without taking her eyes off me, "If the human wishes her children to remain untouched, she will not lift a finger against me. Now go."

I fisted my hands angrily at my sides but said nothing. To use my own children as her shield was the lowest of the low. I suddenly had the irrational urge to bare my teeth at her.

"The king is failing fast," she said as soon as the door closed behind her. "He will be lucky to last more than a few more marks."

My eyes narrowed angrily. "Thaylan will come to save him."

That was the only thing that mattered now.

The queen smirked. "Yes, the mongrel's healers said as much. I, of course, immediately dispatched a messenger to the *Lithviri* informing your brat of the king's imminent demise and urging him to come home at once. Of course, he will arrive only in enough time to bury his father and learn of the execution of his traitorous mother. You understand, don't you? With both parents deceased, the heir—your children—will, of course, belong to me."

"So what are you waiting for?" I demanded bitterly. "It's just you and me down here. The whole of the elven court already believes me guilty of cursing the king to his death thanks to you and your cronies' lies. No one but my friends and children would cry if you just slit my throat right here in a fit of 'rage.' Or are you too much a coward to dirty your own hands? I hate to tell you this, but they're already blacker than pitch, and that shit doesn't wash off."

"I could," she said with a nod, seemingly ignoring my crude taunts, "but that would not even begin to repay me for these past thirteen years of insult and humiliation you and the House of Elerren have afflicted on me and my family name. A thousand years of suffering would not be enough, but that's exactly what you will receive. A thousand years to sit here and rot, knowing that the fault of your husband's death lies solely in your hands for refusing to leave the realm when I asked. Knowing that your children will grow up hating you not only for killing their father but also for the human taint that runs through their veins."

As the queen looked at me with absolute hate in her eyes, I knew that she meant every word, that she really intended to keep me locked up here for a small eternity.

Thaylan! Hurry! my soul screamed with all the desperation I had in me.

CHAPTER 33

As I sat in the darkness screaming my silent warnings to Thaylan over and over until I wondered if I would ever get those words out of my head, I occasionally had paused for a few moments and had tried desperately to sense Sethian's essence deep within me in the place where our souls were bound. Over the years, his presence within me had grown to the point that I had been able to sense him without any real effort, as though viewing someone from the corner of your eye. Now, it was as though a part of me had been cut away and only a gaping wound remained.

I refused to believe that it meant that he was gone. I was certain the queen would have already come down to gloat and dig the knife in just that much more deeper if that had been the case, so I comforted myself in feeling the emotions of my children even though they were currently dominated by anxiety and confusion. I don't think I would have been able to bear it if their emotions had projected physical pain.

Then clear as day, I heard somewhere in the space before me, "I'm here."

The dark outline of a small person suddenly appeared before me, then like an avenging angel, the slightly glowing form of my son was standing before me, long black hair hanging wild and tangled over his shoulders as though he had just come in from a windstorm. I was already hugging him to me before the glow about him completely faded, and we were plunged into darkness again. The blackness was almost painful after that brief illumination.

"We have to hurry to your father!" I said urgently, my voice thick with threatening tears. "The queen had a mage place a death curse on him, and—"

"I know," Thaylan interjected. "I heard your words quite clearly when I reached the edge of the palace."

"I don't know how they managed to get that curse past your barrier around him," I said as I felt rather than saw the air around us begin to warp.

"It will be all right, Mom," he said, though I could hear the uncertainty that he had tried to hide.

Then the darkness all around us began to rapidly lighten until we were abruptly standing next to the bed where Sethian lay as gray and still as a corpse. The healer closest to us backpedaled so quickly that he managed to trip himself up and ended up sprawled in a heap on the floor.

The look of utter shock on the queen's face is something I would remember for the rest of my life. However, it was probably nothing compared to the shock on mine when Thaylan made a strange gesture with one of his hands, and the very air surrounding Limira seemed to peel away in six large, oval-shaped strips and began closing inward on her like petals on an enormous, nearly transparent flower. She only had time to shriek once before the bizarre phenomenon enclosed her completely, and she winked out of existence as though she was never there.

"Now she can't cause us any more trouble," Thaylan said with satisfaction into the dead silence that followed as he turned to Sethian without another word.

He picked up his father's limp hand and fell still, staring intently at Sethian's chest as he furrowed his brow in concentration. I quickly put what had just happened with the queen out of my mind, filing it under the "things to have a *long* talk about with your son later" category in my brain, and stepped closer to the bed.

I saw several of the guards within the room tense up the moment I moved, but after what Thaylan had done to the queen, no one dared say a word or even dared to *move*. Can't say that I blamed them. Fear rather than rank was what commanded them now.

"No..." Thaylan abruptly whispered, his voice sounding preternaturally loud in the silence.

"What?" I demanded anxiously, laying a hand on his shoulder.

"I can't stop it," he said, turning to me with a stricken look in his eyes. "The drain is connected to his very soul. The mere act of another's essence touching it would kill him instantly, never mind me trying to extract it. His life-force is the fuel that sustains it. Another's cannot be used to ease the burden. That's why the healing energies given him by his healers have failed to revitalize him. It will continue to drain him until there is nothing left to drain and the curse can no longer be sustained."

He turned completely towards me and clutched both of my arms. "I can't stop it!" he cried again, this time sounding every bit like the boy he was as tears began to well in his eyes.

Those words stabbed into me as painfully as if I had been run through with one of the guards' swords.

I grabbed his arms in return. "There has to be something, *something* we can do?" I pleaded.

"No one can touch his soul," he insisted with anguish. "Not unless—"

"Yes, there *is*!" I practically screamed over him.

Our soul bond. Our soul bond had to be the answer. It was something that neither Sethian nor I had ever discussed with the children. Sethian had been reluctant to tell Thaylan his theory about why he had been born so different than everyone else in the event that he was wrong. He feared to set Thaylan on a path that he was never meant to take. Thus, we had mutually agreed to keep that aspect of our relationship to ourselves for the time being.

"Your father and I are soul-bound," I said. "Help me Thaylan. Help me connect with his soul again. It's not something a human can do on their own. I'll open my soul completely to him and feed him my life-force until the curse has consumed all of his and ends as it's intended to do."

Thaylan's eyes widened incredibly large. "What! No! Mom, I can't!" he said, shaking his head vigorously. "Even weakened, an elven soul would consume a human's!"

"I know—your father warned me to never do it, but we're out of options. One of us must survive this for you, for your brother and sisters' sakes, and the *Sidhe* need their king more than a Royal Wife."

"But we need our mother," Thaylan said brokenly, releasing my arms only to throw his own around my middle and hug me with a desperation that almost made me lose my resolve.

I hugged him just as tightly and planted a kiss on his forehead. I wished I could hug Anir, Rinya, and Arra once more before I did this in case the worst happened, but we were simply out of time. I compromised by sending them a wave of love through our empathic bonds.

Thaylan released me reluctantly, his eyes suddenly looking way too old and weary for a twelve-year-old. It made my heart clench painfully with guilt.

"Just remember that I love you—all of you," I said with a tremulous smile. I wanted desperately to promise him that everything would work out just fine, but I had never lied to my children. I wasn't about to start now.

I kicked off my slippers and climbed onto the bed, trying not to get tangled up in my long skirt as I laid myself half-draped over his chest and threaded our hands together. "Here we go," I murmured for Thaylan's benefit.

Then I closed my eyes and remembering that overwhelming feeling from long ago when I had completely surrendered to Sethian and our souls had bonded, I sought to replicate that feeling, that total surrender. I sensed more than felt Thaylan guide me towards a tiny thread of Sethian's essence that I had been unable to find before when I had searched while stuck in that dungeon cell.

Once I touched that thread, I had about a split-second to feel the horror of his rapidly fading life-force before the thread suddenly latched onto me, this sudden influx of life energy it had found, and began to instinctually draw its fill more quickly than I had anticipated. It was like trying to stop the downward flow of a waterfall with a twig, and just as both Sethian and Thaylan had warned, the whole of my being was drawn into that flow before I could even think to pull away. As my consciousness faded, my last thought was not of fear, regrets, or even of death. It was of my family and the knowledge that they would certainly prosper with Sethian at their side to guide them.

CHAPTER 34

I was surrounded by warmth, that was the first thing that registered as my consciousness rose from the murky depths of oblivion. It was both comforting and comfortable, and I would have let my mind fall back into that blissful nothingness had I not suddenly felt something warm and soft brush across my lips. It was a struggle, but I forced my eyes open and managed to keep them open after a couple of false starts even though my eyelids seemed to weigh a ton each and my eyes, themselves, stung a little. At first, my vision was one big blur of various flesh-toned colors and yellows, but eventually, everything came into focus. I realized that my head was currently lying on Sethian's bare chest, and he was looking down at me with a very strange look in his eyes.

It wasn't just his expression. There was something different about him, something that my still sleep-fuzzed mind couldn't quite figure out. I lifted my head and looked at him quizzically. There didn't seem to be anything different about his face that I could tell, but at the same time, I knew there was.

Without saying a word, Sethian cupped the side of my face and leaned forward. Thinking that he was going in for a kiss, I started to close my eyes again but then blinked at him in surprise when I felt him press his forehead against mine and close his eyes with a pinched look on his face as though he was struggling not to cry.

Frankly, I was starting to get a little freaked out by the way he was behaving. In all the thirteen years we had been together, I had never once seen him cry, nor did I ever expect to.

"Sethian?" I questioned, grimacing as my voice came out so raspy that it sounded as though I hadn't had a drink of water in days.

"I was beginning to think that you would never awaken," he said thickly. He hugged me more tightly against his body.

"Never awaken?" I echoed in confusion.

He pulled back a bit and studied my face, his eyes swimming with worry. "You don't remember?"

I tried to think back to what I had been doing before going to bed, but my mind was coming up with a big fat nothing. Apparently, there was a lot I was missing because aside from Sethian's strange behavior, from the moment I had awakened, everything had felt a little—off.

I shook my head. "Did I have an accident? Hit my head or something?" I raised my hand to feel along my scalp, but there were no bumps, and nothing felt even remotely tender.

"You have been asleep for almost a moon-cycle," he said.

I sucked in a sharp breath. "What! Why? But I don't feel—"

If I had been unconscious for that many days, then shouldn't I have been so weak that it would have been difficult to talk, much less move? However, other than an parched mouth, initial confusion, and a little residual weakness, I felt no worse than if I had woken up with a slight hangover.

"What's the last thing you remember?"

"I'm not sure," I said, suddenly feeling a little overwhelmed. "My head is still a little muddled. If I've been out of it for so long, it's no wonder I had so much trouble opening my eyes earlier. Just tell me Sethian. Please."

He ran his fingers through my hair. "Do you remember me being ill at all?" he asked.

I furrowed my brow, considering. Yes, I *did* remember sitting in this room for long marks by his bedside, holding a hand that had gone as cold as ice while several healers fussed over him with faces that had become increasingly graver. I dug a little deeper into the memory, and suddenly the queen's infuriatingly smug face flashed into my mind, standing inside the dungeon cell she had condemned me to while she gleefully told me of Sethian's impending death.

"The queen tried to kill you!" I exclaimed, outrage coloring my voice. "That curse…!"

It was all coming back to me now, as though my sudden rage at what the queen had tried to do to my family had cleared all the remaining haze from my mind, allowing my last memories to finally rise to the surface. Thaylan phasing into the dungeon to rescue me, what he did to the queen, his anguish when he realized that he could not save his father—everything.

"Then Thaylan showed me how to save you," I finished more softly.

Sethian took my face into his hands. "And once you did, and the curse broke, he showed me how to save *you*."

"All I remember is blacking out once your soul had

begun to consume mine. What happened after that?"

"I woke up the moment the curse broke. It happened only moments before my soul could consume all your life-energy completely, and I was able to stop it before all hope to save you would have been lost. Because our souls were so intertwined and his so intrinsically linked with yours, Thaylan was able to share some of his own life-force with you, enough so that with our combined efforts, we were able to bring you back from the brink of death.

"I have been lying here with you day and night, every moment I was able, feeding you as much of my life-energy as was safe in the hope that it would help you to recover, but the human soul is different. Unlike with me, I was not certain receiving the life-energy of an elf could help you at all as it appeared you were unable to absorb it well."

"I put my soul through a tremendous shock. Maybe all it needed was rest and time. And giving me some of your life-energy *did* help. Now it makes sense why I didn't wake up still feeling half-dead."

"Nevertheless, you will not be getting out of bed anytime soon," Sethian said sternly.

"Well, right now you're not exactly making it hard to obey you," I teased. I turned and kissed the palm of one of his hands softly. "Is it night or day right now?"

"It is early morning. The children will be up soon and anxious to see their mother. They have been keeping vigil at your bedside along with me as well."

Anger boiled to the surface again. "Limira, she didn't hurt them, did she?"

I could feel an answering anger within Sethian's own emotions as he replied, "Not physically, but Arra witnessed a guard striking you over the head and then Limira had her sent to a relative within the palace who promptly informed her that we were both dead. She won't be forgetting any of this anytime soon."

"Thank goodness Anir and Rinya were with Rinwen when that whole horrible mess started. As far as I know, the queen was never able to get her hands on them."

He shook his head. "Saeria and Rinwen were able to hide them with their father." He paused a moment, flashing me a rather serious look, before continuing a bit hesitantly, "However, Lariel was not so fortunate. She has recovered, but when we discovered her in the dungeons, she had already been badly beaten by one of the queen's guards. We believe it was to lend credibility to the lies about you that Limira had fed the Court."

"Did Thaylan explain to you what he did with her?" I asked.

Sethian's lips stretched into a satisfied grin as he nodded. "He folded her up within the material of one of the many pocket dimensions he has created over the years. She fell into a kind of stasis until I was well enough to deal with her. In the end, she was less than forthcoming with the answers she was willing to give, and with the mage that had delivered such a deadly curse upon me still unknown, I had no choice but to perform a mind extraction on her before he could target us again."

"Why did she do something so stupid? She had to know the consequences of protecting that mage. She had to know how pointless it was to remain silent when you would get the answers from her anyway."

"Treason against the king carries a harsh punishment," Sethian said, but when he did not elaborate further, I didn't press him. I was probably better off not knowing, anyway.

"At least her death was not completely in vain. The information within her mind pointed me to not only a dangerous mage but also to several enemies I had not even been aware of. It seems the queen was only one of many that wanted you removed from the Realm. It was they, and not Limira or her family that sent the many assassins that attacked you over the years, though she did aid a few of them wherever she could. The only one that could be attributed completely to her is the man that attacked you in our bedroom. Unbeknownst to all of us, every guard on duty that night were those in the pockets of her family. By no means did we find all of them, but we have certainly struck a serious blow to their cause."

"The queen once told me that the healers and mages within her people believed that they would be able to safely extract the human genes from their genomes someday pretty soon," I said quietly. "I believe this is why she hated me so much. She saw me as something that would make the 'taint' within the *Sidhe* blood worse. For her, at least, I don't think it was about seizing the throne just for the sake of the throne at all."

I didn't tell him the rest, about how she had tried to convince me to leave the realm voluntarily. The queen was dead. That was tragic enough. It was better to just let sleeping dogs lie on some things.

Before he could comment, a soft knock sounded at the door.

"The healers have arrived, Your Majesty," Lariel called softly through the door.

"Ah, yes," Sethian said. "It is later in the morning than I had initially thought."

"I shall meet with them shortly," Sethian called back to her. Then he suddenly smiled. "In the meantime, I believe there is someone here that would very much like to see you."

Lariel gasped loudly, then the door flew open in the next second, and she was barreling towards the bed. "Emily! Thank the High Powers! You are awake!" she cried as Sethian carefully helped me to sit up to receive her very enthusiastic hug.

While Lariel was busy fussing over me, Sethian used the opportunity to climb out of bed and change his clothes in order to meet with the healers.

"I shall send them in to examine you shortly, as well as the children," Sethian said to me, giving my hand an affectionate squeeze before turning to address Lariel. "After your visit, I need you to go to the royal baths and make certain the pools are hot and ready to receive us."

Her eyes immediately fell to the coverlet. "Yes, Your Majesty," she said with a slight bow.

I couldn't believe it, but Lariel looked a little afraid of Sethian now.

I was definitely missing something big here. I opened my mouth to question them both about it, but Sethian must have seen me frowning at Lariel because he gave me a *look* and shook his head almost imperceptibly as he stood behind her. Right. We would discuss it later. For now, I just wanted to make sure that she really was all right after the ordeal she had endured because of me. The details could wait.

CHAPTER 35

"I could have walked, you know," I said pointedly as Sethian set me down gently at the edge of the largest bathing pool.

"It does not mean you *should,*" he said in all seriousness.

I sighed but conceded the point. He would probably be over-protective of me for a good long while and knowing how stubborn he could get, it was just easier to let him have his way. Besides, I thought with a wry smile, it wasn't as if being pampered was any kind of hardship.

I lifted my nightgown over my head, tossing it carelessly over to the side, and slipped down into the gloriously hot water while Sethian removed his clothes. I sat down on the underwater bench and just leaned back against the pool's wall with my eyes closed, allowing the warmth of the water to begin soaking the weariness from my body. I was surprised at how quickly visiting with my friends and the children had tired me out, but then there had been many tears involved. The emotional toll no doubt had doubly weighed down on a soul so recently drained as mine.

Soon, the water sloshed beside me as Sethian lowered himself down next to me. I opened my eyes and scooted myself into his lap without any urging on his part. My days of being shy were long past me.

"Do you want to tell me why everyone is suddenly treating you like you've become the big, bad monster?" I asked as Sethian began to caress my body with a soapy sponge.

"Your ladies are just a bit unnerved at the moment," he replied quite matter-of-factly.

"It's not just them," I insisted. "The healers were even jumpier every time you got near one of them."

I felt him nod his head behind me. "They are unnerved for the same reason. When you opened yourself so completely to me and our souls merged more perfectly than they ever had before, you inadvertently unlocked a latent power within me, something that has never been seen among my people. I have caught you scrutinizing my face more than once since you awakened. You can sense something is different but cannot quite pinpoint what exactly has changed, correct?"

"Yes, and I've been so annoyed because I couldn't figure it out."

"I am now completely connected to the natural energies of the whole realm. That is the difference you sense when you look at me even though what you see is not what others have seen when they look upon me now."

I really hated it when he explained things so vaguely. It was a bad habit of his.

"What do you mean?" I prompted.

"When I am with you, your soul acts as a buffer, tempering the power that now perpetually flows into and is absorbed by my body from the natural energy streams around me. I shine quite brightly now without the presence of your soul, as brilliantly as the sun when it is high in a clear sky, I am told. It can be rather troublesome—for everyone."

I looked back at him. "Rather than temper it, it just sounds like my soul is a contaminant," I said with a laugh, "like it's getting in the way of the purity of your essence or something."

The sour look Sethian directed at me had me laughing even harder. However, my chuckles soon turned into a startled moan when I felt him reach between my legs and firmly press his fingers against my clit, rubbing in a slow, circular motion. He pressed his lips against mine and greedily swallowed my moans as I tried not to squirm too much. I knew I was still a little too weak for the more vigorous and sometimes wild sex we often enjoyed, and I didn't want to accidentally drive him into a needy frenzy.

Even so, I could feel his rapidly hardening member begin to poke into my lower back. Knowing that I would not have the energy to prolong this, I started to turn on his lap so that I could mount him more easily, but he immediately moved the hand that had been cupping and caressing one of my breasts down to my hip to stop the movement.

Sethian pulled away from the kiss and moved his lips to the crook of my neck. "Stay as you are," he murmured huskily against my skin. "This time I shall do all the work. Just relax and enjoy and let me feel your warmth and your life pulsing around me. I need to feel that you are here with me right now, that you really have come back to me."

Hearing such melancholy words had my throat instantly tightening with emotion so that I was only able to nod in answer. He bit at my neck gently before I felt his lips stretch into a smile against my skin.

He resumed his gentle but vigorous fondling of the hot button between my legs while continuing to slowly kiss, lick and suck a red path from my neck to my shoulder. This slower pace made sudden actions like the pinching of my nipples or the insertion of a couple of fingers into my moist passage much more potent, and soon he had me moaning and writhing on his lap with blissful abandon as his fingers massaged me into my first orgasm.

Despite his desire for me to just sit back and enjoy, I couldn't help thrusting myself up and down on his fingers as I rode out those pleasurable spasms.

"Please Sethian," I begged breathlessly, "I need to feel you inside me."

He needed no further persuasion as he pulled his fingers from within me and gently grabbed my hips to lift me up and onto the cock that was bobbing eagerly in the water. I reached a hand down and wrapped it around his member to help guide it into my passage. I moaned as the head rubbed across the shallow, sensitive spot that Sethian loved to drive me wild with as he entered me. Then he was buried up into me to the hilt, and he once again stilled my hips when I tried to raise myself to begin grinding myself down onto that thick cock.

"Let me," he whispered again into my ear, making me shiver.

I leaned back against his chest and tilted my head

back and to the side to give his lips and especially those teeth better access to my neck. Knowing what I wanted, Sethian began to slowly nip at my neck with quick, shallow bites while starting a slow, upward thrust deep into my recesses. Once he had established a rhythm, his hands moved from my waist to cup both of my breasts, squeezing and fondling them with greater aggression as my fingers clutched at his thighs in time to his thrusts.

Then one of his hands dropped back down to my groin and began aggressively rubbing my clit again until the pressure became too much, and I exploded for the second time with a cry. Sethian continued to thrust up into me even as I rode out the waves of my orgasm, but by the increasing urgency of his thrusts, and the rising excitement that began to flood my being, he was now teetering on the edge of his own ecstasy.

I deliberately clamped down on his member with the muscles of my passage, and with a startled gasp and a final bite to my shoulder, I felt his warmth begin to release within me. I rocked my hips against him as he came, loving the feel of his cock jerking within me.

Sethian pulled my face towards him with a hand beneath my chin and kissed me slowly and passionately, his tongue lazily sliding against mine as if trying to memorize its contours. Making love with Sethian was always earth-shattering, but I could kiss him forever.

There was just something about the way he moved his lips and tongue that was not only pleasurable but also comforting and sexy, making me feel wanted and powerful like nothing else.

Sitting here, surrounded by the warmth of the water and Sethian, himself, after triumphing over so much darkness, with my four beautiful children and three best friends who would do anything to protect us waiting for us back in the royal suite, I realized with a start that I had actually managed to achieve my Happily Ever After. My only regret was that I would never have the opportunity to let my best friend, Anna, back in the human world know that I was alive and well, living within this, my own personal fairytale.

DATE NIGHT

A BONUS SHORT

Elven King Sethian takes his human bride, Emily, to the human realm and tells her the story of how she came to his attention where things quickly heat up.

"I should've known," I said as I walked hand-in-hand with my elven husband towards the still-familiar cluster of buildings of my old university. "When you said you wanted to show me exactly how our fates became intertwined, I admit that I've always pictured it to have been somewhere more picturesque like one of the city's parks or the lake. I guess I'm more of a romantic than I thought."

Sethian smiled down at me fondly as we stepped onto the campus. "Perhaps not. This was only my first step. Yours had not yet come into play at this point in time, my Emily."

Now more curious than ever, I allowed him to slowly lead me towards the center of campus along the shadows of the trees and buildings where our current, shadow-like manifestation of our bodies within the human realm could blend in and evade notice from human eyes.

"I had not realized how daunting my task to find a human bride would be until I saw this…" He swept his free hand in a broad arc before them. "…these seemingly endless streams of humans milling about like a colony of scattered ants. Things had not appeared quite so busy when I had first chosen this area of this particular human city to observe. I couldn't understand how its population had virtually tripled over the past moon-cycle when I had last entered the human realm."

"Ah," I said, "you probably found this campus between semesters."

"Semesters?"

"I guess an easy way to think of it is levels of study. Once one level—or semester—is completed, students take about a moon-cycle off before beginning a new level."

We paused in the shadows against one of the larger buildings between a couple of large, manicured bushes barely wide enough to accommodate us and well away from the bustling crowds.

"Just as we stand here cloaked in the shadow of this building," Sethian continued, "I stood here that day and immediately saw that slipping from shadow to shadow unseen by the surrounding crowds in pursuit of a human that suddenly interested me would not be as easy of an endeavor as I had first thought. I thought it better to wait until nightfall when my shadow-like body would become just part of the natural environment to a human's eyes.

"I settled down onto the ground and propped myself against the brick wall of this very building. Rather than search out a potential mate while I waited for the skies to darken, I used that time to observe the humans in general. I thought it would be interesting to see just how much the social dynamics had changed in the decades since I had last visited the human realm. In the past, there had always been something that had surprised me."

I made a face. "Typical elven patience. How many elven marks did you sit here? Five? Ten?"

His eyes went distant for a few seconds. "Several, as it had only been midday when I had arrived, but it only took about a mark before I found that surprising 'something.' It soon became apparent that humans were more open and relaxed in their courtship, showing far more displays of their affection than had been proper in their society the last time I had visited the human realm or even within the elven court. Not only that, but I witnessed courtship initiated by *both* sexes. I was pleased to see this change. I felt that this mutual openness could only help my own chances of wooing a potential human mate once I had her within the Realm."

I huffed indignantly. "What wooing? My mind may have been hazy and drowning in your elfy magic, but I don't recall any wooing going on that first night *at all*."

"You accepted me didn't you?" Sethian replied pointedly.

"I don't know why I even bother anymore," I groused with a sigh. "I'm starting to realize that the *Sidhe* will never understand a human's concept of time, much less how one perceives the world."

Instead of staring back at me with a slightly perplexed expression as he always did when I tried to explain something from a human's point of view, he nodded sharply, his eyes looking down at me with a gravely serious expression.

"That is why I wished you to walk this path with me today. I knew then on our wedding night that you did not understand my actions, nor, I daresay, your own reactions to me. I was at a loss of how to adequately explain, so I decided to allow time to give you your answers—time with me and time living among the *Sidhe*. Then after almost losing you the way I did, seeing how far you were willing to go for me without a moment's hesitation, I realized that I have wronged you greatly by not attempting to explain at all, even if my words had ended up being in vain. Perhaps now, seeing this world as I saw it on that fateful day, you may have your answer."

I squeezed his hand and smiled at him softly. "So that's what this is really about. I thought that it was really strange that you suddenly decided to bring me to the human realm for our date night after all these years."

Sethian returned my affectionate squeeze before turning his attention back to the river of students walking past, most likely on their way to their dorms or off campus as it wouldn't be long before the sun would begin to set.

"I had also gleaned from the humans' conversations that this was a rather large place of learning," he said. "I thought to return later during the night to search out the human libraries that were likely housed within this multitude of buildings and snatch a few books. For the enormous shift in the status quo I was about to introduce into the elven realm, I knew it would become necessary to have my subjects study certain aspects of the modern human realm. After locating the correct building, I planned to send a few of the royal scholars who would be better equipped to perform the task."

"So that's where that horde of modern books in English came from," I said wryly. "Now I know why the scholars would never tell me."

"Perhaps they did not wish to be thought thieves by the Royal Wife, although in all fairness, we could hardly ask the humans within for them," Sethian replied with a chuckle.

"Point taken," I said, remembering the shadows that had spirited me away to the elven realm and how terrifying they had appeared. "So, you didn't hunt out the library right away. Did you just stay here watching everyone until nightfall?"

Sethian nodded. "Throughout the day, I watched as the crowds periodically waxed and waned but never completely disappeared, at least enough where I was fairly confident I could move out from the shadows and not be seen. It wasn't until the sky had darkened significantly and the stream of humans had thinned to a few groups here and there that I felt comfortable enough to move away from the building. I decided to follow a rather energetic group of four young females and two young males that had just passed me who had been chattering about leaving the campus for home."

He suddenly turned, tugging me away from the building by the hand as we began to retrace our earlier steps.

"I was eager to see where and how these young humans lived," he continued as we slowly made our way off campus. "Therefore, I carefully trailed them at a distance as they left the grounds and walked along a stretch of road until they came upon another cluster of buildings, these surrounded by several of the vehicles that had greatly fascinated me earlier. I wish to take you there now before I continue my tale."

I was filled with a kind of anxious excitement as we silently walked down several streets. It was kind of comforting to see that the overall design of the cars and trucks that drove past, as well as those parked in driveways, hadn't changed all that radically in the thirteen years I had been gone.

As I turned my attention away from scrutinizing the cars to the neighborhood in general, my heart seized painfully in shock when I realized where he must be taking me.

"Sethian..." I whispered, my grip on his hand unconsciously tightening as we rounded the corner and my old apartment complex came into sight.

Over a decade later and it still looked exactly the way I remembered it.

I could feel the weight of Sethian's eyes staring down at me, but I couldn't tear my eyes away from the front of the nearest building. This was where I had lived with my best friend, where I had literally vanished into thin air in the middle of the night so many years ago.

There was likely zero chance that she would still be living in that same tiny apartment, but my heart nevertheless sped up painfully at the thought of her. No matter how much I wanted to see her, I felt I had no right to, not when I could never offer her the same relief.

That Emily was gone forever.

We paused in front of a slightly rusty, iron stairwell along the outside of the first building we came upon. "Unfortunately, the humans I followed immediately climbed to the second floor here before disappearing into one of the many doors along the walkway."

Forcing thoughts of my old friend away, I looked at Sethian sharply. "Please tell me you didn't go into their apartment!"

Ah—there it was, that look of utter bewilderment he always wore that made him look so adorable whenever I did or said something he didn't or *couldn't* understand. These days, I saw it less and less as my thought processes became more—elven, I suppose. It was enough to distract me from my melancholy thoughts.

Sethian shook his head. "No—I slowly explored the various buildings of this complex, but I was disappointed at the stillness of the night around me. I could, of course, hear a few voices behind the doors I passed, but none of the conversations of food or topics that greatly resembled courtly gossip particularly caught my interest. I decided to just return to the place of learning—the university—and resume my observations of those who still remained as well as to begin my search for the library, but..."

His lips suddenly curved up wickedly.

I gasped. "Someone saw you?"

Once again, Sethian shook his head. "A sharp noise abruptly sounded somewhere above me, like a sword falling onto a stone surface, and I instinctually tilted my head up even as my body moved into a defensive stance. However, what I saw was far from the attack I had expected."

Then maddeningly, he began to tug me away from the stairwell without another word. Resigned, I silently allowed him to guide me around to the back of the building, knowing from years of experience that he would resume his tale only when he felt the time was right. It was a trait that all my elven acquaintances shared, and it drove me absolutely insane.

That they seemed to naturally have no sense of urgency, no real sense of time after they reached adulthood, that Queen Limira was able to spend over a decade patiently plotting and planning before setting her endgame in motion, was something that would probably set me apart from the *Sidhe* for the rest of my life.

We continued walking until we reached the second building over and stopped beneath a small balcony that once again made my heart seize with recognition.

"This is where it happened," Sethian murmured, drawing my eyes to him again. "This was the moment that my eyes first gazed upon you, a petite, dark-haired human standing with her back to me on a narrow, third-floor balcony, silhouetted against the light flooding through that window and wrestling with an apparatus that was half-hidden by your body."

His expression was so full of love at that moment that I couldn't help but lean into his chest and wrap my free arm tightly around his waist. He immediately completed the embrace and brought his lips down to mine—a brief kiss, but strong and full of passion all the same.

"I watched you for over a mark as you peered up into the vast universe through that tiny lens," Sethian said, his eyes practically burning with intensity as they caught and held mine, "then for at least another as you sat on the edge of that balcony with your legs dangling between the vertical bars and stared out into the night with such sadness. Watching you here night after night for many human moon-cycles, as well as from the shadows of the trees during your walks in a nearby park, I came to understand the reason for your sadness. I could *feel* it as well as see it in your eyes."

I closed my eyes and pressed my forehead against his chest. "I was alone."

I could sense his nod even as a small wash of his dismay flowed into me through the Bond. "It was a loneliness I knew very well," he said. "Your soul called to me on all those nights. It was then that I decided that you would be the one, that if you accepted me, then perhaps over time, we could fill the emptiness within each other with something just as beautiful as our love for the child we would conceive together."

I lifted my head and stared up at him almost incredulously. "If I *accepted* you? If you were so worried about rejection, then why did you bring me to the elven realm in the scariest way possible, all but guaranteeing it?"

The expression in his eyes was apologetic. "That was your test. Do you remember the choice I gave you on our wedding night?"

I nodded slowly. "To forget and return home or to stay and accept your touch…"

"If you would have chosen to forget, then I would have had your transmutation reversed and personally returned you to the human realm. You would have awoken the next morning thinking everything was a dream."

"I just don't understand elven reasoning sometimes," I said with a groan. "All these years, I thought you were just being an overbearing brute who, as a king, was simply used to getting his own way. Why couldn't you have lured me into the InBetween and tried to court me there like everyone else? Just think! If I hadn't been such a lonely, dreaming idiot, this happiness we found with each other, *our children* would've never happened!"

"Do not think that I was indifferent to your turmoil

on that night," Sethian entreated. "Your distress is the very reason why I made certain that the rules for seeking a human bride were changed this time around."

My eyes widened. "Wait—you mean the *Sidhe* have always stolen human brides the same way I was taken?" I exclaimed.

"It was their test," he replied simply. "As I recall, there are many such stories passed down by the humans over the ages. Even you, yourself, knew what I was at first sight."

"Yeah, but—" I paused, then shook my head.

No good ever came of dwelling in the past, especially on a deed I had long since forgiven him for.

"What's done is done." I rose up on my tiptoes to kiss him softly on the mouth. "Thank you for telling me this, for bringing me here."

Sethian gazed down at me intently for a long moment before turning his head to look up at my old balcony. "Would you like to go inside?"

"Um—no thank you," I replied with a strangled laugh. "The one reason I might've wanted to enter my old apartment is to see my friend, Anna, but no doubt she's long gone. The last thing we should do is scare the crap out of some poor soul just so I can see my old room."

"There are no humans currently living within," Sethian assured me with a grin.

I could feel a sense of anticipation building within him, and for a moment, I thought maybe he had left a gift within the apartment for me to find. This was, after all, despite the heaviness of our conversation, supposed to be a date. I had a momentary vision of a candlelight dinner laid out across the bare floorboards of my old bedroom complete with wine when a different, strong emotion began to trickle across the Bond.

An answering heat instantly began to swell within me. *Oh.*

"I have a better idea," I said, my tone low and seductive. "Since it's spring, there's this clearing near a stream in the park where you stalked me that should be filled with bluebonnets. I've always had this fantasy of making love under the stars surrounded by flowers."

His pupils instantly dilated with desire. "I remember."

Then the world began to fade out before I could even blink as Sethian phased, and this time, it was my own emotions that surged with anticipation. In the aftermath of all the chaos Limira had wrought, between regaining my health and Sethian's duties, there had been very little time to focus on just ourselves.

When the world once again came into focus, we

were standing in a darkened sea of flowers. I looked up at the sky and was pleased to see there wasn't a single cloud in sight and only the barest sliver of a crescent moon.

Then I felt Sethian release my hand and step away. Before I could protest, the entire area instantly lit up with a brilliant, golden light that emanated from Sethian, himself.

"Beauty such as this should be seen in the light," he said simply.

I couldn't help but laugh even as I leaped forward to grab both of his hands. The light from his body faded at my touch, leaving behind spots of yellow across my vision.

"You'll bring people running thinking a UFO landed in the trees," I half-seriously scolded, "and I definitely don't want an audience."

I yelped as Sethian abruptly tumbled me to the ground. Since our bodies were only slightly manifested within the human realm, I could only faintly smell the sweet scent of the surrounding bluebonnets. Then Sethian's lips were pressing hard onto mine, his body a warm, pleasant weight between my legs, and that barely-there fragrance was instantly overwhelmed by Sethian's scent.

"Then I shall bring you again when there is daylight," he whispered huskily against my tingling lips.

I smiled and licked his bottom lip playfully. "It's a date."

While any humans who might happen upon us would likely see nothing in the darkness, Sethian and I could see each other as clearly as if we were under the night sky within the elven realm. It gave the illusion that we were doing something a little naughty as I was still a bit shy about PDAs, much less about actually making love out in an open field.

The way his eyes were fixed on my face as he slowly unlaced my bodice, as though I was something worthy of worship, had me trembling with both excitement and a mixture of more complicated emotions. I could feel tears begin to well up within my eyes as those emotions suddenly became overwhelming. Although we had made love countless times, I still could never quite get used to that look, couldn't quite believe that this beautiful being above me against a backdrop of shimmering stars could love me so deeply.

My breasts now exposed, Sethian smiled before bending down to take one of my nipples into his mouth, sucking hard until it was a firm, aching pebble of sensitive flesh. One of his hands moved down my still-covered belly and began to tug the skirt of my dress upwards until my lower half was revealed.

I gasped as Sethian's fingers dipped beneath my undergarment and began to teasingly rub over my clit with a light, slow touch of his fingertips that had me instantly bucking and moaning. My own fingers were both tangling themselves into his silk-like hair and clutching at the stalks of the bluebonnets beside me that felt as brittle as a flower of ash due to my body's not-quite-manifested state. It made Sethian's touch feel that much more real and intense.

After a final, playful nip to my nipple, he was kissing me again, the thrust and slide of his tongue against mine in sync with the sensual movements of his hand massaging between my legs. I tugged his hair a little harder than I had intended when he abruptly pinched my clit, sending a jolt of pleasure racing up my spine, but that sense of excitement flowing from him across the Bond only seemed to increase with that little bit of added pain.

"Sethian...!" I moaned into his mouth, grabbing his gloriously firm ass through layers of silky material with the hand that had been making a mess of the bluebonnets and squeezing firmly in an attempt to urge him to thrust his hardness against my throbbing core even though I knew it was futile.

When he wasn't lost in a frenzy of lust, Sethian enjoyed slowly licking and caressing every inch of my body until my vision turned white and my entire being was on the brink of exploding. As much as I enjoyed the mind-shattering orgasms that resulted from such thorough, loving attention, this time, I wanted something more aggressive and primal. After everything terrible that had happened recently to my family and friends, I needed to feel alive again, to feel him heavy against me, deep within me, as much as was physically possible. There would be time enough later for worshipful lovemaking—thousands of years' worth.

Thankfully, I knew exactly which button to push.

I moved the hand still threading through his hair to one of his delicate, pointed ears and slowly teased the pad of my index finger along the edge to the ultra-sensitive tip. An instant stiffening of his entire body was my only warning before his mouth was suddenly doing its damnedest to suck the air right out of my lungs while my body jolted as Sethian tore the pair of absurdly delicate, elven equivalent of panties from my body in one rough tug.

Then his mouth was suddenly gone, and before I could do more than blink in bewilderment, he was opening his robes and sloppily pushing his breeches down until his swollen cock was revealed. Another blink and his warmth and weight were stretched over my hot and throbbing body once again, pushing my thighs open wider with an aggressive thrust of his hips. The feel of his silky hardness sliding urgently against my wetness had me arching up and begging him to enter me.

His lust poured into me through the Bond, overwhelming and delicious and everything in between as I felt his thick member fill my passage completely in one, sudden hard thrust, his mouth swallowing my ecstatic cry.

The world became a surreal mosaic of a black, starlit sky. The spill of delicate, blond hair over his shoulder tickled my face, and the preternaturally loud sound of our bodies slapping together in a dance older than even Sethian filled my ears before I closed my eyes and surrendered myself to the wild passion I had deliberately invoked within my elven husband.

I didn't want to think. I didn't want to remember any of the bad we had all endured. For that moment in time, feeling Sethian stoke the fires of my pleasure in the most primal way was all my wounded soul needed, and I loved him more for it.

Then that broiling pleasure exploded within me, and I desperately held Sethian even tighter within my arms as my entire body violently shuddered, my voice hoarsely screaming out his name into the soft, damp skin of his neck. My cry seemed to add to the frenzy of his hips as well as the lips that were sucking firmly on my pulse point, each impossibly deep thrust amplifying my orgasm to new heights until it was Sethian's turn to let out a moan deep in his throat as his seed filled me.

I loved hearing him moan. There were very few instances that could shatter the regal, powerful calm of an elven king, and I felt an immense amount of pleasure knowing that I could give him that relief, that he trusted me to surrender so utterly to his emotions.

It wasn't until Sethian was cuddling me, his lips softly kissing the corner of my eye, that I realized that I was leaking quiet tears. I felt a tinge of embarrassment. I hadn't been this raw and emotional after making love in quite some time, but my mind wasn't so scrambled by pleasure not to understand the reason for my tears.

"I'm okay," I murmured against his chest in answer to his silent question. I lifted my head, and my lips curved up into a genuine smile. "We're all okay, and you gave me the answers about our beginning that I didn't realize I still needed."

I laughed and stretched up to kiss him affectionately. "I even got to make love under the stars! How cheesy is that? I would hope all our future dates go so well." Then wistfully, "Do you think we can lie here and watch the stars all night?"

Sethian's eyes were smiling as he hugged me more tightly against him.

"We can stay here for a millennium."

CLAIMED BY THE ELVEN BROTHERS: DECISION AND FATE

ELVEN KING SERIES BOOK TWO

It started with a dream—a dream of two pine trees with a dead branch fallen between them along the jogging path she often frequented, but when Megan Reyes is driven to seek out the place in reality to rid herself of what was quickly becoming an obsession, instead of the big fat nothing she expects to find, she discovers more than she bargains for when she steps between the pines and is confronted by a very familiar pointy-eared man she last saw in her dreams.

He and his brother have been waiting for her, and what they want will test how far she is willing to go to escape the dullness of her everyday life just for the chance to spice things up.

NOW AVAILABLE

ABOUT THE AUTHOR

Cristina Rayne is a *New York Times* and *USA Today* best-selling author who lives in West Texas with her crazy cat and about a dozen bookcases full of fantasy worlds and steamy romances. She has a degree in Computer Science which totally qualifies her to write romances. As Fantasy is her first love, she feels if she can inject a little love into the fantastical, along with a few steamy scenes, then all the better. She is the author of the *Elven King, The Elven Realms, Riverford Shifters, Dragon Shifters of Elysia, Incarnations of Myth, Lords of the Vampire Underground* paranormal romance series, and the *Fractured Multiverse* science-fantasy series.

For more information:

www.cristinaraynebooks.com

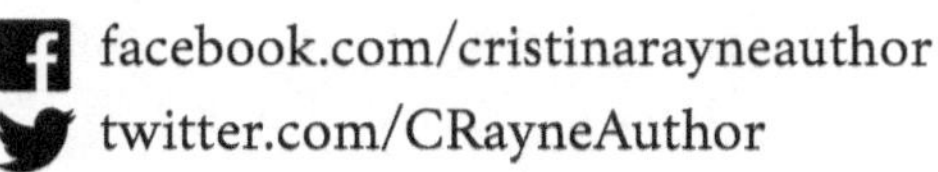

www.ingramcontent.com/pod-product-compliance
Lightning Source LLC
Chambersburg PA
CBHW031422240626
47154CB00001B/162
* 9 7 8 0 6 9 2 2 4 0 7 9 3 *